T0267078

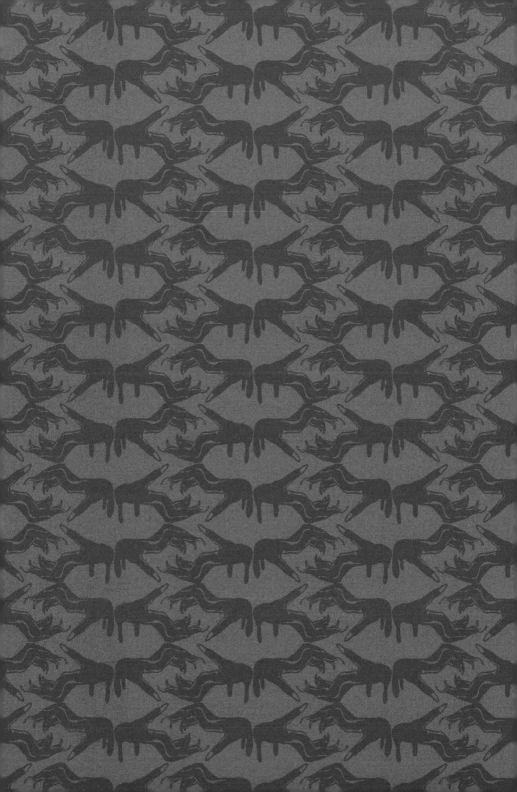

PENNY BLOODS

PENNY BLOODS

Gothic Tales of Dangerous Women

Edited by

NICOLE C. DITTMER

THE BRITISH LIBRARY

This collection first published in 2023 by
The British Library
96 Euston Road
London NW1 2DB

Selection, introduction, edited texts and notes © 2023 Nicole C. Dittmer
Volume copyright © 2023 The British Library Board

Cataloguing in Publication Data
A catalogue record for this publication is available from the British Library

ISBN 978 0 7123 5418 9

Cover design by Mauricio Villamayor with illustration by Mag
Ruhig. Original interior ornaments by Mag Ruhig.
Text design and typesetting by Tetragon, London
Printed in the Czech Republic by Finidr

CONTENTS

INTRODUCTION

In the early nineteenth century serialised texts, known formally as penny publications, or penny fictions emerged from the residue of the first-wave of Gothic literature. Introduced during a time of what Franz J. Potter calls "trade" Gothic, these new serials materialised due to a demand in marketing and the increase in England's working-class literacy.* Written by what literary society considered "hack writers", penny fiction, in its inception, was quickly composed, most notably by James Malcolm Rymer (1814–84) and Thomas Peckett Prest (probable dates 1810–1859), for monetary purposes in lieu of artistic ambition. Following the precedence set by the inexpensive chapbooks, bluebooks, and pamphlets of the 1820s, these new lurid tales emerged as patchwork stories infused with social issues—such as medical, cultural, and legal—and Gothic tropes. As admixtures of such nineteenth-century commentary and Gothic influence, penny serials highlighted the significance of human transgressions, most notably those of women, and how their deviant behaviour was a threat to rigid social structures.

At the emergence of these relatively cheap serials in the late 1820s and early 1830s, they were unofficially labelled "penny bloods" based on their sensationalist content that exhibited violent, and sometimes sanguinary characteristics. Formatted into weekly episodic segments, these initial penny bloods found a home in Edward Lloyd's *Penny Weekly Miscellany*, a magazine that promoted the scandalous tales alongside promotional advertisements

---

* Franz J. Potter. *Gothic Chapbooks, Bluebooks and Shilling Shockers, 1797–1830* (Cardiff: University of Wales Press, 2021): p. 5.

for new fiction. Inclusive of characteristics from eighteenth-century Gothic tales, social discourses, and canonical literature, the early penny fiction contained elements of adventure, the supernatural, horror, and politics. This new literature was considered "trash" by critics and unsettled society as it was feared as a negative influence on the Victorian populace. Amalgamations of exaggerations and melodrama, penny bloods highlighted the monstrous behaviours of the protagonists and glamorised such criminal heroics and exploits of the villains. Later, during the 1860s, the penny bloods metamorphised into the now popular term "penny dreadfuls".* Similar to the earlier bloods, these serials maintained the sensationalism and violence; however, they transitioned to incorporate new features to target juvenile readership.

Penny dreadfuls, also referred to as "awfuls", rebranded their material to align more with the adventurous exploits of their heroes to target young male readers. While including the traditional penny tropes of questionable morals and mercurial characters, the dreadfuls incorporated elements of romance, brave men, women in distress, investigators, and outlaws. These later serials also replaced the lurid black and white images with colour illustrations that highlighted the new content and attracted a larger audience. While the early bloods were suspect as sources of negative influences on social morals and behaviours, the later dreadfuls were a threat to Victorian standards in their promotion of rebellion and criminality. Lasting until the *fin-de-siècle*, penny fiction was both informed by and informed social commentary of the nineteenth century, until it finally dissolved into children's tales.

While these nineteenth-century serials, both bloods and dreadfuls, were marketable, mostly amongst working-class readership, the popularity of these tales determined their weekly segments and publications. There were two types of penny fiction that were published, and both caused their own issues: first was the unpopular, abandoned story and second was the popular, excessive narrative. If a penny tale was substandard and failed in its

---

* See more information in Nicole C. Dittmer and Sophie Raine. *Penny Dreadfuls and the Gothic: Investigations of Pernicious Tales of Terror* (Cardiff: University of Wales Press, 2023).

popularity, the serial would end abruptly, as the author would typically abandon the story, or the publisher would refuse its continued circulation. On
the other hand, if a penny serial achieved such popularity, it would expand
to accommodate the publishing demand, and incorporate writing strategies
that involve excess or padding, such as unnecessary character backstories,
derivative plots that typically end up unresolved, inveigle personas, and
lavish dialogue. This surfeit of content typically conflated the main plot(s)
of the penny serials which led to its own sabotage as the storylines would
become lost amongst the exorbitant material. Considering this abundance
of content, for each chapter of this collection I edit each penny narrative to
eliminate the excess and focus on the primary point of each tale; in this case
it is the dangerous woman.

This collection offers a balance of both popular and obscure penny publications that occurred in between the years 1828 to 1863. All of the included
short tales and edited excerpts of longer narratives, include women that are
designated as monstrous or dangerous, using Gothic tropes and characteristics of the traditional style. For example, each chapter contains stories of
witches, criminals/*femme fatales*, madwomen, and vampires, thereby exhibit-
ing how these serials, while at the end of a supposed Gothic literary decline,
perpetuate the Gothic style and ultimately inform later canonical novels
of the mid-Victorian period and the *fin-de-siècle* (i.e., Charlotte Brontë's
Jane Eyre (1847), Emily Brontë's *Wuthering Heights* (1847), Bram Stoker's
Dracula (1897), and Sheridan Le Fanu's *Carmilla* (1872)). The overall structure of this collection is not categorised according to the type of monstrosity
but is, instead, organised by publication date. While it would make sense to
segment these tales by their monstrous identifiers, the incorporation of tale
by dates create their own overarching story that demonstrates the progression of female monstrosities, and ultimately society's changing perspective of
women (due to such discourses of medical sciences) from the early Victorian
period right through to the *fin-de-siècle*. It is this particular progression of
female monstrosities that the following chapters will trace to illustrate the
nineteenth-century anxieties and fears of the potential dangers of women

in society. In the words of Mary Shelley (1818), "It is true, we shall be monsters, cut off from all the world; but on that account we shall be more attached to one another".* It is this journey of danger and potentially "monstrous" women I invite you to join, indulge in, and leave your world behind, if only for a while, or maybe a bit longer, you decide.

NICOLE C. DITTMER is a Lecturer of Victorian Gothic Studies at The College of New Jersey, Proofreader and editorial board member at the *Studies in Gothic Fiction*, and advisory board member of *Ecocritical Theory and Practice* for Rowman & Littlefield's imprint, Lexington Books. Her works include "Malignancy of Goneril: Nature's Powerful Warrior", published in the collection, *Global Perspectives on Eco-Aesthetics and Eco-Ethics: A Green Critique* (2020); the monograph, *Monstrous Women and Ecofeminism in the Victorian Gothic, 1837–1871* (2022); the edited UWP collection *Penny Dreadfuls and the Gothic: Investigations of Pernicious Tales of Terror* (2023); and the contribution "Victorianism and Ecofeminist Literature" for *The Routledge Handbook of Ecofeminism and Literature* (2022) edited by Douglas Vakoch.

ACKNOWLEDGEMENTS

I would like to thank Jonny Davidson at the British Library for his enthusiasm with this project. I am grateful for his assistance and eagerness to welcome this collection into the BLP family.

I would also like to thank my friends and colleagues of Bliss Hall at The College of New Jersey for their never-ending support and encouragement throughout the years. They have truly been the village of support during my academic journey.

Finally, I would like to dedicate this book to my brother, Sean, who left this world too early.

---

* Mary Shelley. *Frankenstein* (New York: Dover Publications, 2013/1818): p. 105.

1828

THE SKELETON COUNT; OR, THE VAMPIRE MISTRESS

Elizabeth Caroline Grey

Not much is known about *The Skeleton Count* other than the year and place of its publication, the fact that it is one of the first English language vampire tales, and that it is the earliest written narrative of a female vampire. This story of necromancy and vampirism was published in the early nineteenth-century weekly penny paper, *The Casket*, a magazine that promoted serials abound with sensational and Gothic components. Credited as the author of *The Skeleton Count* in 1828, Elizabeth Caroline Grey's (1798–1869) Gothic tale of monstrosity exhibits influences from Mary Shelley's *Frankenstein* (1818) with elements of human reanimation, scientific experimentation, and vengeful mob behaviour from the townsfolk; and as one of the original tales about vampiric women, this Gothic tale further informs texts such as Sheridan Le Fanu's later *Carmilla* (1872).

This short story revolves around two characters, Count Rodolph of Ravensburg, a Faustian character who has made a pact with the Devil and, every night transforms into a vulnerable skeletal figure until the sun rises; and Bertha, a once living, beautiful and virtuous peasant girl who becomes a vampiric companion for the Count. Both characters initially keep their secrets from one another, but eventually their identities are revealed when they are confronted by the villagers and executed. Although Rodolph is depicted as a visually monstrous figure, his behaviour and actions are lessened in comparison to those of Bertha. Once classified as the "angel" of her village, the revivification of Bertha transforms her into an all-consumptive, feral, and destructive monstrosity who is remiss of remorse and expectations of nineteenth-century femininity.

Since this is such a short tale that has a singular plot and does not follow the penny trope of deviation and excess, it is included in its entirety to illustrate the profound danger of women in the early Gothic.

I

*

There is much discussion over the authenticity of Elizabeth Caroline Grey as the author of this tale. Similar to the James Malcolm Rymer versus Thomas Peckett Prest debate, there is an ongoing argument about the authorship of the popular Elizabeth Caroline Grey as the writer of penny fiction. In one instance, Helen R. Smith argues that James Malcolm Rymer is the true author of the work attributed to Grey. See *New Light on Sweeney Todd, Thomas Peckett Prest, and Elizabeth Grey* (2002). Peter Haining, on the other hand, purports that *The Skeletal Count* was in fact written by E.C.G. in 1825 for *The Casket*; however, this claim is still under investigation. See *The Vampire Omnibus* (1995). Finally, Patrick Spedding stipulates that there were numerous writers in the nineteenth century with the name "Mrs. Grey". Due to the myriad of the like-named writers and the deliberate fabrications from such notable deceivers as Andrew De Ternant, the true identities of these penny authors were conflated and misidentified. Spedding, then, dismisses the renowned Elizabeth Caroline Grey as the true author of this, and other, penny tales. See "The Many Mrs. Greys: Confusion and Lies about Elizabeth Caroline Grey, Catherine Maria Grey, Maria Georgina Grey, and Others", *PBSA* 104:3 (2010).

As this debate is ongoing and unresolved, I opt to leave Elizabeth Caroline Grey as the assumed author for this particular tale to bring attention to the problematic issues of penny publication authorship and ownership.

C OUNT Rodolph, after his impious compact with the prince of
darkness, ceased to study alchemy or to search after the elixir of
life, for not only was a long lease of life assured him by the demon,
but the same authority had declared such pursuits to be vain and delusive.
But he still dabbled in the occult sciences of magic and astrology, and frequently passed day after day in fruitless speculation, concerning the origin
of matter, and the nature of the soul. He studied the writings of Aristotle,
Pliny, Lucretius, Josephus, Iamblicus, Sprenger, Cardan, and the learned
Michael Psellus; yet was he as far as ever from attaining a correct knowledge
of the things he sought to unveil from the mystery which must ever enve-
lope them. The reveries of the ancient philosophers, of the Gnostics and
the Pneumatologists, only served to plunge him into deeper doubt, and at
length he determined to pass from speculation to experiment, and put his
half-formed theories to the test of practice.

After keen studies of the anatomy of the human frame, and many operations and experiments on the corpse of a malefactor who had been hanged
for a robbery and murder, and which he stole from the gibbet in the dead of
night, and conveyed to Ravensburg Castle, with the assistance of two wretches
whom he had picked up at an obscure hostelry in the town of Heidelberg,
he resolved to exhume the corpse of someone recently dead, and attempt its
reanimation. The formula of the necromancers for raising the dead did not
suffice for their restoration to life, but only for a temporary revivification; but
in an old Greek manuscript, which he found in the library of the castle, was
an account of how this restored animation might be sustained by means of
a miraculous liquid, for the distillation of which a recipe was given.

Count Rodolph gathered the herbs at midnight, which the Greek manuscript prescribed and distilled from them a clear gold-coloured liquid of very little taste, but most fragrant odour, which he preserved in a phial. Having discovered that a peasant's daughter, a girl of singular beauty, and about sixteen years of age, had died suddenly, and was to be buried on the day following that on which he had prepared his marvellous restorative, he had set out on that day to Heidelberg to obtain the assistance of the fellows who had aided him in removing the corpse of the malefactor from the gibbet, and then returned to Ravensburg Castle, to prepare for his strange experiment.

At the solemn hour of midnight he departed secretly from the castle by a door in the eastern tower, of which he retained the key in his own possession, and bent his step to the churchyard of the neighbouring village. It was a fine moonlight night, but all the rustic inhabitants were in the arms of Morpheus, the leaden-eyed god of sleep, and the violator of the sanctity of the grave gained the churchyard unperceived. He found his hired associates waiting for him in the shadow of the wall, which was easily scaled, and being provided with shovels and a sack to contain the corpse, they set to work immediately. The fresh broken earth was soon thrown off from the lid of the coffin, which the resurrectionists removed with a screw-driver, and then the dead was disclosed to their view.

The corpse of the young maiden was lifted from its narrow resting place, and raised in the arms of the ungodly wretches whom Rodolph had hired, who deposited the inanimate clay on the margin of the grave, which they hastily filled up, and then proceeded to enclose in the sack the lifeless remains of the beautiful peasant girl. Having removed every trace of the sacrilegious theft which they had committed, one of them took the sack on his shoulders, and when he was tired his comrade relieved him, and in this manner they reached the castle. Count Rodolph led the way up the narrow stairs which led to his study chamber in the eastern turret, and having deposited the corpse upon the floor, and received their stipulated reward, the two resurrectionists were glad to make a speedy exit from a place which popular rumour began to associate with deeds of darkness and horror.

Having lighted a spirit lamp, which cast a livid and flickering light upon the many strange and mysterious objects which that chamber contained, and made the pale countenance of the corpse appear more ghastly and horrible, Count Rodolph proceeded to denude the body of its grave-clothes, which he carefully concealed, lest the sight of them, when the young maiden returned to life might strike her with a sudden horror which might prove fatal to the complete success of his daring experiment. He then placed the corpse in the centre of a magic circle which he had previously drawn upon the floor of the study, and covered it with a sheet. He had purchased some ready-made female apparel in the town of Heidelberg, and these he placed on the table in readiness for the use of the young girl, whom he felt sanguine of resuscitating.

Bertha had been, as was evidenced by her stark and cold remains, a maiden of surpassing symmetry of form and loveliness of countenance; no painter or sculptor could have desired a finer study, no poet a more inspiring theme. As she lay stretched out upon the floor of the study she looked like some beautiful carving in alabaster, or rather like a waxen figure of most artistical contrivance. Her long black hair was shaded with a purple gloss like the plumage of the raven, and her features were of most exquisite proportion and arrangement. But now her angelic countenance was livid with the pallid hue of death, the iron impress of whose icy hand was visible in every lineament.

Count Rodolph then took in his hand a magic wand, one end of which he placed on the breast of the corpse, and then proceeded to recite the cabalistic words by which necromancers call to life the slumbering tenants of the grave. When he had concluded the impious formula, and awful silence reigned in the turret, and he perceived the sheet gently agitated by the quivering of the limbs, which betokened returning animation. Then a shudder pervaded his frame in spite of himself, as he perceived the eyes of the corpse slowly open, and the dark dilated pupils fix their gaze on him with a strange and stolid glare.

Then the limbs moved, at first convulsively, but soon with a stronger and more natural motion, and then the young girl raised herself to a sitting posture on the floor of the study, and stared about her in a wild and strange manner, which made Rodolph fear that the object of his experiment would prove a wretched idiot or a raving lunatic.

But suddenly he bethought him of the restorative cordial, and snatching the phial from a shelf, he poured down the throat of the resuscitated maiden a considerable portion of the fragrant gold-coloured fluid which it contained. Then a ray of that glorious intellect which allies man to the angels seemed to be infused into her mind, and beamed from her dark and lustrous eyes, which rested with a soft and tender expression on the handsome countenance of the young count. Her snowy bosom, from which the sheet had fallen when she rose from her recumbent position on the floor, heaved with the returning warmth of renewed life, and the Count of Ravensburg gazed upon her with mingled sensations of wonder and delight.

As the current of life was restored, and rushed along her veins with tingling warmth, the conscious blush of instinctive modesty mantled on her countenance, and drawing the sheet over her bosom, she rose to her feet, with her long black hair hanging about her shoulders, and her dark eyes cast upon the floor. Count Rodolph then directed her attention to the clothing which he had provided, so sanguine of complete success had the daring experimentalist been, and then he withdrew from the study while the lovely object of his scientific care attired herself.

When the Count of Ravensburg returned to his study, Bertha was sitting before the fire, attired in the garments he had provided for her, and he thought that he had never beheld a more lovely specimen of her sex. She rose when he entered, and kissed his hand, as though he were a superior being, and would have remained standing, with head bowed upon her bosom, as if in the presence of a being of another world, had he not gently forced her to resume the seat from which she had risen, and inquired tenderly the state of her feelings upon a return to life so strange and wonderful. But he found that she retained no remembrance of a previous existence, and all her feelings were new and strange, like those of Eve on bursting into conscious life and being from the hand of the Omnipotent. In her mysterious passage from life to death, and from death to new life, she had lost all her previous ideas and convictions, all her experience of the past, all that she had ever acquired of knowledge; and she had become a child of nature, simple and unsophisticated as a denizen of the woods, with all the keen perceptions and untrained instincts of the untutored savage.

The young girl had braided up her flowing tresses of glossy blackness, and on her cheeks dwelt colour that might test a painter's skill, so rich yet delicate its hue, like the rosette tinge of some rare exotic shell, or that which a rose would cast upon an alabaster column. The young count felt himself irresistibly attracted towards the maiden, whom his science had endured with such a mysterious and preternatural existence, and she, on her part, regarded the handsome Rodolph with the wild, yet tender passion of frail humanity, mingled with the gratitude and devotion which she deemed due to one who stood to her in the position of her creator.

Thus the feelings which had so rapidly sprung up in her heart towards the only being of whom she had any conception, partook of a nature of a religious idolatry, but mingled with the grosser feelings of earth, like those which agitated in the bosom of the vestal whose sons founded Rome, or the virgin of Shen-si who was chosen from among all the women of the celestial empire to become the mother of the incarnate Foh.

"Thou art gloriously beautiful, my Bertha!" exclaimed the enamoured count, pressing her in his arms. "Say that thou wilt be mine, and make me thy happy slave; thou should'st be loving as thou art loveable, beautiful child of mystery!"

"Love thee!" returned Bertha, a soft and tender expression dwelling in the clear depths of her dark eyes. "I adore thee, my creator; my soul bows itself before thee, yet my heart leaps at thy glance, though I fear it is presumptuous for the work of thy hands to look on thee with eyes of love."

"Sweet, ingenuous creature!" cried the Count of Ravensburg, kissing her coral lips and glowing cheeks. "It is I who should worship thee! Thou art mine, Bertha, now and forever. Henceforth I live only in thy smile!"

"Forever! Shall I remain with thee forever? Oh, joy incomparable! My heart's idol, I adore thee!" and the beautiful Bertha wound her white arms about his neck, and pressed her lips to his, for in the new existence which she now enjoyed her feelings knew no restraint, and she yielded to every impulse of her ardent nature.

"Come, my Bertha," said the enraptured Rodolph, "this solitary turret must not be thy world; come with me, thy Rodolph, and be the mistress of Ravensburg Castle, as thou art already of its owner's heart."

Passing his arm around the taper waist of the mysterious maiden, Rodolph took up the lamp, and quitting the eastern turret, they proceeded with noiseless steps to his chamber, where the first faint blush of day witnessed the consummation of their desires, nor did the torch of Hymen burn less brightly because no priest blessed their nuptial couch.

The presence in Ravensburg Castle of this young girl, which Rodolph, with that contempt for the opinion of the world which usually marked his actions, took no pains to conceal, because the engrossing topic of conversation in the servants' hall throughout the day, and as Rodolph had never before indulged in any intrigue, either with the peasant girls of the neighbouring village or the courtezans of Heidelburg, the circumstance seemed the more remarkable. But the beautiful Bertha seemed quite unconscious of the equivocal nature of her position in reference to the young count, and though her views of human nature became every moment more enlarged with the sphere of her existence, she still regarded Rodolph as a being of superior mould.

When night again drew his sable mantle over the sleeping earth, Rodolph and the mysterious Bertha sought their couch, and never had shone the inconstant moon on a pair so well matched as regarded physical beauty, or we may add as regarded their strange destiny—one gifted with almost superhuman powers of mind, yet in a few days to undergo so horrible a transformation, and far removed by that strange fate from ordinary mortals; the other endowed with such singular beauty yet doomed to the dreadful existence of one who had passed the boundaries of the grave, and returned to life!

With sonorous and solemn stroke the bell of the castle clock proclaimed the hour of midnight, and then Bertha slowly raised herself from her lover's body and slipping from the bed, attired herself in a half-conscious state, and stole noiselessly from the room.

Her cheeks were pale, and her eyes had the wild and stolid glare which Rodolph had observed when she awakened from the slumber of the grave; she quitted the castle, and after gazing around her, as if uncertain which way to go, she proceeded towards the village.

She stopped opposite the nearest cottage, and then advanced to the window, and shook the shutters; the fastenings being insecure, they opened with little trouble, and a broken pane of glass enabled Bertha to introduce her hand, and remove the fastenings of the window. Then she cautiously opened the window, and entered the room—she ascended the stairs on tiptoe, and entered a chamber where a little girl was in bed and fast asleep. For a moment she shuddered violently, as if struggling to repress the horrible inclination which is the dread condition of a return to life after passing the portals of death, and then she bent her face down to the child's throat, her hot breath fanned its cheek, and the next moment her teeth punctured its tender skin, and she began to suck its blood to sustain her unnatural existence!

For such is the horrible destiny of the vampire race, of whom we have yet further mysteries and secrets to unfold; and such a being was she whom Count Rodolph had taken from the grave to his bed!

Presently the child awoke with a fearful scream, and its father leaping from his bed in the next room, hurried to her succour, but Bertha rushed past him in the dark, and escaped from the house. The peasant found the little girl much frightened, and bleeding at the throat; but she had suffered no vital injury, and having ascertained this fact, he snatched up his matchlock, and hurried after the aggressor.

"A vampire!" exclaimed the peasant, turning pale with horror, as he distinctly saw, by the light of the moon, a young female hurrying from the village at a rapid pace.

The man gave chase to the flying Bertha, and gradually gaining ground, came within gun shot, just as she reached the shelving banks of the river, when raised his weapon to his shoulder, and fired. The report echoed along the banks of the Rhine, and Bertha screamed as the ball penetrated her back, and tumbled headlong into the stream. The peasant hastened back to the village, satisfied that the horrible creature was no more, and the corpse of the vampire floated on the surface of the moonlit river.

The moon was that night at the full, and shed a flood of pearly light over the picturesque scenery of the Rhine, which, throughout its whole course, is a panorama of scenic beauty, every bend revealing some object interesting either for its historical reminiscences or legendary associations. There was the village, but now the scene of a horrible outrage—the castle, thrown into alternate light and shadow by the passing of the light fleecy clouds over the face of the moon—the town of Heidelberg, sloping from the Castle of the Palatine, and spanning the river with its noble bridge—and the Rhine, here shaded by the dark rocks which overhung the opposite bank, and there reflecting the silver light of the moon. The corpse of the vampire floated down the stream for some distance, and then it became arrested in its course by the bending of the river, and lay partly out of the water on the shelving bank.

And now commenced another scene of strange and startling interest—another phase in the fearful existence of the vampire bride! For as the beams of the full moon fell on the inanimate form of that being of mystery and fear, sensation seemed slowly to return, as when the magic spells of the Count of Ravensburg resuscitated her from the grave; her eyes opened, her bosom rose and fell with the warm pulsations of returning life; her limbs moved spasmodically, and then she rose from the bank, and shuddering at the recollection of what had occurred to her, she wrung the water from her saturated garments, and ran towards the castle at a pace accelerated by fear.

Having admitted herself into the castle, she sought the count's chamber with noiseless steps, and having taken off and concealed her wet clothes, she returned to his bed without his being aware that she had ever quitted it. The count was surprised to find that his mistress took no refreshment throughout the day, but he was led to consider it as one of the natural laws of her strange existence, and thought no more about it.

But in the village, the utmost excitement prevailed when it became known that the cottage of Herman Klaus had been visited by a vampire during the night, and his little daughter bitten by the horrible creature. All day long the cottage of the mysterious visitation was beset by the wondering villagers, who crossed themselves piously, and wondered who the vampire could have been, and the services of the priest were called into requisition to prevent the little blue-eyed Minna becoming a vampire after death, as is supposed to be the case with those who have the misfortune to be bitten by one of those horrible creatures, just as a person becomes mad after the bite of a mad dog or cat.

According to the terms of the compact which had been entered into between Count Rodolph and the demon, its conditions did not come into operation until seven days after the signing of the dreadful bond, and as day after day flew on, Rodolph dreaded the necessity of acquainting Bertha with the terrible transformation which he must nightly undergo. But he knew how impossible it would be to keep his hideous and appalling metamorphosis a secret from his mistress, and he reflected that if he made her the confidant of his terrible fate it would be the more likely to remain unknown to the rest of the world. He accordingly nerved his mind to the appalling revelation which he had to make, and on the seventh day after his compact with Lucifer, he disclosed to her his awful secret.

"Bertha," said he, in a sad and solemn tone, "I am about to entrust thee with a terrible secret; swear to me that thou wilt never divulge it."

"I swear," she replied.

"Know, then," continued the count, lowering his voice to a hoarse whisper, "that, by virtue of a compact with the infernal powers of evil and of darkness, I am endowed with a term of life and youth amounting almost to the boon of immortality but to this inestimable gift, there is a condition attached which commences this night, and which I almost tremble to impart to thee."

"Fear not, my Rodolph!" exclaimed his beautiful mistress, twining her round white arms about his neck, "thy Bertha can never love thee less, and her soul the rather clings to thee more intensely for the preternatural gift which links thy destiny more closely to my own. For mine, too, is a strange and fearful existence, which I owe to thee, and therefore shall I cling to thee the more fondly for the kindred doom which allies us to each other while it lifts us far above ordinary mortals."

"Then prepare thy ears for a dread revelation, Bertha," returned the Count of Ravensburg. "Each night of my future existence, at the hour of sunset, my doom divests me of my mortal shape, and I become a skeleton until sunrise on the morn ensuing. Now, thou knowest all, my Bertha, and be it thy care to prevent the dreadful secret from becoming known."

"It shall, my brave Rodolph!" exclaimed Bertha, her eyes glittering with a strange expression, as she thought of the facility which her lover's strange doom would allow for her nocturnal absences from the castle. "No eye but mine shall witness thy transformation, and I will watch over thee until thy return to thy natural shape."

"Thanks, my Bertha!" returned Rodolph, embracing her. "The hour draws nigh when I must relinquish for the night my mortal form; come, love, to our chamber, and see that no prying eye beholds the ghastly change."

Bertha and her lover accordingly repaired to their chamber, and when the luminary of day sank below the horizon, leaving the traces of his splendour on the western sky, the Count Rodolph shrunk to a grisly skeleton, and fell upon the bed. Bertha shuddered as she witnessed the horrid transformation, and they lay down on the bed until midnight, the necessity of secrecy overcoming any repugnance she might otherwise have felt to the horrible contiguity of the skeleton, but when the castle clock proclaimed the hour of midnight with iron tongue, she rose from the bed, and locking the door of the chamber which contained so strange a guest, she stole from the castle to sate her unnatural appetite for human blood.

The moon rose high in the heavens on that night of unfathomable mystery and horror, and her silver beams shone through the chamber window of Theresa Delmar, one of the loveliest maidens in the village of Ravensburg, revealing a snowy neck, and a white and dimpled shoulder, shaded by the bright golden locks which strayed over the pillow. The maiden's blue eyes were concealed by their thin lids and their long silken fringes, and her snowy bosom gently rose and fell beneath the white coverlet as the thoughts which agitated her by day, mingled in her dreams at night. Silence reigned in the thatched cottage, and throughout the village was only occasionally broken by the barking of some watchful house-dog.

But soon after midnight the silence was broken by a slight noise at the chamber window as if someone was endeavouring to obtain an entrance, and the flood of moonlight which streamed upon the maiden's bed was obscured by the form of a woman standing on the windowsill. Still Theresa slumbered on, nor dreamed of peril so near, for the woman had succeeded in opening the window, and in another moment she stood within the room.

With slow and cautious steps she softly approached the bed whereon the maiden reposed so calmly, little dreaming how dread a visitant was near her couch, and then she shuddered involuntarily as she bent over the sleeping girl, and her long dark ringlets mingled with the massed of golden hair which shaded the white shoulder, and the partially exposed bosom of Theresa Delmar. Her lips touched the young girl's neck, her sharp teeth punctured the white skin, and then she began to suck greedily, quaffing the vital fluid which flowed warm and quick in the maiden's veins, and sapping her life to maintain her own!

Still Theresa awoke not, for the puncture made in her throat by the teeth of the horrible creature was little larger than that which would be made by a leech, and the vampire sucked long and greedily, for her long abstinence from blood had sharpened her unnatural appetite. Suddenly Theresa awoke with a start, doubtless caused by some unpleasant transition in her dreams, but she did not immediately cry out, for she felt no pain, and as yet she was scarcely conscious of her danger. But in a few seconds she was thoroughly awake, and her surprise and horror may be more easily imagined than described, when she found bending over her, and sucking her blood, the horrible creature that had but a few nights previously attacked Minna Klaus, and which the child's father thought he had destroyed.

Spell-bound by the glittering eyes of the vampire, she lay without the power to scream, until the appalling horror of her situation became too great for endurance, her quivering nerves were strung to their utmost power of extension, and a wild shriek burst from her lips. Even the horrible creature did not leave its hold, but continued to suck from her palpitating veins the crimson current of her life, until footsteps were heard hastily approaching the chamber, and the lovely Theresa, whose screams seemed to have broken the fascination which had bound her in its thrall, struggled so violently that Bertha was compelled to relinquish her horrid banquet. Springing to the window, she effected her escape, just as heavy blows resounded on the door of the chamber, and her affrighted victim sank insensible on the bed.

"What is the matter, Theresa? Open the door!" exclaimed her terrified parents; but they received no answer.

Then Delmar broke open the door, and he and his wife rushed into the room and found their daughter lying insensible on the bed, with spots of blood on her throat and bosom, and the window wide open.

"The vampire has come to life again, and has attacked our Theresa!" exclaimed her mother. "See the blood-marks on her dear neck! Raise the village, Delmar, to pursue the monster."

"Oh, dear! where am I? Has it gone, mother?" inquired Theresa, as she recovered from her swoon, and gazed in an affrighted manner round the room.

"Yes, it has gone now, dear," said her mother. "What was it like?"

"Aye, what was it like?" added old Delmar. "Perhaps it was not the same one that neighbour Klaus shot at the other night."

"Oh, yes! it was a young woman, and as much like Bertha Kurtel as ever one pea was like another," replied the young girl, shuddering.

"Holy virgin!" exclaimed her mother, crossing herself with a shudder. "Bertha Kurtel a vampire, and returned from the grave to prey upon our Theresa! Oh, horrible!"

Delmar hurriedly dressed himself, and catching up an axe, he hastened to call up Klaus and others to pursue the vampire, and in a few minutes the whole village was in commotion. About twenty men armed themselves with whatever weapon came first to hand, and followed the direction which the vampire had taken when chased by Herman Klaus on a former occasion. They searched every bush all around the village, to which they returned at sunrise without having found any trace of the object of their search. Delmar found his daughter somewhat faint from fright and loss of blood, but not otherwise injured by the vampire's attack. The greatest excitement prevailed in that usually quiet village, and all the morning, groups of men stood about the little street, or clustered round Delmar's cottage conversing in low and mysterious whispers of the dreadful visitation which the village had a second time received.

"What a shocking thing it would be if a pretty girl like Theresa Delmar was to become a vampire when she dies," observed one. "And who knows what may happen now she has been bitten by one of those horrible creatures?"

"And poor little Minna Klaus," said another.

"Ah, and we do not know how long the list may be if we do not put a stop to it," added one of the rustic group. "I have heard Father Ambrose say that they generally attack females and children."

"Who can it be? That is what I want to know," said old Klaus. "Why, Theresa declares it was just like Bertha Kurtel," returned another, shaking his voice to a whisper.

"Bertha Kurtel!" repeated a youth who had loved her who once bore that name. "Bertha a vampire! impossible."

"It is easily ascertained," observed the gruff voice of the village blacksmith. "We have only to take up the coffin and see if she is in it, as she ought to be. If we do not find her we shall know what's o'clock."

"If it was not for her parents' feelings I really should like to be satisfied whether it is Bertha," remarked old Delmar.

"Feelings!" repeated the smith, in a surly tone. "Have we not all got our feelings? Are we to have our wives and children attacked in this manner, and all turned into vampires, and let other people's fine feelings prevent us from having satisfaction for it?"

"There is something in that," observed Delmar, scratching his head with an air of perplexity.

"I would make one if anybody else would go," said Herman Klaus, after pause.

"And I will be another," exclaimed the smith, looking around him. "Now who will go and have a peep in the churchyard to see whose coffin is empty?"

Several expressed themselves ready, and others following their example the smith proceeded to the churchyard, backed by about twenty of the most resolute of the villagers, to reenact the scene which had taken place there but a few nights since. On arriving at the churchyard the smith and another immediately set work to throw the earth out of the grave, which was soon accomplished, and amid the most breathless silence the smith proceeded to remove the lid of the coffin.

"Look here, neighbours," said he, turning pale in spite of himself. "The lid has been removed, and the coffin is empty!"

"So it is!" exclaimed Herman Klaus.

"Then is it not plain that Bertha is the vampire—the horrible creature that sucked the blood of Theresa Delmar and little Minna Klaus?" said the smith, looking round upon the throng which had been swelled during the work of exhumation by idlers from the village.

"But where is she now? that is the question," observed Herman Klaus.

"This must be investigated," said the smith. "We must keep watch for the vampire, and catch it; then we must either burn it, or drive a stake through the creature's body, for they say those are the only methods that will effectually fix a vampire."

The wondering group of peasants returned to the village, and great was the grief of the Kurtels at the horrible discovery that their daughter had become a vampire, and the youth who had so loved Bertha in her human state became delirious on hearing the confirmation of the suspicion which Theresa's assertion had first excited. The ordinary occupations of the villagers were entirely neglected throughout the day, and nothing was talked of but vampires and wehr-wolves, and other human transformations more terrific and appalling than any recorded in the metamorphoses of Ovid. Towards the evening the venerable seneschal of the Count of Ravensburg arrived in the village and had an interview with the Delmars, after which he visited the cottage of Herman Klaus, and a vague rumour spread like wildfire from house to house, to the effect that the vampire was an inmate of Ravensburg Castle.

The communication made by the seneschal to Delmar and Klaus was to the effect that, on the morning following the interment of Bertha Kurtel, a young female exactly resembling her in form, features, voice, and every individual peculiarity, had appeared in a mysterious manner at the castle, and had resided there ever since in the capacity of the count's mistress. No one knew who she was, where she came from, or how she obtained admission into the castle; and the occurrences in the village having reached the ears of the count's retainers and domestics, accompanied with the suspicion that the vampire was the revived Bertha Kurtel, the seneschal had hastened to the village to report his observations. The abstinence of the count's mistress from food was deemed corroborative of the suspicion that she was a vampire, and the seneschal's report caused the utmost excitement among the villagers. Symptoms of hostile intentions soon became visible, and in less than half an hour, more than a hundred men were proceeding in a disorderly manner towards the castle, armed with every imaginable weapon, and swearing to put an end to the vampire.

Count Rodolph and his beautiful mistress were sitting at a window which commanded a view of the road for some distance, the small white hand of Bertha locked in that of her lover, and whispering words of tenderness and love, when their attention was attracted by a disorderly mob approaching from the village.

"What can this mean?" said Rodolph, rising.

"Oh, this is what I have dreaded!" exclaimed Bertha, turning pale, and clasping her hands in a terrified manner: "your studies have caused you to be suspected of necromancy, my Rodolph, they come to attack the castle."

"I fear thou art right, dearest," said the count: "but we will give them a warm reception. Ho! a lawless mob menaces the castle with danger: make fast the gates; bar every door; bid my retainers man the battlements to repel the attack."

"And sunset is approaching," exclaimed Bertha, with a meaning glance at her lover.

"Do thou retire, sweet love, to thy chamber," said Rodolph; "fear thou not for me; I bear a charmed life, and neither sword nor shot will avail against it. If this lawless rabble be not dispersed when the dread moment comes all hope will be lost, and they shall behold the grisly change. Perhaps they may be struck with a sudden panic, and we may be enabled to fly into another country."

Bertha retired after embracing the count, and shut herself up in her chamber. Preparations were immediately made to resist the attack of the insurgent villagers, who continued to advance upon the castle, yelling like savages, and breathing vengeance against the vampire mistress of Count Rodolph.

"Down with the vampire!" was the hoarse and sullen cry which rolled like distant thunder from a hundred throats, and then the mob drew up before the castle gates, and the smith struck them heavily with his ponderous hammer.

The count took an arquebus and fired at the mob, very few of whom were provided with fire-arms; one of the peasants was wounded, and with a shout of rage and defiance a volley of shot, arrows and stones was directed against the beleaguered castle. The smith continued to batter away at the gate, aided by several stalwart fellows with axes, and though several of the mob were killed by the fire of the men-at-arms, those who were endeavouring to force the gate were protected by the overhanging battlements, and continued to ply their implements with unsealed energy.

Count Rodolph turned pale, and shuddered as he listened to the wild cries of the assailants, not from fear, for apart from his invulnerability he was inaccessible to that feeling, but from the horrible ideas engendered from these shouts, having reference to the beautiful Bertha Kurtel. Had her resuscitation from the grave endowed her with the horrible nature of the vampire? Could that lovely creature sustain her renewed existence with the blood of her former companions? Horrible! yet, had she not hinted at something of the kind when he revealed to her the horrors of his own strange doom? It must be so, then; and he shuddered violently at the appalling idea.

"Down with the vampire!" was still the menacing cry which rose from the assailants, who at length succeeded in breaking down the gates, and rushed tumultuously into the courtyard, shouting and brandishing their weapons.

Undismayed by the fire from the battlements, they commenced an attack on the doors and windows of the castle, and now they were all crowded in the courtyard, Count Rodolph thought the moment favourable for a sally. Drawing his sword, and commanding a score of his armed retainers to follow him, he suddenly opened a door leading into the courtyard, and fell furiously on the flank of the assailants. For a moment they were thrown into confusion, but they quickly rallied, when Count Rodolph and his little party were surrounded and compelled to act on the defensive. The ruddy beams of the setting sun were already purpling the distant hills when the peasants marched upon the castle, and as his broad disk sank below the horizon, the aspect of the Count of Ravensburg suddenly underwent a marvellous change, and much as the insurgents had wondered to see arrows glance off from his body, and their swords rebound as if their stroke fell on a giant oak, how much greater was their astonishment when they beheld him suddenly transformed into a fleshless skeleton!

"It is some device of Satan!—he is a sorcerer!" cried the stalwart smith, brandishing his huge hammer. "Come on, mates—down with the vampire!"

"Down with the vampire!" echoed from the mob, and the count's retainers giving way on all sides, as much appalled as the peasants at this horrible metamorphosis, the assailants rushed into the castle by the open door, and marched from room to room, looking in every closet and under every bed, while the terrified Bertha flew from one apartment to another, until she at length sought refuge in the highest apartment of the eastern turret, that chamber which had witnessed her return from death to her renewed state of strange and horrible existence. She had locked and bolted the door of the study, but what availed these obstacles against a furious mob, animated by their success in gaining the castle, and bent upon destruction and revenge? The door cracked, yielded, was forced open, and several men rushed into the little chamber.

"There she is!—here is the vampire!" cried the foremost, and despite her piercing shrieks and earnest supplications for mercy, the wretched Bertha was dragged out of the study, with her long black hair hanging in wild disorder about her shoulders, and beautiful countenance pale with overpowering terror.

"Mercy, indeed! What mercy can we feel for a vampire?" cried the peasants, and the terrified creature was dragged down the turret stairs by one or two of the boldest, for few would venture to come in contact with the dreaded being.

As they reached the foot of the stairs a volume of smoke rolled along the passage, and the crackling of burning wood told them that some of their companions had set fire to the castle.

"Now what shall we do with the vampire?" said her remorseless captors.

"Throw her into the Rhine!" suggested one.

"Tie her up and shoot her!" said another.

"What will be the use of that?" objected a third. "Nothing but fire or a sharp stake will destroy a vampire. Let us shut her up in the castle, and burn her to ashes!"

"Yes, yes! burn the vampire!" shouted a score of voices.

"No, no!—I say, no!" cried the smith. "Let us carry her to the churchyard, put her in her coffin again, and peg her down with a stake, so that she can never rise again."

The suggestion of the smith was approved of, and the wretched Bertha was half-dragged and half-carried, more dead than alive, towards the village church. The flames were bursting forth from all parts of the castle when the lawless spoilers left it, and a red glow hung over its ancient towers; the work of destruction was rapid, and in a few hours nought but the bare and blackened walls were left standing.

On the destroyers of Ravensburg Castle reaching the churchyard, the almost lifeless form of Bertha Kurtel was dragged to the grave, which had been left open, and flung rudely into the coffin. Then a sharp pointed stake was produced, which had been prepared by the way, and the smith plunged it with all the force of his sinewy arms into the abdomen of the doomed vampire. A piercing shriek burst from her pale lips as the horrible thrust aroused her to consciousness, and as her clothes became dabbed with the crimson stream of life, and the smith lifted his heavy hammer and drove the stake through her quivering body, the transfixed wretch writhed convulsively, and the contortions of her countenance were fearful to behold. Thus impaled in her coffin, and while her limbs yet quivered with the last throes of disso-lution, the earth was replaced and rammed down by the tread of many feet.

But those strange and terrible scenes were not yet ended. A young peas-ant of equal curiosity and boldness, and who had been engaged in the attack upon the castle and the horrible tragedy which followed it, was anxious to know more the strange affair of the skeleton, which had been left in the courtyard where it fell, none of the villagers caring to interfere with so ghastly an object. He therefore stole away a little before midnight, and went towards the castle, where the fire was dying out, though a fiery glow was still reflected from the mouldering embers of beams and rafters. He advanced cautiously through the broken gates of the castle, and shuddered slightly as he perceived the skeleton of the Count of Ravensburg still lying on the pavement of the courtyard.

He determined to watch until daylight, and see what became of the grisly relics of mortality, which a few hours before had been the young and hand-some Count of Ravensburg. The hours passed slowly on from midnight to the dawn of another day, and when the rising sun tinged the eastern sky with crimson and gold, a strange spectacle was witnessed by the solitary watcher in the courtyard of Ravensburg Castle.

The skeleton rose slowly from the pavement, and assumed the form of Count Rodolph, just as he appeared at the moment preceding his transformation on the evening before. A cold perspiration bedewed the brow of the peasant, and his hair stood erect with terror, on witnessing this sudden metamorphosis. The count looked up at the dilapidated walls and towers of his castle, and shuddered violently, and crossing the courtyard, passed through the broken gate.

The peasant then hastened to the village, and reported what he had seen, which was a source of much marvel to the rustic inhabitants. The story of the skeleton count, and his vampire mistress, quickly spread all over Germany, but the villagers were no more molested by vampires, for Bertha Kurtel was securely fixed in her coffin, and no ill effects ensued from her attacks upon Theresa Delmar and little Minna Klaus.

THE WILD WITCH OF THE HEATH; OR, THE DEMON OF THE GLEN

Wizard

As one of the most obscure bloods in this collection, very little is known about its publication or its author. Written anonymously by the self-titled Wizard, *The Wild Witch of the Heath* was published in 1841 by T. White. The most notable fact of this penny is that it was inspired by William Shakespeare's *Macbeth* (1606), as the content utilises similar tropes, styles, and characters, while the tale also begins with Act II, Scene I of the play.

Set in sixteenth-century Scotland, *The Wild Witch* begins with the aggressive and injured Viscount Dunbardon who seeks to destroy his enemy and kidnap and marry his daughter, the innocent Isabella. Finding these objectives out of his control, Dunbardon travels to the heath where he requests assistance from three prophetic, rhyming hags. Once they agree upon the conditions, the three witches summon a demon, an imp, and the Wild Witch to assist in Dunbardon's schemes. With the assistance of the witch and her companions, he achieves the kidnapping of Isabella; however, due to the witch's deceptions, Dunbardon is eventually imprisoned by his enemy. Unbeknownst to Dunbardon, the witch is simultaneously working with the hero, Walter Raven, to save Isabella. This tale ends with the pure Isabella delivered safely back to Raven and Dunbardon destroyed by his underworld companions, while the Wild Witch disappears into the void.

Excessive in its descriptions and secondary and tertiary plots, *The Wild Witch* continues the traditions of penny fiction, thus the entire tale is narrowed down for this chapter. As the consummate monstrous woman of this narrative, the Wild Witch is highlighted as the source of potential danger in the following entry.

I N the beginning of the sixteenth century there dwelt in an ancient and fortified castle, situated on the borders of Scotland, a powerful nobleman, known as the Viscount Dunbardon. He was of a cruel, malevolent, and implacable disposition; pride, avarice, ambition, and revenge were his predominant passions. He had recourse to fraud, hypocrisy, and stratagem, whenever they served his purpose; and had long entertained a secret hate, and sworn a deadly revenge, against the Baron Glendovan, a neighbouring noble, whose eminent virtues, which were in such direct opposition to the principles of his haughty foe, rendered him an object of love to all, save the Viscount, whose hatred had arisen to such a fearful height that he would have shrank from no means, however base, whereby he might have effected his purpose; for beside another powerful motive for wishing the death of the Baron, which will be shown in due course, he had long since given imperative orders to his vassals, that all members of the Baron's establishment found near the castle should be made prisoners; by which means he hoped, by bribery, to obtain an easy access to the castle of his enemy.

The Viscount impatiently awaited the return of the messenger the whole of the following day. Still he came not; and though he dispatched several of his favourite and confidential vassals in the direction of his enemy's castle, they all returned after a fruitless search, on the third night from his departure. The Viscount wrapped himself in his plaid, and arming himself with a sword and a brace of pistols, he sallied forth from the castle no one knew whither. When he had proceeded some distance from the castle, the sky, which was before clear and cloudless, suddenly, turned to a pitchy hue.

Loud and terrible peals of thunder shook the earth from its foundation; the forked and vivid lightning angrily darted in long and repeated flashes from the blackened clouds; and, as he reached the heath, he was startled at beholding several wild and uncouth female figures dancing around a huge blazing fire.

He was at first inclined to suppose this strange phenomenon proceeded from the vapours to which that part of the country was subjected; but a nearer approach convinced him that he was mistaken in his conjectures, for when he had approached to within a few yards of the spot where they were standing, he distinctly heard one of the hags in a dreadful tone howl forth the following:—

> "Behold! the Viscount this way stalks.
> With fearful step the murderer walks:
> The blood of one he late hath shed,
> With deep revenge shall crush his head.
> Prepare at once our art to show—
> Strike to his peace the mortal blow;
> Appear at once, and cross his path—
> His wish to grant, and brave his wrath!"

The Viscount stood for some few moments, apparently bewildered at the appearance of this wild group. At length, after some hesitation, he placed his hand upon his sword, and exclaimed in a fierce tone,

"What wild and withered hell-cats have we here? Minions! what is your purpose here, and at this wild hour? Speak! Why have you thus crossed my path? Say!"

"Our purpose here is to warn thee from that bloody track which thou art now pursuing!" exclaimed one of the sisters; "be warned in time, or, if thou wilt persist, be prepared to meet the dreadful fate which awaits thee."

"Peace!" cried the Viscount, drawing his sword; "cease thy accursed trifling, or by ——, I will strike thee dead where thou now standest!"

"Think you, my lord Viscount," continued the hag, without appearing to notice the threat, "that the murderer can attain his object, and overcome the virtuous, without the aid of supernatural agency? We know thy desires, and would forward them. It is for that purpose that we have crossed thee here. What wouldst thou sacrifice to obtain an easy and complete revenge upon thy enemy!"

"Any, oh, any!" replied the Viscount, impatiently; "but the means, the means?"

"Are here!" cried the hag. "Say. Canst thou nerve well thy heart, and steel thy eyes against the terrors to which they will be exposed? If thou canst do this—"

"I can, and much more!" exclaimed the Viscount; "but delay not longer."

The hags now joined hands, and after dancing and making other hideous gestures around the magic circle, they motioned to him to enter the same; which he did; after which they continued to dance until a low, hollow groan was heard, as if proceeding from the most impenetrable depths of the forest. Next followed a loud hissing noise through the air. At the sound of this they ceased their antics, and immediately the sounds were changed into the most delicious music.

"He comes!" cried one of the sisters; "Peace! our labour's done."

Next his ears were assailed by a dreadful peal of thunder. The next moment a huge ball of fire was seen to hover for an instant in the air; the next, and it fell with a loud crash at the feet of the Viscount who had witnessed these strange appearances in silent amazement but who can describe the terror which seized him, when the fiery ball which rolled at his feet, suddenly, and with a loud crash, opened, and a hideous form presented itself before him, and turning to the hags, it commanded in a dreadful tone, to know why it had been summoned.

"We summoned thee at the request of yonder lord, who requires thy aid," answered one the hags.

Turning to the Viscount, the demonic form before him exclaimed, "Bold mortal, we admire thy bravery, and promise to grant all thou shalt ask. What wouldst thou with us?"

The Viscount appeared to hesitate, probably awed by the dreadful aspect of the demon.

"What!" he cried, with a satanic smile, "art thou affrighted at the mere sight of what thou must one day endure? Well! to satisfy thy humour, behold!" With which words his demoniacal form vanished; and, to the astonishment of the bewildered man, a neat, dapper form, clothed in black velvet, stood before him. "Now, poor mortal, thy request?"

"If, then, thy power can grant so much," replied the Viscount, his confidence somewhat reassured by the transformation; "I would have my inveterate foe, the Baron Glendovan, in my power."

"'Tis granted! What more?"

"I would know the conditions upon which this is granted."

"The exchange of thy immortal soul!"

"Begone! I will not accede to thy hellish proposals."

"Cease thy tauntings, and see that thy wishes are complied with; and for thy soul—know that thou hast already endangered that by this conference with us."

"'Tis false, false as hell and thy fiendish self!" exclaimed the Viscount, in a furious tone. "Thus, thus do I defy thee!"

Saying which, he drew forth both his pistols, and fired them at the object before him. A loud fiendish laugh followed this act, and on looking towards the spot from whence it seemed to proceed, he was horror-stricken to behold the messenger whose arrival he had so long and so patiently awaited, lying dead at his feet. He looked in vain for the mysterious forms by which he had been so lately surrounded. No traces of them remained. When he had in some measures recovered from his surprise, he listed the lifeless body, which was yet warm, from the ground, and to his horror and consternation, discovered that his favourite domestic had been shot through the head. No doubt remained on his mind as to who was the murdered; still how could he have stood before him, and invisible?

"'Tis evident," he exclaimed, after a pause, "their fiendish and demoniac laugh was not without cause. Ah, well! their triumph is complete in this; but now to dispose of my faithful slave."

Saying which, he hastily quitted the spot, and, on reaching the castle, selected four of his confidential vassals, and again departed in the direction of the heath.

On arriving there, his astonishment was increased by the disappearance of the body which, but half an hour since, he had left lifeless upon the ground.

"By Heaven," he exclaimed, in the extremity of his surprise, "I—I could have sworn that it was—near this spot. Ah! Merciful heavens!" he continued, "what dreadful sight is this I see? Down, fiends, down! Why do you glare at *me*? Did—d-i-d I not refuse your aid? See! they advance. Save, oh, save me!" Saying which, he fell, exhausted, into the arms of an attendant.

"Are they gone?" he inquired, on his recovery.

"What? who, my lord?"

"The fiends! the fiends!"

"You are fatigued, my lord," exclaimed the terrified domestic; "we have seen no living being but ourselves."

"'Tis well! then am I content;" cried the Viscount; "it was but the force of heated imagination. But lead me from this hateful, damnable spot."

On reaching the castle, and being conducted to his chamber, he commanded to be left alone; and pacing the floor with hurried steps, he continued long to ponder on the strange incidents of the night.

"Fool that I was to be baffled and affrighted by their devilry!" he at length exclaimed; "had I but threatened the lives of those accursed hags, all might have been well. And yet—those fearful words are still ringing in mine ears, and crowd themselves upon my memory; and—. Can it be possible that there is a world beyond that dark and uncertain period which terminates the mortal career? No! it cannot be; 'tis impossible. Yet—but I grow fearful, and start at imaginary horrors. I will have recourse to that soul-stirring and effectual bane to melancholy—wine, and in its potent fumes beguile the past, and defy the impenetrable future. Come death; come torment, and aught else that will—I defy them all, all. Ha! ha! ha!"

*

On quitting Glendovan Castle, D'Arste slowly retraced his steps through the mountain, still pondering on the sudden and mysterious disappearance of the Viscount and revolving within himself on the most probable means by which he might become acquainted with the cause of his absence; when his attention was attracted by the sudden appearance of the WILD WITCH OF THE HEATH, who stood on the brow of the mountain. Her appearance, which was at all times wild and terrific, was now such as would strike terror into the boldest heart. In her right hand she clutched a huge black snake, which emitted volumes of fire from its mouth; and in her left, which was extended towards D'Arste, she held a long, black wand of ebony, around which was coiled another snake of much smaller dimensions than that which she grasped in her other hand. She was attended by her inseparable companion in mischief, and ugly mis-shapen creature, known as the Red Dwarf.

Though naturally a brave man, Pietro indulged in all the superstitions of the times. And on perceiving these uncouth figures, his first impulse was to fly. A moment's meditation, however, convinced him of the folly of this resolution, and he abandoned it accordingly.

"What seeks the brave Pietro here?" at length exclaimed the Dwarf, in a croaking voice.

"Ah! what seekest thou?" responded the Witch.

"Spirit of the mountains," answered D'Arste, "I would ask of thee where Dunbardon's lord, the brave Viscount of yonder castle, is now concealed?"

"Art thou, whose courage prompts thee to question us thus, prepared to behold all that our art can show thee!" croaked forth the Witch.

"I am, I am!" replied Pietro.

Scarcely had he given utterance to the latter sentence, when the moon, moon which was before bright in the heavens, suddenly changed to a blood-like hue, and all was buried in impenetrable darkness, save when the lightning momentarily illuminated the scene. An awful silence prevailed for some moments, which was at length broken by the Dwarf, who cried in a loud tone, "Behold!"

On looking towards the spot where they had before stood, and from whence the sounds seemed to proceed, he beheld the Witch and the Dwarf still in their former positions, and apparently enveloped in a blue sulphurous flame, the intense heat of which compelled him to recede several paces backwards, which action was hailed by the Dwarf with a loud, derisive laugh.

"Behold!" repeated the Witch, waving her wand.

This command was seconded by a loud and long peal of thunder; and, on again looking in the same direction, what was his astonishment to behold the inanimate form of the Viscount laying weltering in his blood! He involuntarily advanced a few paces.

"Hold!" cried the Dwarf: "rash mortal, whither wouldst thou come!"

"The Viscount!" stammered D'Arste. "Should he remain longer in that condition, his death will be the result. Release him, then, I pray you!"

"You sue in vain," replied the Dwarf. "We have, by our power, shown you in his present condition; if you would release him, repair, at midnight, to the old Abbey ruins: the charm is now broken, and you can remove him to the Castle."

"But," continued Pietro, "you have not revealed to me how he—"

"Seek to know no more," interrupted the Dwarf, "or dread the consequences. At midnight, we meet again!"

A loud hissing noise followed this speech; and both the Witch and her companion disappeared from his astonished gaze. He advanced to the spot, where, a moment before, the mystic pair had stood, and which, as we have before stated, was enveloped in flames; but, on examining the foliage by which the spot was surrounded, could not discover even the smallest traces of the effects of the devouring element. He remained for some time upon the spot buried in the gloomy depths of meditation. Arousing himself at length from his reverie, he hastened towards Dunbardon Castle, where he remained until an hour before midnight, at which time he, in company with Angus, the late Governor of the castle, departed, in the direction mentioned by the Dwarf, for the discovery of the Viscount. On arriving at the ruins, D'Arste involuntarily came to a halt.

"Why tarry here?" inquired Angus; "this is not the spot you mentioned as being the place where the Viscount was to be found. Perhaps the time we are wasting here may be precious, and necessary for his recovery. Are you not assured of the place?"

"I am," answered Pietro. "Come on!"

Saying which, they entered the venerable pile, where they discovered the Viscount, stretched upon the ground, apparently lifeless. His sword was still in his right hand, and seemed to be held in the convulsive gripe of death. On his breast was seated the Dwarf, whose horrible and fiendish grin contrasted fearfully with the scene of death and devastation by which all were surrounded.

"Merciful Powers!" exclaimed Angus, "his lordship is dead."

"He is," replied the Dwarf: "approach, and convince thyself."

Angus did so; and clasping the hand of the Viscount, instantly let it fall to the ground, with a cry of horror. He was cold and insensible as the marble tomb. The fearful evidences of decomposition were already visible upon his rigid features. The Dwarf shrugged in his shoulders on beholding this; and he instantly, and in a terrific tone, yelled forth the following words:—

"'Tis time,'tis time the slaves were here,
Spirit of Wrong! appear, appear!"

Scarcely had he spoken these words, when the Witch appeared before them. Her aspect was, if possible, more terrible than before. The same blue, sulphurous flame surrounded her; the same disgusting reptiles entwined her arms. On beholding this unsightly object, Angus started with affright, and would have darted from the spot, had not D'Arste seized him by the arm.

"Whither would ye fly?" he exclaimed. "Shrink not from this single terror. What would ye have done, had ye beheld what I have this day encountered—horrors, the bare mention of which would freeze the current of thy life's blood, harrow up thy soul, and chill life's energy? To thy coward heart, 'twould have been death, worse than death!"

"What would ye with me?" yelled forth the Witch.

"They would witness the reanimation of yonder mass of filth and cor-ruption," replied the Dwarf. "'Twas by my commands they came hither. And—"

"Shall be gratified," interrupted the Witch. "What, ho! Cabello! Appear, appear!"

A tremendous crash of thunder followed this command. Next, was heard loud deafening sounds, which appeared to proceed from a whole forest of wild animals. A moment, and this cry was changed to the most exquisite music. A loud noise succeeded this, and suddenly the earth opened near to where the Viscount lay; and a fiendish monster issued from the aperture. The aspect of this fiend, who was enveloped in flames, was so horrible, that it struck terror even to the marble heart of D'Arste. In its right hand was an enormous trident, which, like itself, appeared to be composed of one dense mass of fire; its body, which was covered with scales, was of a blood-red hue; and its whole aspect was that of the Arch Fiend himself.

"What would ye?" he exclaimed, addressing the Dwarf.

"Bring to life this mortal here!"

"His course must and shall continue longer!"

A low hollow groan was now heard.

"It shall be done!" cried the Fiend.

"Never!" exclaimed an unknown voice.

"Ha!" roared the Demon, "who dares refuse when I say 'Aye!'?"

"Behold!" answered the same voice.

All turned at the sound—all beheld a figure armed with a spear, and clothed in complete armour.

On perceiving this phenomenon, the Demon gave utterance to a wild derisive laugh, which was echoed by the Dwarf.

"So!" he exclaimed, "thou wouldst interrupt us. What, ho! Rhadamanthus, Mephistophiles, Hellwine, appear!"

Scarcely had he concluded this, when the earth again opened, and the three monsters above-named appeared, and with them a whole legion of hellish tormentors, each of whom carried his own peculiar instrument of torture, and instinctively commenced testing the quality of their merciless engines upon the persons of the already trembling Angus and D'Arste, who speedily acknowledged the favour by roaring most lustily for help and mercy. Not heeding either of these, however, they still continued to enjoy the pastime which evidently, by their demoniac grins, afforded them much satisfaction, until their victims fell to the earth, writhing beneath their tortures; and then only did their fiend-master command them to desist.

"'Tis yonder slave," he exclaimed, pointing to the phantom, "who dares to rise in disobedience, and would thwart my plans. To your tender care I confine him. Hence with him!"

The spirits brandished their weapons, and advanced towards the figure. Instantly the armour vanished, and a skeleton form appeared, clothed in white. In its right hand it held a small ebony crucifix, which it extended towards the demons; at the sight of which they all shrank back with terror. Slowly retracing its steps towards the entrance of the ruins, it disappeared from the view of all.

"He has repented of his interference, and quitted our presence, in the abject fear of what may follow," exclaimed the first of the demoniac group. "Shall we delay our project! No!"

Saying which, he approached the spot where lay the prostrate and lifeless form of the Viscount; seized his right hand; muttered a few cabalistic words, and the Viscount, obedient to his power, slowly raised his head.

"Away!" shouted the Witch.

All immediately disappeared; and Angus, D'Arste, the Witch, and Dwarf alone remained.

"What horrible phantoms are these?" gasped the Viscount, on his first beholding the Dwarf and the Witch.

"I know not," stammered D'Arste; "but I believe they are—"

"Thy friends!" screeched the Witch.

"'Tis false!" faintly ejaculated the Viscount; "I know ye now—cheating, cozening fiends!"

"Thy words savour of insult," cried the Witch; "and did we reward thee rightly, we should strike thee dead to the earth; but we will punish thee thus."

And waving her wand thrice over his head, the Viscount started to his feet, perfectly recovered from the effects of his wound.

"Our work is done!" exclaimed the Witch, turning to the Dwarf; "we'll now away!"

"Hold!" cried the Viscount; "tell me—for by thy power thou should'st know—how can I obtain the means of gratifying any wish I may have, without endangering my immortal soul?"

"Meet us on the Heath at the midnight hour of the morrow!" yelled the Dwarf; "and thou shalt know more!"

"I would know all now, here upon this spot!" cried the Viscount, fiercely.

"Thou cannot—shalt not know!" screamed forth the Witch; "our power denies thee that."

"Then die!" shouted he, aiming a blow with his sword.

A loud supernatural laugh followed this action, and, on looking round to discover who had given utterance to the same, he was petrified at the spectacle which presented itself to his astonished gaze. He beheld the Witch and her companion descending into the bowels of the earth, encircled by a large body of fire. Wiping the sweat from his brow, the Viscount commanded D'Arste and Angus to follow him. They quitted the ruins and soon arrived at Dunbardon Castle.

The late Viscount, obeying the instructions of Cabello, now sprang upon the couch whereon she lay, and grasping the golden tassel that had been pointed out, an opening in the floor appeared, and the couch gradually sank down through a trap, leaving the room undisturbed in which it had so lately been, save that neither the Lady Isabella nor the bed on which she reposed were any longer visible.

The piercing shriek that ran through the household when Isabella disappeared, now aroused the whole of the domestics. Bursting into the room, no language can express their surprise when it was found that neither their mistress nor the supposed monk were in the apartment. Walter rushing in, soon participated in the excitement that prevailed, and all was bustle and confusion.

Walter did not hesitate long before he resolved in his mind the course he should adopt. Feeling confident that supernatural powers were at work to counteract his designs, he sought aid from the same source; the rest of the servants with trembling looks and pallid faces, awaited their master's bidding, but as Walter moved not, nor uttered a syllable that might be construed into an order for their departure in search of the abducted bride, they remained perfectly stationary.

It was a fine clear night; the moon flung forth its silvery light over tower and tree, buttress, and battlement, making the sky as clear and light as though the fair Cynthia had stolen more than her usual share of her brother Phoebus's rays, when Walter Raven, girding his cloak more closely around him, for the air was chilly, pursued his path from Dunbardon Castle to the abode of the Wild Witch.

The road, as we have already mentioned, lay through a rugged defile, flanked on either side by long lines of rock, looming out against the horizon in fearful grandeur. He had proceeded thus far, when the usual chant of the Wild Witch was heard welcoming Raven to her abode.

> "Welcome! welcome! noble youth,
> Rich alike in worth and truth;
> I—the Witch—will grant thee all
> Thou dost wish performed, and call
> On all my imps to aid thy cause,
> As guided by fair Virtue's laws.
> I will now ensure thy life
> Against thy hated rival's strife,
> And soon in crushing him essay
> To gain myself triumphant sway.

Come! then, to my wild abode,
And heed not what may check thy road,
Well knowing this, I am your friend,
And that your troubles soon will end;
Come, then, and triumph will be mine,
Whilst Isabelle again is thine."

As these words died away on the breeze, Raven paused, and saw that he had now approached within a few yards of the Witch's abode. A bright blue light, that danced on before him, showed plainly that his visit was not repugnant to the mysterious woman who presided over the place, and soon after the Witch herself appeared, and inquired the reason of his arrival.

Her demeanour was subdued and gentle, and her manner that of one who could at different times, and under different impulses, enact the part of termagant or Griselda as the occasion warranted. She held in her hand the snake-entwined rod by which her enchantments were performed, and at the distance of about three feet from her appeared the Dwarf, whose social qualifications have been already introduced to the reader. He was perched upon a small rise or hillock, on which not a blade of grass was seen to grow, all vegetation being withered by the scorching propensities of those who dwelt in the vicinity.

"I know thine errand Walter," said the Witch, as she perceived him about to answer her first inquiry.

"Indeed!" responded Walter, "then thou can'st find the means doubtless of relieving me from my difficulties."

"That depends upon the concurrence of another being."

"And he is—"

"A tyrant more powerful than I, though executing that power with the worst designs. His name is Cabello, and he is the protective genius of Dunbardon, whom he has secured as his victim, and who has bartered to him his soul itself, for the cravings of ambition."

"I would but know," said Walter, "where my bride, the Lady Isabella is imprisoned, so that I might release her from the captivity in which, as I conjecture, she has been placed by the supernatural means, at the command of the hated Alexander."

"The knowledge thereof would be but of little value," responded the Witch, "did I not give thee the means to overcome the difficulties what you will have to encounter."

"And wilt thou do so?"

"I will!" pursued the other, "what Ho! my faithful Dwarf, I require thy services."

As these words reached the resting place of her dwarfish familiar, his ears pricked up, and his whole countenance underwent an animated change. He rose, and seeming conscious for what purpose he had been summoned, rolled over to the foot of his mistress, prepared to obey her behests.

Striking her rod against the earth, a magic cauldron now rose, boiling with a sulphurous flame that almost stifled Walter, as he watched with amazement its sudden appearance from the earth. Into this the Dwarf poured from a crucible which rose before him various metals in a state of fusion, and stirring up the metallic mixture with her rod, a helmet was soon seen moulded to her hand.

"Take," cried the Witch, "this Magic Casque; it will confer on you the power of invulnerability, sword and dagger will fall as lightly upon thy frame as though the aggressor stabbed the viewless air, or yielding water. By its means you can obtain instant power over those who would thwart your plans of vengeance."

"And where is Isabella imprisoned?"

"In the dungeon beneath Dunbardon Castle."

"And how to obtain admission?" inquired Walter.

"Listen. The entrance is guarded by an invisible spirit, whose power is bounded, but to whom is confided the care of the cell. This talisman," continued the Witch, presenting Raven with a glowing ruby set in pure gold, "will procure you instant ingress to the vault; at its touch the barred doors will immediately fly open, and revolving on its hinges will disclose the form of her whom thou hast called thy bride. Be vigilant, and conquer."

"I will," answered Walter, "and thank thee, too; how can I return this kindness?"

"By being ready when I bid thee to execute my wishes."

"So that they are not at variance with the dictates of my conscience, I will," responded Raven.

"I ask for no more," exclaimed the Witch. "When I have need of thy services, I will take such means as will ensure them; till then, farewell. Morning is breaking, and its ruddy streak warns me that my presence is required elsewhere. Once more, farewell!"

And before Walter had time to return the compliment, the Witch had struck her rod upon the earth; a chasm had opened at her feet, and she, together with the Dwarf, and the strange implements they had used in their incantation, had disappeared, and left no visible trace upon the surface of their former existence.

Walter, pleased, yet horrified with the scenes they had witnessed, and their result, began to turn his footsteps back to the castle, holding the Casque or Helmet firmly grasped in his hand, as a proof that all he had just heard was no delusion. Whilst Walter is thus spell-bound with amazement and expectation, turn we our attention to Dunbardon, whom we left a few pages back sinking with the Lady Isabella, through the chasm that had so suddenly appeared.

Dunbardon, still retaining a firm grasp of the magic tassel, heeded not the swoon of his fair companion of his flight. Downwards they sank through a succession of chambers, until the couch, resting on the surface of the stone floor of a dungeon, ceased to continue its descent. Dunbardon, perceiving now that his journey was concluded, sprang forth, and bearing the senseless girl in his arms, strode towards a barred door that obstructed his view before him.

He now touched a spring on the wall, the existence of which the Demon had rendered familiar to him, and the bed and its appurtenances vibrated a moment, and then, by a mechanical contrivance, the trap rose, and gradually ascended, till the bed appeared in the same position that it formerly occupied in the chamber, with but this difference, that the Lady Isabella, the former beauteous occupant, no longer pressed the pillow.

We have said that Dunbardon's progress was obstructed by a door, which, thickly studded by huge bars of iron, seemed to oppose all his attempts at obtaining admission, but we have to add that Cabello had, by imparting sundry cabalistic words to Dunbardon, prevented any unpleasantness of the sort occurring.

It was now the time when these words were to be called into requisition, and Alexander, resting his burden on his left arm, prepared to give them utterance.

"*Clash ma giel tu releddyl,*" cried the soul-lost Dunbardon; and as these words were uttered, the ponderous portals yielded to the awful words, and revolving on their cumbrous hinges, disclosed a narrow but lofty dungeon, dimly lighted by a small taper lamp that was suspended from the roof, that rose in solemn darkness above the surface of the cell.

The abductor bore the helpless maiden in his arms into the vault which we have described, and placing her with some violence on the ground, she gradually recovered by the shock from her swoon.

"Where am I?" she faintly articulated, as unclosing her pale blue eyes they rested on the person of the late Viscount.

"Here where you will be well provided for," responded that person, in tones as soft as the natural gruffness of his voice would permit; "I love you, Lady Isabella; and, trust me, there are few more constant or devoted in their attachments than Dunbardon."

"*Love,*" almost shrieked the affrighted girl, "and from you, the murderer— the crime-ridden Dunbardon!"

"Aye!" thundered forth the other, "Dunbardon, the proud—the haughty, if you will, but still the powerful Dunbardon—master of thy person—the controller of thy destiny—the avenger of my own wrongs—and the punisher of thy husband's treachery!"

"Are there no lightnings yet in heaven to strike the traducer to the earth?" exclaimed the fair Isabella; "or has that great Power whose might protects the innocent permitted the existence of a wretch like this to wander unscathed through this beautiful world Heaven has created, and to crush the helpless whilst he spares the guilty."

"Peace, raving fool!" roared the late Viscount.

"I will not cease to upbraid you with the wrongs you have committed till this form, weak though it be, falls stricken to the earth. Aye, 'tis well," continued she, seeing Dunbardon involuntarily grasp the hilt of his sword, "strike a woman, 'twill be in unison with the test of thy noble deeds; nay, I care not for thy threats and menaces; the time will soon arrive when heaven will punish thy misdeeds—when providence will turn against yourself the dagger raised to smite another—when thy repentance may be atoned and received, and then thou wilt ponder with sorrow on my words, and reflect on the injuries thou hast done mankind."

"Silence, again, I say, thou taunting slave," pursued Dunbardon, "or I will level thee with the earth, woman though thou art, from which you sprung."

"Nay, frown on, proud and haughty chieftain, but my latest breath shall be spent in proclaiming thy crimes aloud to the whole world, and calling for vengeance on thy devoted head."

"Death and furies!" screamed the infuriated Alexander, "must I crouch before a menial like thyself? must I bow to the mandates of a woman, and seek for no other confessional than that she would afford me? Pshaw! out on't; I will have no more of this fanaticism here, or this shall—" and the withdrawal of a short *kidah*, or stiletto, from his breast, filled up the pause with an action of fearful import.

The Lady Isabella seemed to disregard, however, all attempts to concil-iate her, either by threats or remonstrances. She continued to pour out her vituperations with unabated force, and ceased not until languor compelled her to obtain repose. Dunbardon, seeing this, left her to recover on the stone floor of the dungeon, and slamming to the door, which closed with a spring, returned to the lobby to see if he could discover his partner in crime, D'Arste.

He wandered stealthily on amid the labyrinthine passages of the castle walls, and saw no light, and heard no footstep which might serve to guide

him in the direction which his former companion had taken. At this junc-
ture, whilst he was bewildered with the different thoughts that crowded
round his confused brain, he heard the sound of voices break upon his ear,
and listening anxiously, heard the following dialogue:—

"Pooh! Gerald, I care not for thy surmise," cried one, "thou art in the
wrong, most assuredly."

"Indeed!"

"Aye, indeed! he has gone, vanished, evaporated, if you will, and these
eyes saw him disappear."

"Nonsense, man! you were dreaming, or had been drinking too deeply
when you saw this."

"Drunk I might have been, but it was with horror; and dreaming I might
be, but it must have been with fright. I tell thee the mysterious monk has
gone, shaven crown, gaberdine, and all."

"And with thy wits, too, good Oswald, or my place as steward of the
buttery goes for nought. Gone, forsooth. Stone floors are not marvellously
renowned for pitfalls."

The late Viscount stopped to hear no more, but proceeded onwards with
a firmer step and sterner aspect, assured, as the overhearing of the above
dialogue enabled him to feel, that the mysterious monk, whose brief process
of evaporation had occupied so fully the attention of the speakers, was no
other than D'Arste himself.

Confident of this, and likewise believing that Pietro had only left the hall
to meet with him, his mind became easy upon that score, and hearing the
clock of the old turret toll the hour by three sonorous strokes, he found that
he had already wasted fruitlessly four hours in the pursuit of D'Arste, and
with that discovery he determined to return without delay to the cell where
the Lady Isabella had been imprisoned during the night.

Here for awhile we leave him, and returning to Walter, take up the
thread of the narrative that point when, leaving the Witch with the Magic
Helmet in his possession, he was about retracing his steps to the castle. The
night, which had been hitherto one vast cloudless expanse of azure, thickly

studded with myriads of stars that resembled so many golden specks cast into the abyss of space, now became murky and overcast. Dense clouds weighed down the atmosphere in every direction, and a heavy mist or fog seemed gradually rising from the lochs to meet it. Flakes of fire gleamed at intervals from the marshes by which he was on every side surrounded, and ever and anon huge balls of flame, each more vivid than the last, darted athwart his path, flashing light upon every object, and leaving a glistening train of sparks behind to mark their track. Still he pursued his way, unheeding the wrathful omens that thus crossed him, and confident in the uprightness of his cause, and the honesty of purpose by which he was guided, he slacked not his pace until the crumbling battlements of Dunbardon Castle frowned in all their awful and gigantic majesty before him.

On reaching the eastern postern he was challenged by the sentinel, but as he gave the pass-word, and touched by accident the soldier's halberd with the magic Helmet which he carried in his hand, he was astounded to perceive that by the touch the lance and halberd in the sentinel's hand was shivered into a hundred fragments.

Without pausing to dwell upon the strange nature of circumstance like this, he hurried onwards, and reaching the corridor that led to the dungeons below, he earnestly bent his steps to the spot where the Wild Witch had informed him the Lady Isabella had been incarcerated.

After traversing the numerous intricate passages that led to the vaults, he at last arrived at one which he conjectured was the place of which he was in search. The doors were secured by massive bars of iron in triplets, that seemed to present insurmountable obstacles to his attempts at entrance, but remembering that this cell had been originally contrived by a magician, who, learned in the law of the Egyptians, had applied the knowledge of the magi to the security of this place in a manner that would have reflected the highest credit ever on the wonder-executing Zoroaster himself, he ceased to marvel at the apparent impenetrability of the portal, and prepared himself fully to meet with other obstacles, much more calculated to affright him in the progress, and deter him from the execution, of the task which had been imposed upon him.

Nor in this particular was he at all deceived, as succeeding events quickly proved. A shriek from Isabella gathered his wandering senses to their seat, and restored him once again to himself. He called aloud upon her name; she responded; and now, feeling confident that he was correct in his suppositions, and that this was the place whither she had been conveyed, he drew his sword, placed the Helmet on his head, and, prepared to encounter every difficulty, in the anxious wish to regain his soul's idol, he commenced wrenching the sturdy bars that creaked in their rusty sockets before his eyes.

No sooner had he commenced his operations in this manner, than a small, diminutive figure, from two to three feet high, suddenly rose from the earth to oppose his passage. He was apparelled in complete armour, and accoutered in all the majesty of an armed warrior. His shield shone like burnished gold, and his sword gleamed like lightning as he released it from the silver scabbard by which it had been confined. His features were concealed by a huge visor, that terminated in an embossed point above, and a scrolled crescent beneath. His demeanour, notwithstanding his disadvantageous size, was of a fiery and haughty nature, and from the gentle movement of the head it seemed that the Demon Dwarf was taking a complete, but contemptuous survey of the party before him.

Such was he whom Walter had to encounter, and his quick eye had scarcely been able to note the particulars we have above given, ere the figure commenced a furious onslaught.

The blows showered upon the crest of the Dwarf fell like rain, but possessed, in addition to the attribute of rapid succession, that of harming not. Thrusts were parried upon both sides with vigilance and skill; but the combat remained not long undecided. A blow from the Dwarf fell upon the head of Raven; he yielded to the force, and sank upon one knee, but the invulnerable Helmet had done its work, and the sword of the dwarfed Demon splintered into a thousand fragments, its owner falling, at the same time, through the earth, and vanishing from sight.

Walter for an instant stood aghast at the wonderful result of the Witch's present, but soon recovering his equanimity he laboured hard to force the passage which had been so furiously disputed.

Whilst thus engaged, huge toads with bloated bodies, and eyes like two blazing coals protruding from their heads, stared at him from beneath, jerking their envenomed sweat, over his flesh, and raising on the fall of each drop a burning blister. Still Walter worked unceasing to complete his task.

Apes of a strange and uncouth shape, with forms of unnatural dimension, now sat gibing and gibbering at him from every dark recess. Large black cats, of a size equal to a mastiff, purred against him with their bristled backs, causing the same acute pain as if each hair had been a packing-needle. Faces detached from bodies, and headless forms, endeavoured to divert him from his purpose, but, with the skilful exercise of his sword, he soon put them all to flight.

Additional phantoms, each more hideous than the other, appeared now like visions of faces that he had seen before, in the stone walls that confronted him. Faces whom he had seen, loved, and adored, faces which had gazed up to him with veneration, and valued as dearly as his own life, now faces which—but their glances were but the glances of the moment, another moment, and they changed to features expressing strong, implacable hatred.

These, however, speedily disappeared in their turn, and now his only difficulty was to break open the door.

As he was pondering upon the means by which this could be accomplished, he heard a low plaintive voice proceeding from some dark aperture around him, which, though at first indistinct, gradually grew louder, and merging into that well-known voice of the Wild Witch of the Heath, resolved itself into the following words;

> "Walter Raven! look around,
> Know you tread on magic ground.
> That door your progress will oppose
> Until you've conquered all your foes.

That you may do this without fail,
And render fruitless bar and nail,
This talisman—a magic ring—
Will instant aid and succour bring,
But turn it to the stony walls,
And in that instant each one falls,
Owning in their gloomiest hour,
That even here THE WITCH has power."

No sooner had these airy syllables died away into the air whence they had sprung, than Raven feeling a slight pressure to which he had previously been a stranger on the middle finger of his right hand, looked down and discovered that that finger was clasped by a ring. The golden circlet was most exquisitely fashioned; being as brilliant and elaborate in the beautiful tracery by which the rim was distinguished, as if that moment it had left the hands of some fairy jeweller; a circumstance that Walter considered within himself by no means an improbable one.

In an enamelled border of the most perfect chysolites, was set a ruby of such a fiery lustre, that its reflection was visible in a bright red hue, for some yards round the place where he stood. No sooner had he turned the ruby towards the barred portals, than at that instant they vanished with a loud crash, leaving, however, one behind, still more durable, and apparently still more obdurate. This notwithstanding, speedily followed in the wake of the other, and left Raven a clear and unobstructed passage into the cell. Isabella, roused by the tumult, had sprung forth to meet him; tears of gratitude for her deliverance trickled down her pallid cheek in pearly drops. She thanked him with the tribute of a moistened eye and a bloodless lip; fear had subdued all her faculties, and now the reflux of joy—the flowing in once more of the tide of happiness—was too much for her to withstand. She sank to the earth, oppressed now as much with joy as she had been during her imprisonment bowed down with the weight of sorrow. Walter, whose presence of mind nought could destroy, and nothing lessen, was now reminded, by the approach of footsteps still distant though ringing loudly upon the stone pavement of the dungeon, that someone was approaching, whose power might be exerted anew for their captivity. Not knowing the passage that would secure them a safe retreat to another portion of the castle, Walter began to feel vexed that after so much had been accomplished there still remained so much to be done. In this perplexity he had recourse to the ring. Turning the stone towards the south, and using a little gentle friction, he was surprised to see appear before him the Witch, accompanied by her familiar, the subtle Dwarf.

"What wouldst thou?" exclaimed the Witch, in as bland a tone as the natural roughness of her voice permitted; "are not thine enemies yet o'ercome? are not thy wishes accomplished?"

"Thanks to thee, my kind protectress, they are," responded Raven; "but the Lady Isabella—she who now reclines senseless in my arms—is inadequate to the perils and anxiety of a return to the other portion of the castle by the subterraneous corridors that lead thither, to say nothing of the dangers that seem likely to beset us on the path; may I request again thine aid to free us from this dilemma?"

"Enough! 'tis granted," said the other; "throw thy Magic Helmet on the ground."

This was done.

The Witch continued:—

"Spirits of night! obey my power,
Aid me in this lonely hour.
Take this Magic Helmet here,
And let a car instead appear."

Waving her wand over the Cabalistic Casque, she took a small paper packet from her bosom, and sprinkling upon it a fine red powder, which immediately, upon contact with the ground, burst into a bright red flame, a dense vapour arose, and soon afterwards the Helmet began to increase in size, and change its shape, until it had assumed the outward appearance of a car, or small chariot, at each corner of which a bright blue lambent flame was burning.

"Now," said the Witch, "step within this flying vehicle; in another instant you will reach your own chamber."

Raven did as he was directed, and still bearing the senseless Isabella in his arms, he nerved himself for what might follow. The Witch struck the ground with her stick, and the car at that instant ascended.

The floor seemed to sink beneath them; the ceiling parted to admit their entry, and soon after closed when they had passed it; and encircled as they were by the vapour arising from the flames, it seemed as if they were cleaving on eagles' wings through the fields of space.

They rose still upwards, till on gazing round, Raven saw that he was once more secure in his own chamber. Here they stopped, and Walter, placing the beauteous form, yet clasped in his arms, on the couch before him, he turned around to look upon the car, and found it had disappeared. In its place, however, appeared the Dwarf.

"Hast thou anything further to require of myself or my mistress?" inquired the mannikin.

"Nothing!" answered Raven, "save that thou wilt inform me of Dunbardon's designs against me and this castle."

"Listen!" cried the Dwarf; and at that moment a wild, unearthly strain broke upon his ear, which took the form of words:—

> "Dunbardon, bent on war and strife,
> Would take your own and consort's life,
> But Providence protects you both,
> And disregards the tyrant's oath.
> Within that dungeon whence you came
> Will he be 'prisoned just the same;
> A punishment awaits him there
> More dire, more dread, than man can bear.

His sad existence then will cease,
And yours will straight begin in peace.
So now farewell! When aid is wanted,
But turn the ring—that aid is granted."

Walter turned round to acknowledge his gratitude for the protection thus afforded him, but the sound had ceased, and the Dwarf had disappeared.

The Lady Isabella, with Walter Raven, after a tour around the southern parts of Europe, returned to Scotland with her health much improved from the change, and Glendovan and Strathallan inviting them to make the Hall their temporary residence, they passed the remainder of their days in the enjoyment of love and tranquillity.

There is but one more whom it behoves us to mention, and though no longer influencing mortals, to this day it is said her appearance is common in the Highlands. On the shafts of lightning, on the wings of the wind, on the forked glare of the thunderbolt, may be still seen, as the harbinger and pilot of the coming storm,

THE WILD WITCH OF THE HEATH.

THE FEMALE BLUEBEARD: OR, THE ADVENTURER

Eugène Sue

Written by the popular novelist Marie-Joseph "Eugène" Sue (1804–1857), this narrative, derived from the folkloric Bluebeard, was originally a French text, titled *L'Aventurier ou la Barbe-bleue* before it was translated into the English *The Female Bluebeard*. Published by W. Strange in 1845, this text was available as both a large 306-page single volume or as a twenty-part serial magazine segment.

This tale of *La Barbe-bleue*, or the Female Bluebeard, tells the story of woman who uses an evil and violent façade to protect her royal husband. Like her namesake, the notorious Female Bluebeard, who is only known as Angelina to her close confidants, is rumoured to have murdered her past three husbands in cold blood. In her state of supposed widowhood, Angelina is believed to have intimate relationships with three unlikely suitors: Youmaale, a Carib cannibal; Hurricane, a pirate captain; and Arrache'lâme, the boucanier. Hearing such tales of the Female Bluebeard's grandiosity, wealth, and status, the impulsive Chevalier de Croustillac vows that his devotion, appearance, and ability to raise incapable women to their expected domestic status will win her heart and hand in marriage. During his interaction with Angelina and her numerous companions, Croustillac is teased and taunted with tales of her deviance and lechery. Although it is later disclosed that the Female Bluebeard's behaviour is that of a ruse to protect her husband's true identity, the initial chapters of this penny demonstrate the social belief that women have the potential for true monstrosity and danger towards the domestic structure.

Similar to other penny narratives, Sue's tale is filled with secondary plots, superfluous details, and an epilogue that considerably extends the length of the overall text. The following excerpt, then, is edited to offer a concise focus on the introduction of *La Barbe-bleue* and her initial interactions with Croustillac that exhibit her as the monstrous Gothic woman.

THE brilliant and pure moon diffused a light almost equal to that of the European sun, and allowed visitors to that neighbourhood to distinguish perfectly, at the summit of a lofty rock, surrounded by wood on all sides, a habitation built with bricks, and of a strange and novel style of architecture.

It could only be reached by a narrow path, forming a kind of special line round a cone. This path was bordered on one side by almost perpendicular masses of granite, on the other by a precipice, of which, even during the clearest day, the bottom was not to be seen. The way was worthy of the reputation of the inhabitant.

This dangerous path terminated on a platform crossed by a wall of thin but wide bricks; itself very thick, and pierced with loopholes.

Behind this apology for a glacis rose the walls of the *enceinte* of the habitation, into which one entered by a very low oaken door.

This door communicated with a vast square court, which contained the outhouses and other domestic offices. This court once crossed, a vaulted passage was reached which led to the very sanctuary itself; the pavilion occupied by La Barbe-bleue.

The house rose on the opposite slope to that by which you ascended to the pinnacle of the mount.

This slope, much less rapid, and divided into several terraces and natural ridges, was composed of five or six immense steps, which on all sides terminated in tremendous precipices.

By a phenomenon rather frequent in volcanized islands, a pond, about two acres in extent, occupied that of the space of one of the upper steps.

The water was limpid and pure, and the house of La Barbe-bleue was only separated from this little lake by a narrow strip of sandy soil, as smooth and apparently as polished as silver, beneath the blue tint of the moon.

The house was composed of only one storey. At the first aspect, it appeared constructed only of the bark of trees; its bamboo roof, at an angle of forty-five degrees, projected five or six feet beyond the outer wall, leaning against the trunks of palm-trees thrust into the ground, and forming a species of gallery or verandah round the house.

A little above the level of the lake, a lawn of turf came down, swelling in a gentle bosom-like slope, as fresh and as sweetly green as the most beautiful of English meadows; this unexampled rarity for the West Indies, was owing to the invisible but still perceptible irrigation which diffused themselves on all sides from the pond, and spread around this little park a delicious freshness.

To this lawn, ornamented here and there by pots of equinoctial flowers, succeeded a garden composed of massive trees of various rare varieties; the slope was in part so rapid that their stem was not to be seen, but only their summits dotted with the most varied and elegant tints; then, again, after the trees, came a lower step, a vast wood of orange and citron trees, heavy under the weight of flowers and fruits. This seen from aloft appeared a carpet of odoriferous snow, sprinkled with golden globules.

In the extreme verge of the horizon of the moment, the lofty trunks of bananas and cocoa-nut trees formed a prodigious hedge, and crowned the precipice, at the bottom of which terminated the subterranean passage.

Let us now enter one of the most private apartments of the mansion, and, we shall there find a young woman, from twenty to three-and-twenty years of age; with, however, features so infantile, a form so *mignone*, a freshness so juvenile, that one would hardly suppose her sixteen.

Dressed in a muslin tunic with wide sleeves, she is half reclined on a sofa of Indian stuff, brown, with flowers of gold, her forehead leans upon her hand, which half disappears in a forest of heavy curls of hair, of the most perfect auburn colour. This young woman is *coiffée* almost *a la Titus*; a mass of silky rings fell in profusion over her neck and snowy shoulders, and framed her delicious little finger—round, firm, and rosy of that of a lovely child.

A large volume, bound in red morocco, placed on the edge of the divan, where she was seated, is open before her.

The young woman read with attention by the light of three perfumed candles, supported by a silver-gilt candelabra, of which the chasing, exquisite and elegant, surrounded the royal arms of Great Britain, enamelled and raised in relief.

The eyelashes of the pretty reader were so long, that, projecting, they cast a slight shade on her cheeks, in which were cradled two dimples, most exquisitely graceful; her nose was straight and delicate, her purple mouth was smaller than her fine blue eyes, and her physiognomy was characterised by a ravishing expression of innocence and candour.

From the lower part of her tunic of fine muslin, peeped out two little Cinderella feet, covered by white silk stockings, and Moorish slippers of cherry-coloured satin, flowered with silver, so small that one could have hidden them both in the hollow of one's hand.

The position of this young woman left the imagination to divine the most exquisite, moulded limbs, though her figure was small.

Thanks to the width of her sleeve, which had fallen back, a spectator could have gazed upon an arm—round, polished as ivory, and marked near the elbow by a charming little dimple. The hand which turned over the book is worthy of the arm, and her long nails had all the shining brightness of the agate. The ends of her fingers were tinted by so lively a scarlet, that one would have supposed them coloured by Indian *henné*.

The *ensemble* of this delicious creature recalled the ideal beauty of classic Psyche, adorable realisation of that fugitive moment of perfect beauty, which passes with the first flower of youth. Certain organisations, however, preserve this juvenile primitiveness; and as we have said, though at most not more than three and twenty, La Barbe-bleue was one of those privileged creatures.

For this was the so much talked of and redoubtable Female Bluebeard! We shall no longer, therefore, hide from the reader the name of this lovely inhabitant of the Devil's Mount; and we will further add, that she was called Angelina! Alas! this celestial name, this candid physiognomy, was it not strangely in opposition to the diabolical reputation enjoyed by this young widow of three husbands, and who had living as many lovers as she had husbands?

The progress of events will allow us to condemn or acquit La Barbe-bleue. At a slight noise which she heard in the neighbouring room, Angelina raised her head, like a gazelle on the watch; she immediately rose sitting on the sofa, and pushed back her heavy curls from her ivory brow.

At the moment she rose, crying, "It is him," a man raised the tapestry, and was about to enter the room.

Iron catches not more quickly at the loadstone, than did Angelina run to meet the newcomer. She threw herself into his arms, pressed him to herself with a sort of tender fancy, covered him with caresses, and passionate kisses, crying with joy:—

"My tender friend, my good Jacques."

This first effusion of joy over, the newcomer caught Angelina in his arms, as one would take a child, and regained the sofa with his precious burthen.

Then Angelina seated herself on one of Jacques' knees, took one of his hands in hers, put her pretty white arm round his neck, drew him towards her, and gazed upon him fondly and eagerly.

Alas!—alas! the gossips of Martinique, had they really at bottom truth in their statements, with regard to the morality of La Barbe-bleue?

The man whom she welcomed with this ardent familiarity had copper skin; he was tall and stalwart, elegant and robust; his very agreeable features had a forest of jet-black hair that surrounded his forehead; his eyes were large, and of a velvet black; beneath thin, red and moist lips, shone the whitest teeth. His beauty, on the whole, both manly and charming; his combined strength and elegance recalled the noble portions of the Indian Bacchus, or of Antinoüs.

The costume of the man which certain *flibustiers* adopted very generally. He wore a close coat of dark granite velvet, with worked-gold buttons; large Flemish pantaloons of similar stuff, and ornamented with the like buttons, which ornamented them down the side, it being supported by a belt of orange silk, in which was passed a richly worked dagger; in fine, large gaiters of white leather *picquées*, and embroidered with silk in a thousand different colours, *a la Mexicaine*, reached above the knee, and shewed off a leg of the finest proportions.

Nothing could be more piquant, nothing more pretty, than the contrast presented by Jacques and Angelina when thus grouped. On one side, blonde hair, alabaster complexion, rosy cheeks, infantine grace and beauty; on the other, a bronzed tint, ebony hair, and a bold and manly mien.

The whiteness of Angelina's frock was thrown out forcibly by the sombre colour of the clothes of Jacques, and once could better appreciate the lovely and supple shape of La Barbe-bleue. Her large blue eyes fixed on the black eyes of the man, the young woman amused herself by stroking down the embroidered collar of Jacques' shirt, the easier to admire the colour of his neck, which in colour and form would have rivalled the best Florentine caste.

After prolonging, during some time, this strange interview in silence, Angelina gave Jacques a noisy kiss under the ear, took his head between her two little hands, disarranged his massive black hair, gave him a tap on the cheek, and cried—

"That's how I love you, Monsieur Hurricane."

At a slight noise which was heard behind the tapestry that served as a door, Angelina said:

"Is that you, Mirette? What are you doing there?"

"Mistress, I have just brought some flowers, and I am engaged in arranging them."

"She hears us," said Angelina, with a mysterious sign.

Then she burst again into a laugh, and childishly amused herself by disarranging the hair of Monsieur Hurricane.

M. l'Ouragon, since we must call him by this name, bore the gentle caprices of Angelina most patiently, and looked upon her lovingly.

He then said, smiling:—

"Child! because you are always sixteen you think everything is allowed you."

Then he added, with sigh of grave raillery:—

"Who now, to see that little rosy form, so ingenuous, so young, so smiling, that I hold thus upon my knees, would believe her the most wicked creature in all the West Indies?"

"And who would take this man, who speaks thus gently, to be the fierce Captain Hurricane, the terror of both English and Spaniards," cried Angelina, bursting into a loud laugh.

We think it right to advise the reader, that the Hurricane and the widow expressed themselves in the best and most elegant French, without the least foreign accent.

"There is, however, some difference between us," replied the latter smiling. "It is not me who is accused of horrible and mysterious adventures, and who is called La Barbe-bleue."

At these words, which should have raised in her mind the most sinister souvenirs, the little widow, with a gesture full of mutinous coquettishness, gave the most tender of fillips under the nose of Captain Hurricane, shewed him, by a gesture, the door of the neighbouring room, as a warning that he could be heard, and said, with a malicious, pouting air—

"That, sir, is to teach you to speak to me of the dead."

"Fie! the monster!" said the Captain, actually roaring with laughter; "and remorse, madame, do you, then, feel none whatever?"

"You give me a kiss by way of remorse, and I shall then feel some."

"Lucifer assist me; one must be a woman to be so wicked. Ah! my dear, you are well named. You make one shudder! If we were to sup now."

Angelina struck on a gong, and a young *métisse*, who had heard the preceding conversation, entered. She wore a frock of white muslin with scarlet stripes, and had silver rings on her arms and legs.

"Mirette, have you finished arranging the flowers in there?" said the pretty Barbe-bleue?"

"Yes, mistress," replied the young woman, with a profound courtesy, her arms at the same time folded over her bosom.

"You were listening to us?"

"No, mistress."

"But it is all the same if you were. When I speak it is to be heard. Let us have supper directly, Mirette."

Then, turning to the captain, La Barbe-bleue said:—

"What wine do you drink?"

"Why, I will take some Xeres, well iced. It is a fancy I have to-day."

Mirette went out, and returned in an instant after to lay the table.

"Apropos," said l'Ouragon, "I had quite forgotten to inform you of a great event."

"What is it?—one of my defuncts coming back again?" said Angelina, eagerly.

"Why, something of that sort," said the filibuster, calmly.

"What! Ah, Monsieur Jacques, Monsieur Jacques, none of your horrible jokes," replied Angelina, with a frightened air.

"Well, my dear, it is not a defunct, a spectre, but a live suitor, who is anxious to become your husband."

"He wishes to marry me?"

"He wishes to marry you."

"Ah, the miserable fellow! then he is quite tired of life," cried Angelina, with a renewed burst of laughter.

Mirette, at these words, crossed herself devoutly, without ceasing from observing the two other girls, who brought in bottles of Bohemian glass, covered by golden arabesques, and piles of plates of magnificent Japan porcelain.

The Barbe-bleue was silent for a moment.

"My lover is of this country?"

"No, indeed! for despite your riches, *ma chère,* I will defy you to find a fourth husband, thanks to your infernal reputation."

"But where then, does this marrying man come from, my dear Jacques?"

"He comes from France."

"From France? He comes from France to marry me? *Diable!*"

"Angelina," said Jacques, with a serio-comic air, "you know that I do not like to hear you swear."

"I beg pardon, Monsieur l'Ouragon," said the young woman, casting down her eyes with a most hypocritical air of repentance; "that little exclamation only signified that I thought the news rather surprising which you brought. It appears, then, that my reputation is beginning to reach to Europe."

"Do not flatter yourself with that piece of vanity, my dear. It is on board the Unicorn that this worthy Paladin has heard speak of you; and, at the mere enumeration of your riches, he has become in love—ay, and madly in love, with you. This will, I hope, lower your pride a little."

"The impertinent fellow; and what kind of man is he, Jacques," said the pouting beauty.

"The Chevalier Croustillac," replied l'Ouragon, with a desperate attempt at gravity.

"That is the name of—my suitor."

And the pretty widow once more gave way to a noisy laugh, which nothing could stop, and her companion soon joined in her mirth.

They were scarcely calmed, when Mirette again entered, preceding two other *métisses*, who carried a table splendidly laid out with vermillion plate. On each separate piece were cut and enamelled the royal arms of England.

The two slaves placed the table near the divan; the captain rose to take a seat; while Angelina knelt on the border of the sofa, uncovering the plates one after another, and prying into the contents with the gestures and modes of a hungry puss.

"Are you hungry, Jacques? I am ravenous," said Angelina; and doubtless, to prove the truth of her assertion, she opened her coral lips, and shewed two rows of the most ravishing little teeth, which she clashed together several times.

"Angelina, my dear, you have been decidedly very badly brought up," said the Captain, helping her to a slice of dorade, with ham and gravy of a most tempting flavour.

"Captain l'Ouragon, if I receive you at my table, it is not to be scolded," said Angelina, making an almost imperceptible but *mutine* grimace at him. Then she added, while bravely attacking the slice of dorade, and pecking at her bread like a bird—

"Isn't it so, Mirette? If he scolds me, I will not receive him?"

"No, mistress," said Mirette.

"And that I will give his place to Arrache'lâme, the boucanier?"

"Yes, mistress."

"Or to Youmaale, the Carib?"

"Yes, mistress."

"Do you see that, sir?" said Angelina.

"Go, go, my dear. I am not jealous than that, I pardon you. Help me to what is before you. What is that, Mirette?"

"Ah, mistress, it is priques fried in the fat of wood-pigeon."

"Quite as good, at least, as the fat of quails," said l'Ouragon; "but you must just add the least trifle of citron-juice while the fry is still hot."

"Do you see him, the gourmand? But, our marrying man, we forget him. Give me to drink, Mirette."

The *flibustier*, pirate though he was, was quicker than the girl, and poured out some Xeres wine, iced, for Angelina.

"I must love you indeed, my dear, to drink this, I that prefer the wines of France."

And La Barbe-bleue drank very resolutely the fingers deep of Xeres wine, which gave a fresh colour to her lips, her blue eyes, and animated her ruddy cheeks with a scarlet tint.

"But come, my marrying man, my suitor," continued she—"how will he do? Is he a nice fellow? Is he worthy to join the others?"

Mirette, despite her passive submission, could not help shuddering when she heard her mistress speak in this manner, though the poor slave was, doubtless, sufficiently accustomed to these abominable jokes, and, doubtless, to even greater enormities.

"Well, Mirette, what is the matter with you?"

"Nothing, maitresse."

"Yes, you have something the matter."

"No, maitresse."

"Perhaps you may be sorry to see me remarried. Oh, it will not last long; be satisfied, my child."

Then, turning to L'Ouragon—

"And the Chevalier de—de—what is it you call him?"

"The Chevalier de Croustillac."

"You have seen him?"

"No, no; but knowing his project, and knowing that, in despite of every-thing, and despite the representations of the good Father Griffon he vis-ited, he had reached as far as this, I requested Youmaale the Carib," said l'Ouragon, regarding Angelina in a very marked manner, "to send him a little announcement to induce him to give up his projects."

"And you gave this order, sir, without giving me notice. And if I had wished not to refuse this pretender? for, in fine, Croustillac, that must be the name of a Gascon, and I have never yet been married to a Gascon."

"Yes, indeed, it is the most famous of Gascons whoever gasconded on the earth; and, with this, an unimaginable figure and unexampled assurance—moreover, plenty of courage."

"And the warnings of Youmaale?" inquired Angelina, with a pretty little pout.

"Was of no earthly use, it glided over the immovable soul of this paladin, like a ball on the scales of the crocodile. He started this morning bravely, at the point of day, across the forest, with his rose-coloured silk stockings, his rapier by his side, and a switch in his hand, to drive away serpents. He is doubtless in the wood at this moment, for the road to the Morne-au-Diable is not known to everybody."

"Ah, Jacques, an idea!" cried the widow, with joy. "Bring him hither to amuse ourselves at his expense—to torment him. Ah! he is in love with my treasures and not with me. Ah! he wants to marry me, this brave knight-errant. We shall see it fast enough. *En bien!* you do not laugh at my project, Jacques! What is the matter with you? In the first place, sir, you must know that I am not to be contradicted; I quite enjoy the idea of having my Gascon here. If he is not bit by the serpents, or devoured by the tiger-cats, I shall have him here to-morrow. You go to sea to-morrow; well, tell the Carib, or Arrache'lâme, to bring him to me."

L'Ouragon, instead of partaking the gaiety of La Barbe-bleue, according to his custom, was serious, pensive, and seemed to reflect profoundly.

"Jacques! Jacques! do you not hear me?" cried Angelina, stamping her pretty little foot with impatience: "I must have my Gascon! I have set my mind on it, and I must have him."

Jacques did not answer, but he described, with the thumb of his right hand, a circle round his head, and looked at the young woman with a significant air.

She understood this mysterious sign.

Her face immediately assumed an air of sadness and fear; she arose hastily, ran to l'Ouragon, kneeled before him, and cried, in a touching voice—

"You are right—my God, you are right! I am mad to have the thought. I understand you."

"Rise—calm yourself, Angelina," said Jacques. "I do not think this man is to be feared; but, you know, it is a stranger—and he might come from England or France, and—"

"I tell you I must have been mad—that I was joking, my good Jacques. I had forgotten what I ought never to have forgotten. It is horrible!"

The fine eyes of this beautiful young creature were filled with tears; she bowed her head, and took his hand over which she wept during some moments.

L'Ouragon kissed tenderly the forehead and the hair of Angelina, and said with tenderness—

"I am very vexed to have awakened these cruel recollections. I should have said nothing about it to you, but should have assured myself that there was no danger in bringing you this imbecile fellow as a plaything, and then—"

"Jacques, my good friend," cried Angelina, sadly interrupting him, "my dear *amant*, do you still think of anything of the kind? For a childish caprice, to expose, to endanger all that I love dearest in the world!"

"Come, come, calm yourself," said Jacques, raising her and seating her beside him, "do not frighten yourself; Father Griffon has taken information concerning this Gascon; he appears to me only ridiculous. For greater safety, I will to-morrow go to him at Macouba, and have a talk on the subject, and then I will tell Arrache'lâme, who will precisely be hunting that way, to try and discover the poor devil in the forest, where doubtless he has wandered and lost himself. If he be dangerous," said her companion, making signs to Angelina, for the slaves still waited at table, "if he be dangerous, the boucanier will know how to rid us of him, and to cure him completely of the wish to know you; if not, as you have scarcely any amusement here, he will bring him to you."

"No, no! I will not have him!" said Angelina. "For all the thoughts that come into my head are of mortal sadness; my disquietude increases."

Seeing that Jacques no longer ate, she rose; the *flibustier* imitated her, saying—

"Be reassured, my Angelina, there is nothing, I assure you—nothing to be feared. Come into the garden, the night is fine, the moon splendid; tell Mirette to bring my lute, to drive away these painful ideas. I will sing you some of these Scottish ballads that you love so well."

Saying these words, he passed an arm round the waist of Angelina, and holding her thus embraced, they proceeded down some steps which led into the garden.

When about to leave the room, La Barbe-bleue turned her head, and said to her slave,—

"Mirette, bring that lute into the garden; light the alabaster lamp in my bedroom. I shall not want you anymore. Do not forget to tell Cora and her

64

two girls that to-morrow's her day of service;" and she disappeared, learning on the arm of Jacques.

This last order of Angelina arose from the fact of her having, since her last widowhood, divided the service of her slaves into three alternate days.

Having executed the orders of her mistress, Mirette discreetly retired, and said to the other two slaves, with a wicked smile:—

"Mirette, light the lamp for the Captain; Coro, for the Boucanier; and Noun, for the Carib."

The two old slaves shook their heads in a most knowing manner, and then all three went out, after having carefully bolted and barred the doors which led to the outer-buildings of the private house of La Barbe-bleue.

The saloon, where Croustillac had to wait some minutes, was furnished with a luxury of which our adventurer had previously no idea; superb ancient pictures, magnificent porcelain vases, curiosities of clock-work of the most precious character, crowded all the articles of furniture, as precious by the materials as by the work; a lute and a theory, of which the ivory and gold ornaments were of an extraordinary fineness in sculpture, drew the attention of Croustillac, who was ravished to find that his *future wife* was a musician.

"Mordioux!" said the Chevalier to himself, "can it be possible that the mistress of so many precious things is beautiful as the light. No! no! it would be too much joy, though I must say I merit the happiness."

Let the reader judge his astonishment, not to say his utter ravishment, when, shortly after, he saw the Female Bluebeard in the person of Angelina.

The little widow was dazzling in youth, grace, beauty, and dress; clothed and coiffed *à-la-mode* of the age of Louis XIV, she wore a robe of sky-blue waved silk, the *corsage* of which seemed perfectly embroidered with diamonds, pearls, and rubies, so well in taste were the stones disposed.

Croustillac, despite his audacity, started back at the sight of this astounding apparition.

65

In his whole life, he had never met a woman so ravishingly pretty, so royally clothed; he could not believe his eyes, and gazed upon La Barbe-bleue with a perfectly confused and astonished air.

We must say, to the praise of the Chevalier, that he had an instant and praiseworthy return of modesty, unfortunately as rapid as it was severe. He immediately thought that so charming a creature might hesitate to marry so complete an adventurer as himself; but recollecting the impertinent and boasting confidence of the Boucanier, he said to himself that one man was worth another, and thus soon regained his imperturbable assurance.

Croustillac made, one after another, three of his most respectful bows, then he rose up to his whole height to show off the nobility of his shape, advanced one of his long legs, drew up the other a little in the rear, placed his hand upon his hips with a conquering air, holding his beaver in his right hand, and leaning his left hand on the hilt of his sword.

Doubtless he was about to address some gallant compliment, to La Barbe-bleue, for already he had carried his hand to his heart, opening his wide mouth at the same time, when the little widow, not being able to restrain a violent desire to laugh which the heteroclite figure of the Chevalier caused her, gave a free course to her noisy hilarity.

This explosion of gaiety shut the mouth of Croustillac, and he endeavoured to smile, hoping thus to please La Barbe-bleue.

This gallant attempt at gaiety translated itself into so grotesque a grimace, that Angelina, who had fallen in a sitting posture on the sofa, forgot all *convenance* and all dignity, and abandoned herself rashly to laugh like a mad creature—not a laugh only, but a complete roar; her fine blue eyes, always so brilliant, were veiled by joyous tears, her round cheeks were coloured by a lively scarlet, and their charming dimples were deepened to such a point, that the widow might have hid the whole of the rosy end of her little fingers in them.

Croustillac, very embarrassed, remained immovable before the pretty laugher, sometimes frowning with an angry air, sometimes on the other hand, seeking to dilate his long and meagre face into a forced and dolorous smile.

During these successive plays of the physiognomy, which were not of a character to put an end to the hilarity of La Barbe-bleue, the Chevalier said to himself, *in petto*, that, for a murderess, the widow had not so very terrible and awful an aspect.

Nevertheless, the vanity of our adventurer accommodated itself, with some difficulty, to the singular effect which his presence had produced. In default of better reasons, he finished by saying to himself, that, above all things, one must strike the imagination of the women, that they must first be astonished, that they must be revolutionised, and that, on this point, his first interview with La Barbe-bleue was everything that could be desired.

When he saw that the widow was in some measure calmed, he addressed her resolutely in the bombastic vein.

"I am sure," said he, "that you laugh, madam, at all the desperate attempts which I make to restrain, in vain, my poor heart, which fires *nolens volens* to your feet. It is that drags me hither, and I have only followed it in spite of myself—yes, madam, in spite of myself."

Croustillac paused.

"I said to him, 'La! la! finely, my heart—finely! It is not sufficient to please a divine beauty to be passionately in love.' But, my little, or, rather, my great hair-brained heart answered me ever by dragging me towards you with all its might, as if he had been of steel, and the Morne-au-Diable an immense loadstone. 'My heart,' said I, answering myself, 'be still, maître; sender and valiant as you are, from the love which you feel will be generated the love which will be felt.' But pardon, madam—the language of my heart appears to me furiously impertinent; it is, doubtless, this impertinence which makes you laugh again."

Croustillac paused.

The widow was nearly suffocated.

"No! monsieur, no! your presence renders me gay because you resemble, in the last degree—ha, ha, ha!—in the strangest manner in the world, my second husband; you have absolutely the same nose—ha, ha, ha!—and when I saw you enter, I thought I saw a spectre—ha, ha, ah!—who came to reproach me—ha, ha, ha!—with his cruel end—ha, ha, ha!"

Here the laughter of Angelina redoubled in its force.

"Ha, ha, ha! that was all."

The Chevalier was not ignorant of the antecedent facts which the Barbe-bleue was reproached with, but he could not conceal his profound astonishment, on hearing a creature so charming and innocent-looking avow herself a homicide, with so much incredible audacity.

Angelina still laughed.

Nevertheless, the Chevalier, regaining his habitual *sang-froid*, answered, in as gallant a manner as possible,—

"I am too happy, madam," said he, with a low bow, "to recall to your mind one of the departed—to awaken, by my presence, one of your souvenirs, whatever it may be. Only," added Croustillac, with a still more gallant air, "there are other resemblances which I should wish to have with your defunct husband, the memory of whom excites so much hilarity in you."

"That is to say, my friend, that you have decidedly the intention of marrying me?" said the Barbe-bleue. "Is it not so?"

At this blunt question the Chevalier remained a moment perfectly stupefied.

Angelina continued.

"I was prepared for it; Arrache-l'âme, whom by abbreviation I call my little Rache-l'âme, has prepared me for the fact, has told me of your good intentions towards me. But perhaps he only caused me a false joy. My expectations are, perhaps, to be disappointed," added the widow, looking at the Chevalier in a coquettish manner.

Croustillac advanced from one surprise to another. He was astounded.

"How?" cried he, "the Boucanier told you, madam, did he, that I—"

"That you came all the way from France on purpose to marry me. Is it not true? Come, speak frankly; do not deceive me now. In the first place, I do not like to be contradicted in my wishes. I warn you, if I have once taken it into my head that you are to be my husband, you shall be my husband."

Croustillac opened his eyes to the utmost and fullest extent.

"Madame, I implore you, do not take me for a ninny, for a stork, for a mere stupid ass, if I remain voiceless—speechless. It is emotion and astonishment which pervades my whole system."

Croustillac paused, and looked all round to assure himself that he was not the plaything of some fantastic and absurd dream.

"May I be snapped up like a mosquito, if I was any way prepared for such a reception."

"Eh, mon Dieu! there is no necessity for so much ceremonious nonsense," continued the widow; "I have been told that you have a great desire to marry me; is it true?"

"As true, madam, as that you are the most dazzling beauty that in all my existence I have ever met," cried the Chevalier, with the utmost impetuosity, carrying his hand to his heart, and saluting her profoundly.

"Truly, then—quite truly!—you are quite decided to take me for your wife—for your spouse?" cried the little widow, joyously clapping her hands together.

"I am so decided on that point, adorable and lovely widow, that my only fear now is, that I may not still realise this wish; which, on my part, I confess, is a most exorbitant desire—a Titanian dream, and—"

"But silence, I tell you!" said La Barbe-bleue, interrupting our friend Croustillac, with the most childish *naïveté*. "What is the use of all these fine words? I cannot see the value of them. You ask me for my hand; and pray why should I not bestow it upon you?"

"How, madam!" exclaimed the enraptured Croustillac, "can I believe you? Ah! come, beautiful islander, I have had many glorious triumphs in my life; princesses have confessed to me their flame, queens have sighed when gazing on me—but never, madam, you may applaud yourself—you may boast of carrying to their loftiest height, my surprise, my joy, and my gratitude. Repeat once more, I conjure you—repeat once more those charming words. You do, then, consent to take me for your husband—you agree to marry Polyphemus de Croustillac."

"I will repeat it to you as long as you like, for nothing is more simple. You will readily understand that I have far too much difficulty in finding husbands not to catch greedily at the offer."

Croustillac winced.

"Ah! madam," answered he, gallantly, "at the risk of passing for a very impertinent individual, you will allow me formally to contradict your assertion. No, no—I can never think that you have any difficulty in finding husbands. I will say more. I am convinced that you have only had, since your last widowhood, the difficulty of choice. But it is all quite simple; you do not think proper to choose. You had too much good taste, madam," added Croustillac, audaciously; "you were waiting—"

"I might deceive you, and allow you to believe this, Chevalier; but you are too gallant a man, too honourable a man, for me to attempt to impose upon you. At the point at which we now are," continued Angelina, with a gracious and confidential air, "considering the familiar terms on which we are not, I may tell you all. Listen, then."

Croustillac bowed.

"The first time that I was married, I had but to choose for myself, it is true. Ah! mon Dieu! the suitors presented themselves in vast crowds, and I chose— and chose well; that I can assure you. On the occasion of my second marriage, it was no longer the same thing. People had talked of the singular death of my first husband," added the widow, with a malicious smile, "and suitors began to reflect a little before proposing. However, as I am not quite a fool, by force of graciousness, of coaxing, and coquetting, I finished by catching a second spouse. Alas, it was not, however, without great and wondrous difficulty!"

The widow paused.

Croustillac listened.

"But for the third—ah! for the third, you cannot have the remotest idea of the trouble which I had to succeed. Word of an honest woman, it was enough to drive me mad outright with vexation."

"Ah, madam! had Polyphemus de Croustillac but been there!" said the Chevalier, with a sigh of deep and heavy regret.

"Doubtless, Chevalier; but you see, unfortunately, you were not there. People had talked of the death of the first; judge, then, if they did not say something about the death of the second. People began to be on their guard against me," added the widow, shaking her pretty little head with an expression of ingenuous melancholy. "But what will you, the world is so much of a busybody, so scandalous, and men are such very strange animals—"

"The world is a fool! the world is an imbecile egotist!" cried the Croustillac, full of the deepest pity for the victim of public calumny. "Men are fools and ninnies who believe all the old women's tales which are told them."

"What you now observe is very true, my friend, and you are not one, I see, of this disposition."

"Friend!—she calls me friend," muttered to himself the transported Croustillac.

La Barbe-bleue appeared to wait his answer.

"No, indeed, I am not at all of that disposition, I assure you."

"Doubtless," replied the widow, with much apparent satisfaction, "you—what a difference, indeed. Why, you quite spoil me in accepting my proposition so very kindly and readily."

"Say rather, madam, that I am ravished beyond the utmost bounds of human happiness."

"Yes, yes! you really spoil me," added the widow, with an enchanting smile, and casting a grateful look at the Chevalier at the same time. "I assure you, indeed, you do quite spoil me, you are so easy, so accommodating. Alas! one day, how shall I ever replace you, my friend?"

Croustillac shuddered.

"Replace me?"

"Yes, after you, my friend!"

"After me, madam?"

"Doubtless, after you."

"Madam, I do not, cannot, will not understand," cried the Chevalier, somewhat hotly.

"Nevertheless, it is very simple: how can I ever hope again to find anyone who will agree to marry me so easily and readily as you have done. Oh, no, no! men like you, Chevalier, are indeed rare."

"But what is this, madam, about 'after me'?" cried the Chevalier, almost stunned by this singular hypothesis, "you already think of my successor?"

"Yes, friend, yes!" replied the enchanting, but singular widow, with a most sentimental and die-away air, and the most touching glance in the world. "Yes, indeed, for when you are no more, it will be necessary for me to set about, seeking, asking, finding a fifth husband. Only think of it, what enormous difficulties, what terrible prejudices to overcome. Perhaps even I might not succeed. Judge yourself: a widow for the fourth time. You shall quite forget this; nevertheless, you must know that it is a fact. After you, I shall in truth be a widow for the fourth time."

Angelina shook her head, as if the idea did really cause her some regretful anticipations.

"I do not forget all this, madam," said the Gascon, somewhat cooled in his ardour, and asking himself, if he were not dealing with a mad woman. "I cannot, of course, forget that in case I enjoy the inestimable honour of marrying you, you will be a widow for the fourth time, if you should chance to lose me. Only, it appears to me that you assign a very brief period to my happiness."

"Alas, yes, friend!" said the widow, with quite an air of emotion: "a year, a year,—it is very short; one year, it passes so quick, when one truly loves," added she, throwing on him a perfectly assassinating look.

"One year, madam—one year!" cried the Chevalier, with horror and surprise.

Soon, however, reflecting that the words of La Barbe-bleue might merely conceal a trap, and that she doubtless wished to try him in order to judge of his courage, he cried in a chivalric tone—

"Well, madam, let it be so—let my happiness last but a year, a month, a week, a day, an hour, a minute—it matters not. I will brave all, if I only can say that I have been happy enough to obtain your hand."

"You are indeed a true knight," cried the widow, apparently ravished with her conquest. "This is well agreed on, then—only I will just warn my little Rache-l'âme, for form's sake, merely—for married or not, I shall always be for him what I have hitherto been."

Croustillac made a slight grimace.

"But, madam," said our hero, with some slight evidence of embarrassment, "might *I* be allowed—would it be indiscreet, to ask you what you have been to this hunter of wild bulls—and what is truly his position with regard to you? or rather, would you be kind enough to explain to me why you feel yourself under any necessity of informing him of your intentions with regard to your humble servant?"

"Certainly, and to whom should I tell it if not to you. Now, friend, I will confess to you that little Rache-l'âme is one of my best-beloved."

Here Croustillac made so singular a grimace, coughing at the same time twice or thrice, that Angelina burst into a fit of laughter.

Croustillac, a moment thunderstruck, soon collected himself, and made a reflection full of wisdom and prudence.

"I am a fool, that is quite satisfactory. She had a kind of taste for this rude and gross personage, the sight of me has decided her to sacrifice him to me, only she wishes to do so in a proper manner—unhappy Boucanier that you are. Only, why in the devil's name does she speak to me of a successor, and tell me that in about a year's time, or perhaps less, she must look out for a fifth husband."

"Ah! here is my friend Rache-l'âme, come in at the very proper moment," said the widow; "let us speak to him of our matrimonial projects, and then we can sup together, like three friends."

"By Heavens!" thought Croustillac, seeing the Boucanier enter, "here is a little woman who can boast, at all events, of being a most decided original."

Croustillac turned towards Rache-l'âme, scarcely knowing in what manner to address him.

*

When the Boucanier entered, the Chevalier scarcely knew him.

Croustillac had just finished this reflection, when the little widow addressed her friend, the Boucanier, pointing, at the same time, to our adventurer, with a triumphant glance.

"Well, sir," said she, ingenuously, "Monsieur the Chevalier demands my hand. You see now, after all, that I was not wrong when I declared that I would find a fourth husband. Of course, as you may well think, I have at once closed with my suitor's offer. It was by far too good an occasion to be lost."

The Boucanier did not answer at first, but appeared to reflect gravely.

Croustillac mechanically placed his hand on the hilt of his sword, not to be taken at a disadvantage, in case the chasseur, exasperated by the pangs of jealousy, might have some notion of resorting to violence.

What, then, was the surprise of our adventurer, when he heard the answer of Arrache-l'âme, as he lolled negligently on a comfortable sofa.

"I always told you, *ma belle*, what our friend Ouragon has always told you—'Marry! ten thousand devils—marry, if you can find the opportunity;' for you, suitors are indeed rare, for no one knows what the deuce you do with them; what is certain is, that they do not last you very long. As for me, I have long had some suspicion of your little tricks. I have seen you more than once preparing certain beverages with your little snow-white hands."

"Oh, fie! fie! what a shocking gossip and talker you are," said Angelina, pettishly, and menacing the indiscreet Boucanier with her little finger.

"But the question, my dear, is—is it true?" continued Arrache-l'âme. "What is the secret of that grey powder, of which I only gave a pinch to my engagé, whom my dogs afterwards devoured? Come, now, what is this infernal preparation?"

"Well, madam, this grey powder," inquired Croustillac; "might one learn its wonderful properties?"

"Oh, the indiscreet man!" cried Angelina, looking at the Boucanier with a somewhat angry air. "Monsieur le Chevalier will take me for a complete child; what shall I appear in his eyes, if he is made aware that I amuse myself with such puerilities?"

Croustillac began to feel a decided conviction of the madness of La Barbe-bleue.

"Fear nothing on this subject, madam," said the adventurer boldly. "I shall be delighted, I swear it to you, to have some new proof of your infantine candour. Come, worthy Nimrod, how about this same grey powder?"

"Come now, truly, I shall be really quite ashamed," said Angelina, lowering her eyes to the ground, and pouting most prettily and seductively.

"Figure to yourself, then," said the Boucanier, "that I made my engagé take only a pinch of this powder in a glass of water, and—"

"Well?" exclaimed Croustillac, who began to feel a deep and personal interest in the relation.

"Well, during two whole days he had such attacks of gaiety, that he was in one constant succession of horse laughs from even to morning, and from morn to evening."

"So far," said Croustillac, with a look at Angelina, "I see no great harm done."

"Wait awhile, wait awhile," said the Chasseur; "you must not think that this amused him in the least—my engagé; he suffered like one of the damned, his eyes started out of his head, and he said, laughing all the while like a foolish person, that there was no torture equal to that which he endured! The third day, the pain was violent that he fell into fainting fits, and he long afterwards felt the effects, I can tell you, of madam's grey powder. You must not, therefore, be surprised if you hear that the second husband of madam, whom you see there, was as gay as a chaffinch, and died quite joyously."

"Oh! mon Dieu—one cannot now play a harmless trick, without being told of it again," said Angelina, tossing herself in a chair like a little capricious girl.

"Holloa! camarade, she calls this a harmless trick," said Maître Arrache-l'âme—"just think that, thanks to madam's grey powder, her second defunct laughed so strongly and violently, that he bled through his nose and ears. But then, as to the laughing part, he laughed as if he were witnessing the finest comedy in the world—which did not prevent him, however, from saying, like my engagé, that he would rather have been burnt over a slow fire than have endured such gaiety as this; and at length he died, laughing most horribly all the while, and swearing like one of the lost souls."

"There, now, you are very far advanced," said the terrible SHE-BLUEBEARD, shrugging her shoulders. Then approaching the ear of the Gascon, she said:—

"Friend, be satisfied, I have lost the secret of this horrid grey powder."

The Chevalier, wishing to smile in return, made a most sinister grimace. He had quitted France at the moment when the frightful *affaire des poisons* was in all its height, and no one spoke of ought save "powder of succession," "powder of old age," "powder of widowhood," &c. Several names of female poisoners were cited with terror; therefore the gaiety-powder of the Barbe-bleue could not but raise very lugubrious ideas in the mind of the Chevalier.

Croustillac, indeed, was sorely puzzled, and said to himself, gazing at Angelina with astonishment—"Can this lively creature dabble in chemistry and laboratories? Can this horrible tale be true?"

"Well, what is the matter, brother?" said the Boucanier, struck by the silence of Croustillac.

No answer.

"See, now, you have quite terrified him!" exclaimed the widow, with a pout.

"No, beautiful lady! no, by no means," replied Croustillac; "I was only just thinking to myself that it must be terribly pleasant to die thus of laughing. It is quite a new and delectable idea."

"Faith! and you are right, brother," said Arrache'lâme; "at all events, that death is far better than that of the third husband;" and the Boucanier gave a look of unmitigated horror at the insensible widow.

"It appears, then, that the death of this poor fellow was even a more serious affair than that of the other?" said Croustillac, affecting to assume quite a careless and indifferent air.

"As to this story, camarade, I will not tell it you; indeed, I will not; it will alarm you. You will be afraid," and the Boucanier shook his head gravely and sorrowfully.

"I afraid!" and the Gascon shrugged his shoulders. "Polyphemus de Croustillac was never afraid!"

The Barbe-bleue leaned to the ear of the Chevalier, and whispered him—"Let him alone, my friend," said she; "this story now is worth hearing at all events, and wont I regularly catch my little Rache-l'âme?"

Angelina then turned round sharply to the indiscreet Buccaneer.

"Well, now, come, tell it—tell it, I say; do not stay half-way on so fine a road. You see plainly that the Chevalier listens with all his ears; come, speak, I do not wish him to buy, as the saying is, a *chat en poche.*"

"You mean to say a *tigresse en poche*," replied the Boucanier, laughing. "Well, my gentleman," continued he, turning to and addressing Croustillac, "figure to yourself that this lady's third husband was a fine dark fellow, about thirty-six years of age, a Spaniard by birth, but we caught him at Havanna."

"Eh, *mon Dieu!* tell it quick, Arrache-l'âme, you see the Chevalier is quite impatient."

"It was not grey powder this time, that this one tasted," continued the Boucanier; "but a drop—a single drop of some pretty green liquor, contained in the smallest flask that ever I saw in my life, since it was cut out of a single ruby."

"But that's quite simple," said Angelina; "the force of this liquid is such that it would dissolve or break every flask which should not be made of a single ruby or diamond."

Croustillac was silent.

"Judge, after this, Chevalier," said the hunter, "of how agreeable this liquor must have been to our third husband—poor man! Certainly I am neither very tender nor very easily terrified; but after all, one has some difficulty in using oneself to seeing a man, who looks at you with green eyes, luminous, and set so deeply in their orbits, that they had all the effect of glow-worms at the bottom of a hole."

"The fact is," said Croustillac, who could not control a slight shudder—"the fact is, that the first time this must appear rather singular."

"That is nothing, my friend."

"The devil it is."

"Listen to the end," said the widow, in whispered tones, as if quite satisfied with herself.

Croustillac bowed.

The Boucanier continued.

"It was only his ordinary state, poor dear man! to have his eyes like glow-worms; but the time that it became horrible, was when one day Madame gave a gala to I, the Ouragon, the Cannibal. She dipped a small colibri feather in the ruby flagon, and calling to her side the unfortunate Spaniard, passed the feather over his eyes."

"Well?"

These words, uttered by the Chevalier without any other end than that of proving to the inhabitants of the Morne-au-Diable that he was determined not to be their dupe, produced on the little Barbe-bleue the most singular effect.

Casting a terrified glance at the Boucanier, she addressed Croustillac haughtily, and said:—

"I am by no means joking, sir; you came here with the intention of marrying me; I offer you my hand; I will presently tell you in what conditions. If they suit you, we will conclude this matter in eight days; there is a chapel here, and the reverend Father Griffon, of the parish of Macouba, will come here and unite us. If my propositions do not suit you, you will quit this house, to which you should have never come."

While La Barbe-bleue spoke, her physiognomy was gradually losing its joking and delighted air; she became by degrees sad and melancholy, and presently almost menacing in the express which pervaded her features.

"A comedy!" continued she. "If I could for a moment think that you looked upon all this as child's play, you should not remain one minute—nay, not one second, in this house!" said she, in a trembling voice, that betrayed singular and powerful emotions, glancing alternately at the Chevalier, and from him to the Boucanier.

"No—nonsense! the Chevalier has no idea of taking all this for a comedy!" exclaimed Maître Arrache'lâme, casting on the irritated Gascon a scrutinising glance.

Croustillac, by nature impatient and quick, experienced a strong feeling of real annoyance at not being able to penetrate what was true and what was false or feigned in this singular adventure, which almost confounded him. He therefore cried—

"Oh! mordioux, madam, what would you that I should think?" said he. "I meet this worthy Boucanier in the forest; I impart to him the desire that I have to know you; he tells me, as frankly as you yourself have just done me the honour to inform me, that he has the inestimable happiness of being in your good graces."

"Well, sir?"

"Madam—up to this time, all proceeds, I might say, well. But now, the Boucanier endeavours to make me believe, in collision with you, that I am destined to make a fourth defunct, and to succeed to the man who died from over-laughing; or, at all events, to him whose eyes served as torches to illumine your festivities."

"I assure you it is the truth, and nothing but the truth," drily observed the Boucanier.

"How—it is the truth!" exclaimed Croustillac, recovering his vivacity, for a moment numbed. "Are we, then, in the fabled land of dreams! or do you really take the Chevalier de Croustillac for a ninny? Do you take me for one of those turkey-buzzards who believe in the devil and his conjurations? I am not a mere goose; no, and I ask not even twenty-four hours to fathom the mystery which all these follies is intended to conceal."

Angelina became very pale, cast on the Boucanier a fresh look of anguish and undefinable terror, and then replied to the Chevalier with ill-concealed and restrained anger—

"And who tells you, monsieur," said the Female Bluebeard, with an effort at playfulness, "that all which passes here is natural? Do you know why I, young and rich, offered you my hand from the very first moment that I saw you? Are you aware at what price I shall place this union? You think yourself an *esprit-fore*, a man of vigorous intellect; but what tells you that there are not certain phenomena which pass the reach of your intelligence? Do you know, in the least, who I am? Are you cognisant of where you are? Are you aware by the means of what strange mystery it is I offer you my hand? A comedy, indeed!—a comedy!" exclaimed La Barbe-bleue, with bitterness, again glancing at the Boucanier with a frightened air. "May you never be forced to acknowledge that there is no child's play in it, monsieur! You must not think, after all, that your good angel, at all events, had any hand in bringing you here."

Croustillac remained silent.

"And, above all, who is it has yet told you, Monsieur de Croustillac, that you will ever leave this place?" inquired Maître Arrache-l'âme, with a sinister meaning in his tones.

The Chevalier retreated a step, placed his hand upon his sword-hilt, shuddered, and said—

"Mordioux! No violence, I beg. At all events, if it to be so, madame et monsieur—"

"If it be so—what would you?" said La Barbe-bleue to the angry Gascon, with a smile, which appeared to him of the most implacable cruelty.

Croustillac now recollected, at rather a late moment, the fact of the doors which were closed behind him; his mind referred back to the thick vaults which he had had to traverse to reach the diabolical habitation; he saw himself at the mercy of the widow, the Boucanier, and their numerous slaves.

He now repented sincerely, and for the first time really, having thus blindly engaged in this enterprise, after all the warnings of the Père Griffon.

Croustillac, however, when contemplating the enchanting and innocent face of La Barbe-bleue, could not believe this young woman capable of an atrocious and bloody act of perfidy; nevertheless, the singular confessions which she had made, the terrible reports which were scattered about concerning her, the menaces of the Boucanier, commenced having an effect on the Chevalier.

The impression of the Female Bluebeard's really diabolical character began to gain ground with our friend Croustillac, despite his better reason.

A young girl now entered, and announced that supper was served.

During the duration of our adventurer's sombre reflections, Angelina had carried on, in a low voice, a conference of some seconds with her friend the Boucanier; she was no doubt satisfied with the result, and above all reassured; for little by little her forehead cleared up, and her usual gracious smile returned to her lips.

"Come, come! brave Paladin," said she, gaily to the Chevalier, "do not, I beg you, be frightened at me. Take me not for the prince of darkness, and let me pray you now to do honour to the modest supper which a poor widow is too happy to offer you."

Saying these words, she most graciously offered her hand to the Chevalier de Croustillac.

Despite the sprightliness and the quite ideal grace of the mysterious widow, despite the jovial sallies of the Boucanier, the supper passed off somewhat sadly for Croustillac; his habitual *nonchalance* and assurance began to give way to the most lively disquietude. The more Angelina appeared to him charming, the more she displayed all her seductive powers, the more the luxury which surrounded her was dazzling, the more did the adventurer feel his mistrust increase.

Despite their absurdity, the strange stories of the Boucanier returned incessantly to the imagination of Croustillac, as well as the stories of the grey powder which killed with over-laughing, and the liquor of the ruby flask, which changed the eyes into burning lamps. Though these recitals had no more reality than the recollection of an evil dream, the Gascon, in the fear of partaking of some infernal ragout, could not prevent himself from being uncomfortable at the viands which were presented to him.

He watched the widow and her friend the Boucanier with the most jealous attention; in their manners was given not the slightest evidence of impropriety; Rache-l'âme behaved precisely towards La Barbe-bleue with that fitting familiarity which a husband shows to his wife before strangers.

"But then," said the Chevalier to himself, impatiently, "how does this reserve tally with the cynicism of the little widow, who so cavalierly avows that the Carib and the *flibustier* divide her good graces with the Boucanier, without the latter testifying the slightest jealousy."

The Gascon asked himself again, what could be the aim and end of La Barbe-bleue in offering him her hand—at what price did she place this union? Despite his tremendous conceit, he had still too much perspicacity not to have remarked the lively and sincere emotion of the widow, when she testified her indignation at the adventurer having believed her capable of joking, or playing a comedy, in offering him her hand.

In this Croustillac was not deceived.

La Barbe-bleue had been painfully and severely moved; she would have been in despair to have thought that the Chevalier took for a play or a comedy all that was passing at the Morne-au-Diable.

She reassured herself, on seeing the vague and uneasy disquietude which animated the countenance of the Chevalier, despite his utmost efforts to the contrary.

In fact, he lost himself in repeated and vain conjectures as to the truth.

Never had Polyphemus Amador de Croustillac been placed in so strange a position, that the idea of a supernatural influence or power was presented to his mind. Despite himself, he asked if all he saw and all he heard could, by any possibility, be human?

The more strongly, because he, for the first time, felt the influence and inexplicable anguish of superstitious terrors, was Croustillac struck.

He dare not, however, to avow, even to himself, that much more energetic, wise, and learned men than he, had in his own age, and very recently, put faith in the actual motive power of the demon.

Besides, our adventurer had been hitherto by far too indifferent on all matters of religion, not thoroughly to believe in the reality of the devil at the last.

This first and loftier fear but crossed the mind of the Chevalier rapidly, and for an instant, but it was fated to have for the future a salutary and ineffaceable impression.

Croustillac, however, gradually regained his courage, as he saw the pretty widow do honour to the supper heartily, proving herself by far too *friande* for, at all events, a spirit of darkness.

Supper concluded, the three guests rose and re-entered the *salon*, where Barbe-bleue addressed the Chevalier in a very solemn voice,

"To-morrow," said she, "I will inform you on what conditions it is that I offer you my hand; if you refuse, you must immediately quit the Morne-au-Diable. To give you a very striking proof of the confidence I have in you, I consent that you pass the night in the interior of the house, though I never before allowed this favour to a stranger. Arrache'lâme will conduct you to the chamber which is prepared for you."

Saying these last words, the widow courtseyed, and entered her own private room.

Croustillac remained thoughtful and absorbed, without making any answer.

"Well now, brother," said the Boucanier, addressing him, "positively, how do you like her!"

"Pray, monsieur, what is your intention in putting this question to me? Is what you ask a sarcasm?" cried the Chevalier, impatiently.

"My only intention in asking, is to learn your real opinion of our hostess."

"Hum! hum! Without wishing in any way to speak ill of the absent, you will confess that she is a woman somewhat difficult to class on a single interview," replied Croustillac, with considerable bitterness. "You will, therefore, not be surprised if I take some little time to reflect before I give my opinion. To-morrow, I will answer you, if, in the meantime, I can succeed in answering myself."

"In your place now," said the Boucanier, "had I to choose, I would not reflect at all. I would accept with my eyes shut all she proposed me, and marry her at once; for, faith, one knows not who lives and who dies. Tastes change with age, days follow days, and yet they are not alike."

"Ah, ca! mordioux! where the devil are you going at this rate with your proverbs and your parables," cried the angry Gascon. "Why, then, in God's name, you speak thus, why do you not marry her?"

"I?"

"Yes, you."

"Because I have no wish to die of over-laughing, or to be changed into a burning lamp."

"And why should I wish it any more than you, pray?" exclaimed the Adventurer.

"Yes. Why should I have any more wish than you, to see the red man signing my wedding contract, as this extraordinary woman has it?"

"Then do not marry her. You are your own master, and best judge of your own affairs."

"Certainly, I am the best judge, and I will marry her if I choose—mordieux!" cried Polyphemus, who began to fear that he was about to lose his reason amid this chaos of strange thoughts.

"Come, brother, calm yourself," said the Boucanier, "do not be angry; I assure you, you were wrong to be so. Have I not kept my word with you? The prettiest woman in the world offers you her hand, her heart, and her treasures. What would you more?"

"I wish to fathom all that is passing here; I wish to understand all that has happened to me these last two days; all that I have seen and heard this evening," cried Croustillac, exasperated. "I want to know whether I am in a dream, or whether I am awake."

"Do not, I beg, be angry, brother; perhaps to-night you may dream a dream that will enlighten you. I hope so. But come, not; the chace has been rough to-day; it is late."

*

Angelina, seated in the apartment we have before described, addressed the Boucanier.

"Unfortunately, this man is less foolish and less credulous than we took him to be. I only hope that he may not prove dangerous," and Angelina shuddered.

"No, no; reassure yourself," said the Boucanier. "He only wished to play the *esprit fort*; but our two tales struck him most violently; he will recollect this evening as long as ever he lives, and what is better, he will speak of it far and wide. Believe me, all the exaggeration which he will relate will once more restore youth to the mysterious recitals which are current of the Morne-au-Diable."

"Ah!" cried the widow, still frightened with the recollections, "when this adventurer said that all this was but a comedy, and that he clearly saw through all our appearances, despite my better judgment, I was frightened."

"There is nothing to fear, I tell you, Madame La Barbe-bleue," continued the Boucanier, gaily, at the same time placing himself on his knees before Angelina, and gazing at her tenderly; "your diabolical reputation will suffer no diminution; it is too well established to be easily removed; but confess that I am possessed of a rich imagination, and that my grey powder and green liqueur worked marvels—"

"And, my red man, who signs the contract?" exclaimed Angelina, once more bursting into a fit of laughter. "Do you really count that for nothing?"

"That is right now—that is how I love you, laughing and foolish," said the Boucanier; "when I see you sad and dreamy, I begin to fear me that this retreat weighs upon your spirits."

"Will you be quiet, now, Monsieur Arrache'lâme? You do not mean to say that I have the air of being annoyed near you. Are you jealous of your rivals? Ask them if I love them better than you. Have you not procured me the delight and feast of this Gascon, to whom I owe the most delicious attack of gaiety? In fact, I was quite vulgar, and uproarious."

"I am sure that this poor devil is still in some horrible dream. Ah, but to-morrow we will give him a guide, and send him away once more to Macouba."

1 8 4 6 – 7

THE STRING OF PEARLS;
OR, THE SAILOR'S GIFT

James Malcolm Rymer

Undoubtedly one of the most popular penny serialisations, James Malcolm Rymer's *The String of Pearls* is a dreadful tale that's credited for introducing one of the most notorious serial killers into Gothic folklore, and is renowned for its creation of Sweeney Todd, the murderous butcher. Initially released as a serial in *People's Periodicals and Family Magazine* from 21 November 1846 to 20 March 1847, this blood was re-serialised and extended later as *The String of Pearls; or, The Barber of Fleet Street* by Edward Lloyd from 1 February 1850 to 30 November 1851. Since its inception, the authorship of this publication has been a source of contention, as both Thomas Peckett Prest and James Malcolm Rymer have been suspect. It is only within the last few decades that clarity has been offered on this conflict by Helen R. Smith's *New Light on Sweeney Todd, Thomas Peckett Prest, James Malcolm Rymer and Elizabeth Caroline Grey* (2002). While others still debate the Rymer-Prest ownership, Smith provides enough evidence for this collection to recognise Rymer as the sole proprietor. While written as a Victorian melodrama informed by the *Newgate Calendar* with its criminal activities and adventurous side-plots, *The String of Pearls* is a critical piece of literature that features a key monstrous female figuration in Gothic literature: Mrs. Lovett.

The tale is set in 1785 and begins with the disappearance of Lieutenant Thornhill. This sailor was tasked with delivering a string of pearls to Joanna Oakley by Mark Ingestrie, who was assumed to be lost at sea. Thornhill's disappearance was soon investigated by Colonel Jeffrey and Thornhill's dog, Hector, who were quickly introduced to Sweeney Todd and his barbershop. Concurrently, other plots are developed: Mark Ingestrie, disguised as Jarvis Williams, finds employment with Mrs. Lovett's pie-shop; Joanna faces internal conflict as she questions Ingestrie's lack of communication and disappearance; Tobias Ragg's introduction as Todd's apprentice, and later

87

confinement to the asylum, to name a few. Meanwhile, investigators search for the malodorous odours beneath St. Dunstan's church. It is later discerned that Sweeney Todd murders citizens in his ingenuitive barber's chair where he feeds the corpses through a subterranean passage to the cellar of Lovett's shop for transformation into pies. The tale ends with resolution for Mark, Joanna, and Tobias, while Sweeney Todd meets his demise at Newgate while Lovett succumbs to poison before her arrest.

As the multi-plotted *String of Pearls* is extensive in individual stories and details, the following chapter primarily focuses on the charismatic draw of Mrs. Lovett and her pie-shop, as she is depicted as the angelic and domestic Victorian woman while hiding the monstrous villain who constructs human tissue into food for social consumption.

HARK! Twelve o'clock at midday is cheerily proclaimed by St. Dunstan's church, and scarcely have the sounds done echoing throughout the neighbourhood, and scarcely has the clock of Lincoln's-inn done chiming in with its announcement of the same hour, when Bell-yard, Temple-bar, becomes a scene of commotion. What a scampering of feet is there, what a laughing and talking, what a jostling to be first; and what an immense number of manoeuvres are resorted to by some of the throng to distance others!

And mostly from Lincoln's-inn do these persons, young and old, but most certainly a majority of the former, come bustling and striving, although from the neighbouring legal establishments likewise there come not a few; the Temple contributes its numbers, and from the more distant Gray's Inn there come a goodly lot.

Is it a fire? is it a fight? Or anything else sufficiently alarming and extraordinary to excite the junior members of the legal profession to such species of madness? No, it is none of these, nor is it there a fat cause to be run for, which, in the hands of some clever practitioner, might become quite a vested interest. No, the enjoyment is purely one of a physical character, and all the pacing and racing—all this turmoil and trouble—all this pushing, jostling, laughing, and shouting, is to see who will get first to Lovett's pie-shop.

Yes, on the left-hand side of Bell-yard, going down from Carey-street, was, at the time we write of, one of the most celebrated shops for the sale of veal and pork pies that London ever produced. High and low, rich and poor, resorted to it; its fame had spread far and wide; and it was because the first batch of those pies came up at twelve o'clock that there was such a rush of the legal profession to obtain them.

Their fame had spread even to great distances, and many persons carried them to the suburbs of the city as quite a treat to friends and relations there residing. And well did they deserve their reputation, those delicious pies; there was about them a flavour never surpassed, and rarely equalled; the paste was of the most delicate construction, and impregnated with the aroma of a delicious gravy that defies description. Then the small portions of meat which they contained were so tender, and the fat and the lean so artistically mixed up, that to eat one of Lovett's pies was such a provocative to eat another, that many persons who came to lunch stayed to dine, wasting more than an hour, perhaps, of precious time, and endangering—who knows to the contrary—the success of some lawsuit thereby.

The counter in Lovett's pie-shop was in the shape of a horseshoe, and it was the custom of the young bloods from the Temple and Lincoln's-inn to sit in a row upon its edge while they partook of the delicious pies, and chatted gaily about one concern and another.

Many an appointment was made at Lovett's pie-shop, and many a piece of gossiping scandal was there first circulated. The din of tongues was prodigious. The ringing laugh of the boy who looked upon the quarter of an hour he spent at Lovett's as the brightest of the whole twenty-four, mingled gaily with the more boisterous mirth of his seniors; and oh! with what rapidity the pies disappeared!

They were brought up on large trays, each of which contained about a hundred, and from these trays they were so speedily transferred to the mouths of Mrs. Lovett's customers that it looked like a work of magic.

And now we have let out some portion of the secret. There was a Mistress Lovett; but possibly our readers guessed as much, for what but a female hand, and that female buxom, young and good-looking, could have ventured upon the production of those pies. Mrs. Lovett was all that; and every enamoured young scion of the law, as he devoured his pie, pleased himself with the idea that the charming Mrs. Lovett had made that pie especially for him, and that fate or predestination had placed it in his hands.

And it was astonishing to see with what impartiality and with tact the fair pastry-cook bestowed her smiles upon her admirers, so that none could say he was neglected, while it was extremely difficult for anyone to say he was preferred.

This was pleasant, but at the same time it was provoking to all except Mrs. Lovett, in whose favour it got up a sort of excitement that paid extraordinarily well, because some of the young fellows thought, and thought it with wisdom too, that he who consumed the most pies would be in the most likely way to receive the greatest number of smiles from the lady.

Acting upon this supposition, some of her more enthusiastic admirers went on consuming the pies until they were almost ready to burst. But there were others again, of a more philosophic turn of mind, who went for the pies only, and did not care one jot for Mrs. Lovett. These declared that her smile was cold and uncomfortable—that it was upon her lips, but had no place in her heart—that it was the set smile of a ballet-dancer, which is about one of the most unmirthful things in existence.

Then there were some who went even beyond this, and, while they admitted the excellence of the pies, and went every day to partake of them, swore that Mrs. Lovett had quite a sinister aspect, and that they could see what a merely superficial affair her blandishments were, and that there was "a lurking devil in her eye" that, if once roused, would be capable of achieving some serious things, and might not be so easily quelled again. By five minutes past twelve Mrs. Lovett's counter was full, and the savoury steam of the hot pies went out in fragrant clouds into Bell-yard, being sniffed up by many a poor wretch passing by who lacked the means of making one in the throng that were devouring the dainty morsels within.

Towards the dusk of the evening in that day, after the last batch of pies at Lovett's had been disposed of, there walked into the shop a man most miserably clad, and who stood for a few moments staring with weakness and hunger at the counter before he spoke.

Mrs. Lovett was there, but she had no smile for him, and instead of its usual bland expression, her countenance wore an aspect of anger, as she forestalled what the man had to say, by exclaiming,—

"Go away, we never give to beggars."

There came a flash of colour, for a moment, across the features of the stranger, and then he replied,—

"Mistress Lovett, I do not come to ask alms of you, but to know if you can recommend me to any employment?"

"Recommend you! recommend a ragged wretch like you!"

"I am a ragged wretch, and, moreover, quite destitute. In better times I have sat at your counter, and paid cheerfully for what I have wanted, and then one of your softest smiles had been ever at my disposal. I do not say this as a reproach to you, because the cause of your smile was well-known to be a self-interested one, and when that cause has passed away, I can no longer expect it; but I am so situated that I am willing to do anything for a mere subsistence."

"Oh, yes, and then when you have got into a better case again, I have no doubt, but you have quite sufficient insolence to make you unbearable; besides, what employment can we have but pie-making, and we have a man already who suits us very well with the exception that he, as you would do if you were to exchange with him, has grown insolent, and fancies himself master of the place."

"Well, well," said the stranger, "of course there is always sufficient argument against the poor and destitute to keep them so. If you will assert that my conduct would be of the nature you describe it, it is quite impossible for me to prove the contrary."

He turned and was about to leave the shop, when Mrs. Lovett called after him, saying—"Come in again in two hours."

He paused a moment or two, and then, turning his emaciated countenance upon her, said, "I will if my strength permits me—water from the pumps in the streets is but a poor thing for a man to subsist upon for twenty-four hours."

"You may take one pie."

The half-famished, miserable-looking man seized upon a pie, and devoured it in an instant.

"My name," he said, "is Jarvis Williams: I'll be here, never fear, Mrs. Lovett, in two hours; and notwithstanding all you have said, you shall find no change in my behaviour because I may be well-kept and better clothed; but if I should feel dissatisfied with my situation, I will leave it and no harm done."

So saying, he walked from the shop, and after he was gone, a strange expression came across the countenance of Mrs. Lovett, and she said in a low tone to herself,—"He might suit for a few months, like the rest, and it is clear we must get rid of the one we have; I must think of it."

There is a cellar of vast extent, and of dim and sepulchral aspect—some rough red tiles are laid upon the floor, and pieces of flint and large jagged stones have been hammered into the earthen walls to strengthen them; while here and there rough pillars made by beams of timber rise perpendicularly from the floor, and prop large flat pieces of wood against the ceiling, to support it.

Here and there gleaming lights seem to be peeping out from furnaces, and there is a strange, hissing, simmering sound going on, while the whole air is impregnated with a rich and savoury vapour.

This is Lovett's pie manufactory beneath the pavement of Bell-yard, and at this time a night-batch of some thousands is being made for the purpose of being sent by carts the first thing in the morning all over the suburbs of London.

By the earliest dawn of the day a crowd of itinerant hawkers of pies would make their appearance, carrying off a large quantity to regular customers who had them daily, and no more thought of being without them than of forbidding the milkman or the baker to call at their residences.

It will be seen and understood, therefore, that the retail part of Mrs. Lovett's business, which took place principally between the hours of twelve and one, was by no means the most important or profitable portion of a concern which was really of immense magnitude, and which brought in a large yearly income.

To stand in the cellar when this immense manufacturer of what, at first sight, would appear such a trivial article was carried on, and to look about as far as the eye could reach, was by no means to have a sufficient idea of the extent of the place; for there were as many doors in different directions, and singular low-arched entrances to different vaults, which all appeared as black as midnight, that one might almost suppose the inhabitants of all the surrounding neighbourhood had, by common consent, given up their cellars to Lovett's pie factory.

There is but one miserable light, except the occasional fitful glare that comes from the ovens where the pies are stewing, hissing, and spluttering in their own luscious gravy.

There is but one man, too, throughout all the place, and he is sitting on a low three-legged stool in one corner, with his head resting upon his hands, and gently rocking to and fro, as he utters scarcely audible moans.

He is but lightly clad; in fact, he seems to have but little on him except a shirt and a pair of loose canvas trousers. The sleeves of the former are turned up beyond his elbows, and on his head he has a white night-cap.

It seems astonishing that such a man, even with the assistance of Mrs. Lovett, could make so many pies as are required in a day; but the system does wonders, and in those cellars there are various mechanical contrivances for kneading the dough, chopping up the meat, &c., which greatly reduce the labour.

But what a miserable object is this man—what a sad and soul-stricken wretch he looks! His face is pale and haggard, his eyes deeply sunken; and, as he removes his hands from before his visage, and looks about him, a more perfect picture of horror could not have been found.

"I must leave to-night," he said, in coarse accents—"I must leave to-night. I know too much—my brain is full of horrors. I have not slept now for five nights, nor dare I eat anything but the raw flour. I will leave to-night if they do not watch me too closely. Oh! if I could but get into the streets—if I could but once again breathe the fresh air! Hush! what's that? I thought I heard a noise."

He rose, and stood trembling and listening; but all was still, save the simmering and hissing of the pies, and then he resumed his seat with a deep sigh.

"All the doors fastened upon me," he said, "what can it mean? It's very horrible, and my heart dies with me. Six weeks only have I been here—only six weeks, I was starving before I came. Alas, alas! How much better to have starved! I should have been dead before now, and spared all this agony!"

"Skinner!" cried a voice, and it was a female one—"Skinner, how long will the ovens be?"

"A quarter of an hour," he replied, "a quarter of an hour, Mrs. Lovett. God help me!"

"What is that you say?"

"I said, God help me! surely a man may say that without offence."

A door slammed shut, and the miserable man was alone again.

"How strangely," he said, "on this night my thoughts go back to early days, and to what I once was. The pleasant scenes of my youth recur to me. I see again the ivy-mantled porch, and the pleasant green. I hear again the merry ringing laughter of my playmates, and there, in my mind's eye, appears to me, the bubbling stream, and the ancient mill, the old mansion-house, with its tall turrets, and its air of silent grandeur. I hear the music of the birds, and the winds making rough melody among the trees. 'Tis very strange that all these sights and sounds should come back to me at such a time as this, as if just to remind me what a wretch I am."

He was silent for a few moments, during which he trembled with emotion; then he spoke again, saying,—

"Thus the forms of those whom I knew, and many of whom have gone already to the silent tomb, appear to come thronging round me. They bend their eyes momentarily upon me, and, with settled expressions, show acutely the sympathy they feel for me.

"I see her, too, who first, in my bosom, lit up the flame of soft affection. I see her gliding past me like the dim vision of a dream, indistinct, but beautiful; no more than a shadow—and yet to me most palpable. What am I now—what am I now?"

He resumed his former position, with his head resting upon his hands; he rocked himself slowly to and fro, uttering those moans of a tortured spirit, which we have before noticed.

But see, one of the small arch doors opens, in the gloom of those vaults, and a man, in a stooping posture, creeps in—a half-mask is upon his face, and he wears a cloak; but both his hands are at liberty. In one of them he carries a double-headed hammer, with a powerful handle, of about ten inches in length.

He has probably come out of a darker place than the one into which he now so cautiously creeps, for he shades the light from his eyes, as if it was suddenly rather too much for him, and then he looks cautiously round the vault, until he sees the crouched-up figure of the man whose duty it is to attend to the ovens.

From that moment he looks at nothing else; but advances towards him, steadily and cautiously. It is evident that great secrecy is his object, for he is walking on his stocking soles only; and it is impossible to hear the slightest sound of his footsteps. Nearer and nearer he comes, so slowly, and yet so surely towards him, who still keeps up the low moaning sound, indicative of mental anguish. Now he is close to him, and he bends over him for a moment, with a look of fiendish malice. It is a look which, despite his mask, glances full from his eyes, and then, grasping the hammer tightly in both hands, he raises it slowly above his head, and gives it a swinging motion through the air.

There is no knowing what induced the man that was crouching upon the stool to rise at that moment; but he did so, and paced about with great quickness.

A sudden shriek burst from his lips, as he beheld so terrific an apparition before him; but before he could repeat the word, the hammer descended, crushing into his skull, and he fell lifeless without a moan.

*

"And so Mr. Jarvis Williams, you have kept your word, and come for employment," said Mrs. Lovett to the emaciated, careworn stranger.

"I have, madam, and hope that you can give it to me: I frankly tell you that I would seek for something better, and more congenial to my disposition if I could; but who would employ one presenting such a wretched appearance as I do? You see that I am all in rags, and I have told you that I have been half starved, and therefore it is only some common and ordinary employment that I can hope to get, and that made me come to you."

"Well, I don't see why we should not make a trial of you, at all events, so if you like to go down into the bakehouse, I will follow you, and show you what you have to do. You remember that you have to live entirely upon the pies, unless you like to purchase for yourself anything else, which you may do if you can get the money. We give none, and you must likewise agree never to leave the bakehouse."

"Never to leave it?"

"Never, unless you leave it for good, and for all; if upon those conditions you choose to accept the situation, you may, and if not you can go about your business at once, and leave it alone."

"Alas, madam, I have no resource; but you spoke of having a man already."

"Yes; but he had gone to some of his very oldest friends, who will be quite glad to see him, so now say the word: Are you willing or are you not, to take the situation?"

"My poverty and my destitution consent, if my will be adverse, Mrs. Lovett; but of course, I quite understand that I leave when I please."

"Oh, of course, we never think of keeping anybody many hours after they begin to feel uncomfortable. If you are ready, follow me."

"I am quite ready, and thankful for a shelter. All the brightest visions of my early life have long since faded away, and it matters little or, indeed, nothing what now becomes of me; I will follow you, madam, freely upon the condition you have mentioned."

Mrs. Lovett lifted up a portion of the counter which permitted him to pass behind it, and then followed her into a small room, which was at the back of the shop. She then took a key from her pocket, and opened an old door which was in the wainscoting, and immediately behind which was a flight of stairs.

These she descended, and Jarvis Williams followed her, to a considerable depth, after which she took an iron bar from behind another door, and flung it open, showing to her new assistant the interior of that vault which we have already very briefly described.

"These," she said, "are the ovens, and I will proceed to show you how you can manufacture the pies, feed the furnaces, and make yourself generally useful. Flour will always be let down through a trapdoor from the upper shop, as well as everything required for making the pies but the meat, and that you will always find ranged upon shelves either in lumps or steaks, in a small room through this door, but it is only at particular times you will find the door open; and whenever you do so, you had better always take out what meat you think you will require for the next batch."

"I understand all that, madam," said Williams, "but how does it get there?"

"That's no business of yours; so long as you are supplied with it, that is sufficient for you; and now I will go through the process of making one pie, so that you may know how to proceed, and you will find with what amazing quickness they can be manufactured if you set about them in the proper manner."

She then showed how a piece of meat thrown into a machine became finely minced up, by merely turning a handle; and then how flour and water and lard were mixed up together, to make the crusts of the pies, by another machine, which threw out the paste, thus manufactured, in small pieces, each just large enough for a pie.

Lastly, she showed him how a tray, which just held a hundred, could be filled, and, by turning a windlass, sent up to the shop, through a square trapdoor, which went right up to the very counter.

"And now," she said, "I must leave you. As long as you are industrious, you will get on very well, but as soon as you begin to be idle, and neglect the orders that are sent to you by me, you will get a piece of information which will be useful, and which, if you are a prudent man, will enable you to know what you are about."

"What is that? you may as well give it to me now."

"No; we but seldom find there is occasion for it at first, but, after a time, when you get well fed, you are pretty sure to want it."

So saying, she left the place, and he heard the door, by which he had entered, carefully barred after her. Suddenly then he heard her voice again, and so clearly and distinctly, too, that he thought she must have come back again; but, upon looking up at the door, he found that that arose from the fact of her speaking through a small grating at the upper part of it, to which her mouth was closely placed.

"Remember your duty," she said, "and I warn you that any attempt to leave here will be as futile as it will be dangerous."

"Except with your consent, when I relinquish the situation."

"Oh, certainly—certainly, you are quite right there, everybody who relinquishes the situation, goes to his old friends, whom he has not seen for many years, perhaps."

"What a strange manner of talking she has!" said Jarvis Williams to himself, when he found he was alone. "There seems to be some singular and hidden meaning in every word she utters. What can she mean by a communication being made to me, if I neglect my duty! It is very strange, and what a singular-looking place this is! I think it would be quite unbearable if it were not for the delicious odour of the pies, and they are indeed delicious—perhaps more delicious to me, who has been famished so long, and has gone through so much wretchedness; there is no one here but myself, and I am hungry now—frightfully hungry, and whether the pies are done or not, I'll have half a dozen of them at any rate, so here goes."

He opened one of the ovens, and the fragrant steam that came out was perfectly delicious, and he sniffed it up with a satisfaction such as he had never felt before, as regarded anything that was eatable.

"Is it possible," he said, "that I shall be able to make such delicious pies? at all events one can't starve here, and if it is a kind of imprisonment, it's a pleasant one. Upon my soul, they are nice, even half-cooked—delicious! I'll have another half-dozen, there are lots of them—delightful! I can't keep the gravy from running out of the corners of my mouth. Upon my soul, Mrs. Lovett, I don't know where you get your meat, but it's all as tender as young chickens, and the fat actually melts away in one's mouth. Ah, these are pies, something like pies!—they are positively fit for the gods!"

Mrs. Lovett's new man ate twelve threepenny pies, and then he thought of leaving off. It was a little drawback not to have anything to wash them down with but cold water, but he reconciled himself to this. "For," as he said, "after all it would be a pity to take the flavour of such pies out of one's mouth—indeed, it would be a thousand pities, so I won't think of it, but just put up with what I have got and not complain. I might have gone further and fared worse with a vengeance, and I cannot help looking upon it as a singular piece of good fortune that made me think of coming here in my deep distress to try and get something to do. I have no friends, and no money; she whom I loved is faithless, and here I am, master of as many pies as I like, and to all appearance monarch of all I survey; for there really seems to be no one to dispute my supremacy.

"To be sure, my kingdom is rather a gloomy one; but then I can abdicate it when I like, and when I am tired of those delicious pies, if such a thing be possible, which I really very much doubt, I can give up my situation and think of something else.

"If I do that I will leave England forever; it's no place for me after the many disappointments I have had. No friend left me, my girl false, not a relation but who would turn his back upon me! I will go somewhere where I am unknown and can form new connections, and perhaps make new friendships of a more permanent and stable character than the old ones, which have all proved so false to me; and, in the meantime, I'll make and eat pies as fast as I can."

*

From what we have already had occasion to record about Mrs. Lovett's new cook, who ate so voraciously in the cellar, our readers will no doubt be induced to believe that he was a gentleman likely enough soon to tire of his situation.

To a starving man, and one who seemed completely abandoned even by hope, Lovett's bakehouse, with an unlimited leave to eat as much as possible, must of course present itself in the most desirable and lively colours; and no wonder, therefore, that banishing all scruple, a man so pleased, would take the situation with very little enquiry.

But people will tire of good things; and it is a remarkably well-authenticated fact that human nature is prone to be discontented.

And those persons who are well acquainted with the human mind, and who know well how little value people soon set upon things which they possess, while those which they are pursuing, and which seem to be beyond their reach, assume the liveliest colours imaginable, adopt various means of turning this to account.

Napoleon took good care that the meanest of his soldiers should see in perspective the possibility of grasping a marshal's baton.

Confectioners at the present day, when they take a new apprentice, tell him to eat as much as he likes of those tempting tarts and sweetmeats, one or two of which before had been a most delicious treat.

The soldier goes on fighting away, and never gets the marshal's baton. The confectioner's boy crams himself with Banbury cakes, gets dreadfully sick, and never touches one afterwards.

And now, to revert to our friend in Mrs. Lovett's bakehouse.

At first everything was delightful, and, by the aid of the machinery, he found that it was no difficult matter to keep up the supply of pies by really a very small amount of manual labour. And that labour was such a labour of love, for the pies were delicious; there could be no mistake about that. He tasted them half cooked, he tasted them wholly cooked, and he tasted them overdone; hot and cold, pork and veal with seasoning, and without season-ing, until at last he had had them in every possible way and shape; and when the fourth day came after his arrival in the cellar, he might have been seen sitting in rather a contemplative attitude with a pie before him.

It was twelve o'clock: he heard that sound come from the shop. Yes, it was twelve o'clock, and he had eaten nothing yet; but he kept his eyes fixed upon the pie that lay untouched before him.

"The pies are all very well," he said, "in fact of course they are capital pies; and now that I see how they are made, and know that there is nothing wrong in them, I of course relish them more than ever, but one can't live always upon pies; it's quite impossible one can subsist upon pies from one end of the year to the other, if they were the finest pies the world ever saw, or ever will see. I don't say anything against the pies—I know they are made of the finest flour, the best possible butter, and that the meat, which comes from God knows where, is the most delicate-looking and tender I ever ate in my life."

He stretched out his hand and broke a small portion of the crust from the pie that was before him, and he tried to eat it.

He certainly did succeed, but it was a great effort; and when he had done, he shook his head, saying, "No, no! damn it, I cannot eat it, and that's the fact—one cannot be continually eating pie; it is out of the question, quite out of the question, and all I have to remark is, damn the pies! I really don't think I shall be able to let another one pass my lips."

He rose and paced with rapid strides the place in which he was, and then suddenly he heard a noise, and, looking up, he saw a trapdoor in the roof open, and a sack of flour begin gradually to come down.

"Hilloa, hilloa!" he cried, "Mrs. Lovett, Mrs. Lovett!"

Down came the flour, and the trapdoor was closed.

"Oh, I can't stand this sort of thing," he exclaimed. "I cannot be made into a mere machine for the manufacture of pies. I cannot, and will not endure it—it is past all bearing."

For the first time almost since his incarceration, for such it really was, he began to think that he would take an accurate survey of the place where this tempting manufacture was carried on.

The fact was, his mind had been so intensively occupied during the time he had been there in providing merely for his physical wants, that he has scarcely had time to think or reason upon the probabilities of an uncomfortable termination of his career; but now, when he had become quite surfeited with the pies, and tired of the darkness and gloom of the place, many unknown fears began to creep across him, and he really trembled, as he asked himself what was to be the end of all.

It was with such a feeling as this that he now set about taking a careful and accurate survey of the place, and, taking a little lamp in his hand, he resolved to peer into every corner of it, with a hope that surely he should find some means by which he should effect an escape from what otherwise threatened to be an intolerable imprisonment.

The vault in which the ovens were situated was the largest; and although a number of smaller ones communicated with it, containing the different mechanical contrivances for the pie-making, he could not from any one of them discover an outlet.

But it was to the vault where the meat was deposited upon stone shelves, that he paid the greatest share of attention, for to that vault he felt convinced there must be some hidden and secret means of ingress, and therefore of egress likewise, or else how came the shelves always so well stocked with meat as they were?

This vault was larger than any of the other subsidiary ones, and the roof was very high, and, come into it when he would, it always happened that he found meat enough upon the shelves, cut into large lumps and sometimes into slices, to make a batch of pies with.

When it got there was not so much a mystery to him as how it got there; for of course, as he must sleep sometimes, he concluded, naturally enough, that it was brought in by some means during the period that he devoted to repose.

He stood in the centre of this vault with the lamp in his hand, and he turned slowly round, surveying the walls and the ceiling with the most critical and marked attention, but not the smallest appearance of an outlet was observable.

In fact, the walls were so entirely filled up with the stone shelves, that there was no space left for a door; and, as for the ceiling, it seemed to be perfectly entire.

Then the floor was of earth; so that the idea of a trapdoor opening in it was out of the question, because there was no one on his side of it to place the earth again over it, and give it its compact and usual appearance.

"This is most mysterious," he said; "and if ever I could have been brought to believe that anyone had the assistance of the devil himself in conducting human affairs, I should say that by some means Mrs. Lovett had made it worth the while of that elderly individual to assist her; for, unless the meat gets here by some supernatural agency, I really cannot see how it can get here at all. And yet here it is, so fresh, and pure, and white-looking, although I never could tell the pork from the veal myself, for they seemed to me both alike."

He now made a still narrower examination of this vault, but he gained nothing by that. He found that the walls at the backs of the shelves were composed of flat pieces of stone, which, no doubt, were necessary for the support of the shelves themselves; but beyond that he made no further discovery, and he was about leaving the place, when he fancied he saw some writing on the inner side of the door.

A closer inspection convinced him that there were a number of lines written with lead pencil, and after some difficulty he deciphered them as follows:

"Whatever unhappy wretch reads these lines may bid adieu to the world and all hope, for he is a doomed man! He will never emerge from these vaults with life, for there is a hideous secret connected with them so awful and so hideous, that to write it makes one's blood curdle, and the flesh to creep upon my bones. That secret is this—and you may be assured, whoever is reading these lines, that I write the truth, and that it is as impossible to make that awful truth worse by any exaggeration, as it would be by a candle at midday to attempt to add lustre to the sunbeams."

Here, most unfortunately, the writing broke off, and our friend, who, up to this point, had perused the lines with the most intense interest, felt great bitterness of disappointment, from the fact that enough should have been written to stimulate his curiosity to the highest possible point, but not enough to gratify it.

"This is, indeed, most provoking," he exclaimed; "what can this most dreadful secret be, which it is impossible to exaggerate? I cannot, for a moment, divine to what it can allude."

In vain he searched over the door for some more writing—there was none to be found, and from the long straggling pencil mark which followed the last word, it seemed as if he who had been then writing had been interrupted, and possibly met the fate that he had predicted, and was about to explain the reason of.

"This is worse than no information. I had better have remained in ignorance than have so indistinct a warning; but they shall not find me an easy victim, and, besides, what power on earth can force me to make pies unless I like, I should wish to know."

As he stepped out of the place in which the meat was kept into the large vault where the ovens were, he trod upon a piece of paper that was lying upon the ground, and which he was quite certain he had not observed before. It was fresh and white, and clean too, so that it could not have been long there, and he picked it up with some curiosity.

That curiosity was, however, soon turned to dismay when he saw what was written upon it, which was to the following effect, and well calculated to produce a considerable amount of alarm in the breast of anyone situated as he was, so entirely friendless and so entirely hopeless of any extraneous aid in those dismal vaults, which he began, with a shudder, to suspect would be his tomb;

"You are getting dissatisfied, and therefore it becomes necessary to explain to you your real position, which is simply this: you are a prisoner, and were such from the first moment that you set foot where you now are; and you will find that, unless you are resolved upon sacrificing your life, your best plan will be to quietly give in to the circumstances in which you find yourself placed. Without going into any argument or details upon the subject, it is sufficient to inform you that so long as you continue to make the pies, you will be safe; but if you refuse, then the first time you are caught sleeping your throat will be cut."

This document was so much to the purpose, and really had so little of verbosity about it, that it was extremely difficult to doubt its sincerity.

It dropped from the half-paralysed hands of that man who, in the depth of his distress, and urged on by great necessity, had accepted a situation that he would have given worlds to escape from, had he been possessed of them.

"Gracious Heavens!" he exclaimed, "and am I then indeed condemned to such a slavery? Is it possible that even in the very heart of London I am a prisoner, and without the means of resisting the most frightful threats that are uttered against me? Surely, surely, this must all be a dream! It is too terrific to be true!"

He sat down upon that low stool where his predecessor had sat before, receiving his death wound from the assassin who had glided in behind him, and dealt him that terrific crashing blow, whose only mercy was that it at once deprived the victim of existence.

He could have wept bitterly, wept as he there sat, for he thought over days long passed away, of opportunities let go by with the heedless laugh of youth; he thought over all the chances and misfortunes of his life, and now to find himself the miserable inhabitant of a cellar, condemned to a mean and troublesome employment, without even the liberty of leaving that to starve if he chose, upon pain of death—a frightful death which had been threatened him—was indeed torment!

No wonder that at times he felt himself unnerved, and that a child might have conquered him, while at other moments such a feeling of despair would come across him, that he called aloud to his enemies to make their appearance, and give him at least the chance of a struggle for his life.

"If I am to die," he cried, "let me die with some weapon in my hand, as a brave man ought, and I will not complain, for there is little indeed in life now which should induce me to cling to it; but I will not be murdered in the dark."

He sprang to his feet, and running up to the door, which opened from the house into the vaults, he made a violent and desperate effort to shake it.

But such a contingency as this had surely been looked forward to and provided against, for the door was of amazing strength, and most effectually resisted all his efforts, so that the result of his endeavours was but to exhaust himself, and he staggered back, panting and despairing, to the seat he had so recently left.

Then he heard a voice, and upon looking up he saw that the small square opening in the upper part of the door, through which he had been before addressed, was open, and a face there appeared, but it was not the face of Mrs. Lovett.

On the contrary, it was a large and hideous male physiognomy, and the voice that came from it was croaking and harsh, sounding most unmusically upon the ears of the unfortunate man, who was then made a victim to Mrs. Lovett's pies' popularity.

"Continue at your work," said the voice, "or death will be your portion as soon as sleep overcomes you, and you sink exhausted to that repose which you will never awaken from, except to feel the pangs of death, and to be conscious that you are weltering in your blood.

"Continue at your work and you will escape all this—neglect it and your doom is sealed?"

"What have I done that I should be made such a victim of? Let me go, and I will swear never to divulge the fact that I have been in these vaults, so I cannot disclose any of these secrets, even if I knew them."

"Make pies," said the voice, "eat them and be happy. How many a man would envy your position—withdrawn from all the struggles of existence, amply provided with board and lodging, and engaged in a pleasant and delightful occupation. It is astonishing how you can be dissatisfied!"

Bang! went the little square orifice at the top of the door, and the voice was heard no more. The jeering mockery of those tones, however, still lingered upon the ear of the unhappy prisoner, and he clasped his head in his hands with a fearful impression upon his brain that he surely must be going mad.

"He will drive me to insanity," he cried; "already I feel a sort of slumber stealing over me for want of exercise, and the confined air of these vaults hinders me from taking regular repose; but now, if I close an eye, I shall expect to find the assassin's knife at my throat."

He sat for some time longer, and not even the dread he had of sleep could prevent a drowsiness creeping over his faculties, and this weariness would not be shaken off by any ordinary means, until at length he sprang to his feet, and shaking himself roughly like one determined to be wide awake, he said to himself mournfully,—

"I must do their bidding or die; hope may be a delusion here, but I cannot altogether abandon it, and not until its faintest image has departed from my breast can I lie down to sleep and say—Let death come in any shape it may, it is welcome."

With a desperate and despairing energy he set about replenishing the furnaces of the oven, and when he had got them all in a good state he commenced manufacturing a batch of one hundred pies, which, when he had finished and placed upon the tray and set the machine in motion which conducted them up to the shop, he considered to a sort of price paid for his continued existence, and flinging himself upon the ground, he fell into a deep slumber.

It would have been clear to anyone, who looked at Sweeney Todd as he took his route from his own shop in Fleet-street to Bell-yard, Temple Bar, that it was not to eat pies he went there.

No; he was on very different thoughts indeed intent, and as he neared the shop of Mrs. Lovett, where those delicacies were vended, there was such a diabolical expression upon his face that, had he not stooped like grim War to "Smooth his wrinkled form," ere he made his way into the shop, he would, most unquestionably, have excited the violent suspicions of Mrs. Lovett, that all was not exactly as it should be, and the mysterious bond of union that held her and the barber together was not in that blooming state that it had been.

When he actually did enter the shop, he was all sweetness and placidity.

Mrs. Lovett was behind the counter, for it seldom happened that the shop was free of customers, for when the batches of hot pies were all over, there usually remained some which were devoured cold with avidity by the lawyers' clerks, from the offices and chambers in the neighbourhood.

But at nine o'clock, there was a batch of hot pies coming up, for of late Mrs. Lovett had fancied that between half-past eight and nine, there was a great turn-out of clerks from Lincoln's Inn, and a pie became a very desirable and comfortable prelude to half-price at the theatre, or any other amusements of the three hours before midnight.

Many people, too, liked them as a relish for supper, and took them home quite carefully. Indeed, in Lincoln's Inn, it may be said, that the affections of the clerks oscillated between Lovett's pies and sheep's heads; and it frequently so nicely balanced in their minds, that the two attractions depended upon the toss-up of a halfpenny, whether to choose "sang amary Jameses" from Clare Market, or pies from Lovett's.

Half-and-half washed both down equally well.

Mrs. Lovett, then, may be supposed to be waiting for the nine o'clock batch of pies, when Sweeney Todd, on this most eventful evening, made his appearance.

Todd and Mrs. Lovett met now with all the familiarity of old acquaintance.

"Ah, Mr. Todd," said the lady, "how do you do? Why, we have not seen you for a long time."

"It has been some time; and how are you, Mrs. Lovett?"

"Quite well, thank you. Of course, you will take a pie?"

Todd made a horrible face, as he replied, "No, thank you; it's very foolish, when I knew I was going to make a call here, but I have just had a pork chop."

"Had it the kidney in it, sir?" asked one of the lads who were eating cold pies.

"Yes, it had."

"Oh, that's what I like! Lor' bless you, I'd eat my mother, if she was a pork chop, done brown and crisp, and the kidney in it; just fancy it, grilling hot, you know, and just popped on a slice of bread, when you are cold and hungry."

"Will you walk in, Mr. Todd?" said Mrs. Lovett, raising a portion of the counter, by which an opening was made, that enabled Mr. Todd to pass into the sacred precincts of the parlour.

The invitation was complied with by Todd, who remarked that he hadn't above a minute to spare, but that he would sit down while he could stay, since Mrs. Lovett was so kind as to ask him.

The extreme suavity of manner, however, left Sweeney Todd when he was in the parlour, and there was nobody to take notice of him but Mrs. Lovett; nor did she think it necessary to wreathe her face in smiles, but with something of both anger and agitation in her manner. She said, "And when is all this to have an end, Sweeney Todd? you have been now for these six months providing me such a division of spoil as shall enable me, with an ample independence, once again to appear in the salons of Paris. I ask you now when this is to be?"

"You are very impatient!"

"Impatient, impatient? May I not well be impatient? do I not run a frightful risk, while you must have the next of the profits? It is useless your pretending to tell me that you do not get much. I know you better, Sweeney Todd; you never strike, unless for profit or revenge."

"Well?"

"Is it well, then, that I should have no account? Oh God! if you had the dreams I sometimes have!"

"Dreams?"

She did not answer him, but sank into a chair, and trembled so violently that he became alarmed, thinking she was very, very unwell. His hand was upon a bell rope, when she motioned him to be still, and then she managed to say in a very faint and nearly inarticulate voice, "You will go to that cupboard. You will see a bottle. I am forced to drink, or I should kill myself, or go mad, or denounce you; give it to me quick—quick, give it to me: it is brandy. Give it to me, I say: do not stand gazing at it there, I must, and I will have it. Yes, yes, I am better now, much better now. It is horrible, very horrible, but I am better; and I say, I must, and I will have an account at once. Oh. Todd, what an enemy you have been to me!"

"You wrong me. The worst enemy you ever had is in your head."

"No, no, no! I must have that to drown thought!"

"Indeed! can you be so superstitious? I presume you are afraid of your reception in another world."

"No, no—oh no! you and I do not believe in a hereafter, Sweeney Todd; if we did, we should go raving mad, to think what we had sacrificed. Oh, no—no, we dare not, we dare not!"

"Enough of this," said Todd, somewhat violently, "enough of this; you shall have an account to-morrow evening; and when you find yourself in possession of £20,000, you will not accuse me of having been unmindful of your interests; but now, there is someone in the shop who seems to be enquiring for you."

Mrs. Lovett rose, and went into the shop. The moment her back was turned, Todd produced the little bottle of poison he had got from the chemist's boy, and emptied it into the brandy decanter. He had just succeeded in this manoeuvre, and concealed the bottle again, when she returned, and flung herself into a chair.

"Did I hear you aright," she said, "or is this promise but a mere mockery; £20,000—is it possible that you have so much? oh, why was not all this dreadful trade left off sooner? Much less would have been done. But when shall I have it—when shall I be enabled to fly from here forever? Todd, we must live in different countries; I could never bear the chance of seeing you."

"As you please. It don't matter to me at all; you may be off to-morrow night, if you like. I tell you your share of the last eight years' work shall be £20,000. You shall have the sum to-morrow, and then you are free to go where you please; it matters not to me one straw where you spend your money. But tell me now, what immediate danger do you apprehend from your new cook?"

"Great and immediate; he has refused to work—a sign that he has got desperate, hopeless and impatient; and then only a few hours ago, I heard him call to me, and he said he had thought better of it, and would bake the nine o'clock batch, which, to my mind, was saying, that he had made up his mind to some course which gave him hope, and made it worth his while to temporise with me for a time, to lull suspicion."

"You are a clever woman. Something must and shall be done. I will be here at midnight, and we shall see if a vacancy cannot be made in your establishment."

"It will be necessary, and it is but one more."

"That's all—that's all, and I must say you have a very perfect and philosophic mode of settling the question; avoid the brandy as much as you can, but I suppose you are sure to take some between now and the morning."

"Quite sure. It is not in this house that I can wean myself off such a habit. I may do so abroad, but not here."

"Oh, well, it can't matter; but, as regards the fellow downstairs, I will, of course, come and rid you of him. You must keep a good lookout now for the short time you will be here, and a good countenance. There, you are wanted again, and I may as well go likewise."

Mrs. Lovett was a woman of judgement, and when she told Sweeney Todd that the prisoner was getting impatient in the lower regions of that house which was devoted to the manufacture of the delicious pies, she had guessed rightly his sensations with regard to his present state and future prospects.

We last left that unfortunate young man lying upon the floor of the place where the steaming and tempering manufacture was carried on; and for a time, as a very natural consequence of exhaustion, he slept profoundly.

That sleep, however, if it rested him bodily, likewise rested him mentally; and when he again awoke it was but to feel more acutely the agony of his most singular and cruel situation. There was a clock in the place by which he had been enabled to accurately regulate the time that the various batches of pies should take in cooking and upon looking up to that he saw that it was upon the hour of six, and consequently it would be three hours more before a batch of pies was wanted.

He looked about him very mournfully for some time, and then he spoke.

"What evil destiny," he said, "has placed me here? Oh, how much better it would have been if I had perished, as I have been near perishing several times during the period of my eventful life, than that I should be shut up in this horrible den and starved to death, as in all human probability I shall be, for I loathe the pies. Damn the pies!"

There was a slight noise, and upon his raising his eyes to that part of the place near the roof where there were some iron bars and between which Mrs. Lovett was wont to give him some directions, he saw her now detested face.

"Attend," she said; "you will bake an extra batch to-night, at nine precisely."

"What?"

"An extra batch, two hundred at least; do you understand me?"

"Hark ye, Mrs. Lovett. You are carrying this sort of thing too far; it won't do, I tell you, Mrs. Lovett; I don't know how soon I may be numbered with the dead, but, as I am a living man now, I will make no more of your detestable pies."

"Beware!"

"Beware yourself! I am not one to be frightened at shadows. I say I will leave this place, whether you like it or not; I will leave it; and perhaps you will find your power insufficient to keep me here. That there is some frightful mystery at the bottom of all the proceedings here, I am certain, but you shall not make me the victim of it!"

"Rash fool!"

"Very well, say what you like, but remember I defy you."

"Then you are tired of your life, and you will find, when too late, what are the consequences of your defiance. But listen to me: when I first engaged you, I told you you might leave when you were tired of the employment."

"You did, and yet you keep me a prisoner here. God knows I'm tired enough of it. Besides, I shall starve, for I cannot eat pies eternally; I hate them."

"And they so admired!"

"Yes, when one ain't surfeited with them. I am now only subsisting upon baked flour. I cannot eat the pies."

"You are strangely fantastical."

"Perhaps I am. Do you live upon pies, I should like to know, Mrs. Lovett?"

"That is altogether beside the question. You shall, if you like, leave this place to-morrow morning, by which time I hope to have got someone else to take over your situation, but I cannot be left without anyone to make the pies."

"I don't care for that, I won't make another one."

"We shall see," said Mrs. Lovett. "I will come to you in an hour, and see if you persevere in that determination. I advise you as a friend to change, for you will most bitterly repent standing in the way of your own enfranchisement."

"Well, but—she is gone, and what can I do? I am in her power, but shall I tamely submit? No, no, not while I have my arms at liberty, and strength enough to wield one of these long pokers that stir the coals in the ovens. How foolish of me not to think before that I had such desperate weapons, with which perchance to work my way to freedom."

As he spoke, he poised in his hand one of the long pokers he spoke of, and, after some few minutes spent in consideration, he said to himself, with something of the cheerfulness of hope, "I am in Bell-yard, and there are houses right and left of this accursed pie-shop, and those houses must have cellars. Now surely with such a weapon as this, a willing heart, and an arm that has not yet quite lost all its powers, I may make my way from this abominable abode."

The very thought of thus achieving his liberty lent him new strength and resolution, so that he felt himself to be quite a different man to what he had been, and he only paused to consider in which direction it would be best to begin his work.

After some reflection upon that head, he considered that it would be better to commence where the meat was kept—that meat of which he always found abundance, and which came from—he knew not where; since, if he went to sleep with little or none of it upon the shelves where it was placed for use, he always found plenty when he awoke.

"Yes," he said, "I will begin there, and work my way to freedom."

Before, however, he commenced operations, he glanced at the clock, and found that it wanted very little now to seven, so that he thought it would be but common prudence to wait until Mrs. Lovett had paid him her promised visit, as then, if he said he would make the pies she required, he would, in all probability, be left to himself for two hours, and, he thought, if he did not make good progress in that time towards his liberty, it would be strange indeed.

He sat down, and patiently waited until seven o'clock.

Scarcely had the hour sounded, when he heard the voice of his tormentor and mistress at the grating.

"Well," she said, "have you considered?"

"Oh, yes, I have. Needs must, you know, Mrs. Lovett, when a certain person drives. But I have a great favour to ask of you, madam."

"What is it?"

"Why, I feel faint, and if you could let me have a pot of porter, I would undertake to make a batch of pies superior to any you have ever had, and without any grumbling either."

Mrs. Lovett was silent for a few moments, and then said, "If you are supplied with porter, will you continue in your situation?"

"Well, I don't know that; but perhaps I may. At all events, I will make you the nine o'clock batch, you may depend."

"Very well. You shall have it."

She disappeared at these words, and in about ten minutes, a small trapdoor opened in the roof, and there was let down by a cord a foaming pot of porter.

"This is capital," cried the victim of the pies, as he took half of it at a draught. "This is nectar for the gods. Oh, what a relief, to be sure. It puts new life into me."

And so it really seemed, for shouldering the poker, which was more like a javelin than anything else, he at once rushed into the vault where the meat was kept.

"Now," he said, "for a grand effort at freedom, and if I succeed I promise you, Mrs. Lovett, that I will come round to the shop, and rather surprise you, madam. Damn the pies!"

We have before described the place in which the meat was kept, and we need now only say that the shelves were very well stocked indeed, and that our friend, in whose progress we have a great interest, shovelled off the large pieces with celerity from one of the shelves, and commenced operations with the poker.

He was not slow in discovering that his work would not be the most easy in the world, for every now and then he kept encountering what felt very much like a plate of iron; but he fagged away with right good will, and succeeded after a time in getting down one of the shelves, which was one point gained at all events.

"Now for it," he said, "Now for it; I shall be able to act—to work upon the wall itself, and it must be something unusually strong to prevent me making a breach through it soon."

In order to refresh himself, he finished the porter, and then using his javelin-like poker as a battering ram, he banged the wall with the end of it for some moments, without producing any effect, until suddenly a portion of it swung open just like a door, and he paused to wonder how that came about.

All was darkness through the aperture, and yet he saw that it was actually a little square door that he had knocked open; and the idea then recurred to him that he had found how the shelves were supplied with meat, and he had no doubt that there was such a little square door opening at the back of every one of them.

"So," he said, "that mystery is solved; but what part of Mrs. Lovett's premises have I got upon now? We shall soon see."

He went boldly into the large cellar, and procured a light—a flaming torch, made of a piece of dry wood, and returning to the opening he had made in the wall, he thrust his head through it, and projected the torch before him.

With a cry of horror he fell backwards, extinguishing the torch in his fall, and he lay for a full quarter of an hour insensible upon the floor. What dreadful sight had he seen that had so chilled his young blood, and frozen up the springs of life?

When he recovered, he looked around him in the dim, borrowed light that came from the other vault, and he shuddered as he said, "Was it a dream?"

Soon, however, as he rose, he gave up the idea of having been the victim of any delusion of the imagination, for there was the broken shelf, and there the little square opening, through which he had looked and seen what had so transfixed him with horror.

Keeping his face in that direction, as if it would be dreadful to turn his back for a moment upon some frightful object, he made his way into the larger cellar where the ovens were, and then he sat down with a deep groan.

"What shall I do? Oh, what shall I do?" he muttered. "I am doomed—doomed."

"Are the pies doing?" said the voice of Mrs. Lovett. "It's eight o'clock."

"Eight, is it?"

"Yes, to be sure, and I want to know if you are bent upon your own destruction or not? I don't hear the furnaces going, and I'm quite sure you have not made the pies."

"Oh, I will keep my word, madam, you may depend. You want two hundred pies at nine o'clock, and you will see that they shall come up quite punctually to the minute."

"Very good. I am glad you are better satisfied than you were."

"I am quite satisfied now, Mrs. Lovett. I am quite in a different mood of mind to what I was before. I can assure you, madam, that I have no complaints to make, and I think the place has done me some good; and if at nine o'clock you let down the platform, you shall have two hundred pies up, as sure as fate, and something else, too," he added to himself, "or I shall be of a very different mind to what I now am."

We have already seen that Mrs. Lovett was not deceived by this seeming submission on the part of the cook, for she used that as an argument with Todd, when she was expatiating upon the necessity of getting rid of him that night.

But the cleverest people make mistakes at times, and probably when the nine o'clock batch of pies makes its appearance, something may occur at the same time which will surprise a great many more persons than Mrs. Lovett and the reader.

But we must not anticipate, merely saying with the eastern sage what will be will be, and what's impossible don't often come to pass; certain it is that the nine o'clock batch of two hundred pies were made and put in the ovens; and equally certain is it that the cook remarked, as he did so,—

"Yes, I'll do it—it may succeed; nay, it must succeed; and if so, woe be to you, Mrs. Lovett, and all who are joined with you in this horrible speculation, at which I sicken."

It was five minutes to nine, and Mrs. Lovett's shop is filling with persons anxious to devour or to carry away one or more of the nine o'clock batch of savoury, delightful, gushing gravy pies.

Many of Mrs. Lovett's customers paid her in advance for the pies, in order that they might be quite sure of getting their orders fulfilled when the first batch should make its gracious appearance from the depths below.

"Oh! It's only five minutes to nine, don't you see? What a crow there is, to be sure. Mrs. Lovett, you charmer, I hope you have ordered enough pies to be made to-night. You see what a lot of customers you have."

"Oh! There will be plenty."

"That's right. I say, don't push so; you'll be on time, I tell you; don't be pushing and shoving in that sort of way—I've got ribs."

"And so have I. Last night, I didn't get to bed at all, and my old woman is in a certain condition, you see, gentlemen, and won't fancy anything but one of Lovett's veal pies, so I've come all the way from Newington to get one for—"

"Hold your row, will you? and don't push."

"For to have the child marked as a pie as its—"

"Behind there, I say; don't be pushing a fellow as if it was half-price at a theatre."

Each moment added some newcomers to the throng, and at last any strangers who had known nothing of the attractions of Mrs. Lovett's pie-shop, and had walked down Bell Yard, would have been astonished at the throng of persons there assembled—a throng, that was each moment increasing in density, and becoming more and more urgent and clamorous.

One, two, three, four, five, six, seven, eight, nine! Yes, it is nine at last. It strikes by old St. Dunstan's church clock, and in weaker strains the chron-ometrical machine at the pie-shop echoes the sound. What excitement there is not to get the pies when they shall come! Mrs. Lovett lets down the square, moveable platform that goes upon pulleys into the cellar; some machinery, which only requires a handle to be turned, brings up a hundred pies in a tray. These are eagerly seized by parties who have previously paid, and such a smacking of lips ensues as never was known.

Down goes the platform for the next hundred, and a gentlemanly man says,

"Let me work the handle Mrs. Lovett, if you please; it's too much for you, I'm sure."

"Sir, you are very kind, but I never allow anybody on this side of the counter but my own people, sir; I can turn the handle myself, sir, if you please, with the assistance of this girl. Keep your distance, sir: nobody wants your help."

How the waggish young lawyers' clerks laughed as they smacked their lips, and sucked in the golopshious gravy of the pies, which, by the by, appeared to be all delicious veal this time, and Mrs. Lovett worked the handle of the machine all the more vigorously, that she was a little angry with the officious stranger. What an unusual trouble it seemed to be to wind up those forthcoming hundred pies! How she toiled, and how the people waited; but at length there came up the savoury steam, and then the tops of the pies were visible.

They came up upon a large tray, about six feet square, and the moment Mrs. Lovett ceased turning the handle, and let a catch fall that prevented the platform receding again, to the astonishment and terror of everyone, away flew all the pies, tray and all, across the counter, and a man, who was lying crouched down in an exceedingly flat state under the tray, sprang to his feet.

Mrs. Lovett shrieked, as well she might, and then she stood trembling, and looking as pale as death itself. It was the doomed cook from the cellars, who had adopted this mode of escape.

The throngs of persons in the shop looked petrified, and after Mrs. Lovett's shriek, there was an awful stillness for about a minute, and then the young man who officiated as cook spoke.

"Ladies and Gentlemen—I fear that what I am going to say will spoil your appetites; but the truth is beautiful at all times, and I have to state that Mrs. Lovett's pies are made of *human flesh*!"

How the throng of persons recoiled—what a roar of agony and dismay there was! How frightfully sick about forty lawyers' clerks became all at once, and how they spat out the gelatinous clinging portions of the rich pies they had been devouring. "Good gracious!—oh, the pies!—confound it!"

"'Tis false!" screamed Mrs. Lovett.

"You are my prisoner madam," said the man who had obligingly offered to turn the handle of the machine that wound up the pies, at the same time producing a constable's staff.

"Prisoner!"

"Yes, on a charge of aiding and abetting Sweeney Todd, now in custody, in the commission of many murders."

Mrs. Lovett staggered back, and her complexion turned a livid colour.

"I am poisoned," she said. "Good God! I am poisoned," and she sank insensible to the floor.

When Mrs. Lovett was picked up by the officers, she was found to be dead. The poison which Sweeney Todd had put into the brandy she was accustomed to solace herself with, when the pangs of conscience troubled her, and of which she always took some before the evening batch of pies came up, had done its work.

That night Todd passed in Newgate, and in due time a swinging corpse was all that remained of the barber of Fleet Street.

The youths who visited Lovett's pie-shop, and there luxuriated upon those delicacies, are youths no longer. Indeed, the grave has closed over all but one, and he is very, very old, but even now, as he thinks of how he enjoyed the flavour of the "veal," he shudders, and has to take a drop of brandy.

Beneath the old church of St. Dunstan were found the heads and bones of Todd's victims. As little as possible was said by the authorities about it; but it was supposed that some hundreds of persons must have perished in the frightful manner we have detailed.

WAGNER, THE WEHR-WOLF

George W. M. Reynolds

One of the most renowned penny bloods of the nineteenth century, *Wagner, the Wehr-Wolf*, written by George W. M. Reynolds (1814–79), was serialised from 7 November 1846 to 24 July 1847 in *Reynolds's Miscellany* and finally published in a full volume by John Dicks. Incorporating elements from Faustian lore and classic Gothic literature, Reynolds places an anti-heroine, Nisida of Riverola, and a werewolf, the titular Fernand Wagner, at the heart of this tale.

This story begins with the elder Wagner abandoned by his granddaughter, Agnes, and approaching death. Prior to his termination, Wagner is offered the Faustian "deal with the devil" to extend his life and resurrect his youth, although the payment is his transformation into a werewolf, once a month, which he accepts. The story continues with another family, the noble Riverolas whose tale begins with the death of the Count and the introduction of his two children Nisida and Francisco. Nisida, introduced with the inability to speak or hear, partakes in an intimate relationship with Wagner, albeit unaware of his monstrous transformation. While Wagner's lycanthropic metamorphosis is not the focus of this narrative, it functions as foil to Nisida's true "monstrous" nature. Playing the role of the innocent noble lady, Nisida is a deceptive criminal mastermind who fakes her injuries to avoid any suspicion of her wrongdoings. Witnessing the death of her mother by the hands of her father, Nisida is voluntarily driven to silence and observation so that she may enact revenge on those who wrong both her and Francisco.

Wagner, the Wehr-Wolf possesses traditional issues of excess as other penny narratives, and since this was a popular serialisation, it expands into multiple chapters that branch into varied plotlines and character histories. Similarly, Nisida's storyline, as it also branches out extensively, will not be included in its entirety. The purpose for this chapter is to include an excerpt that demonstrates her ferocity and danger to those deemed as a personal, or familial threat.

GRIFFIN & DUVERCIER

O UR tale commences in the middle of the month of November 1520, and at the hour of midnight.

In a magnificently furnished chamber, belonging to one of the largest mansions of Florence, a nobleman lay at the point of death.

The light of the lamp suspended to the ceiling played upon the ghastly countenance of the dying man, the stern expression of whose features was not even mitigated by the fears and uncertainties attendant on the hour of dissolution. He was about forty-eight years of age, and had evidently been wondrously handsome in his youth: for though the frightful pallor of death was already upon his cheeks, and the fire of his large black eyes was dimmed with the ravages of a long-endured disease, still the faultless outlines of the aquiline profile remained unimpaired.

Two persons leant over the couch to which death was so rapidly approaching. One was a lady of about twenty-five: the other was a youth of nineteen. The former was eminently beautiful; but her countenance was marked with much of that severity—that determination—and even of that sternness, which characterised the dying nobleman. Indeed, a single glance was sufficient to show that they stood in the close relationship of father and daughter. Her long, black, glossy hair now hung dishevelled over the shoulders that were left partially bare by the hasty negligence with which she had thrown on a loose wrapper; and those shoulders were of the most dazzling whiteness.

The wrapper was confined by a broad band at the waist; and the slight drapery set off, rather than concealed, the rich contours of a form of mature but admirable symmetry. Tall, graceful, and elegant, she united easy motion with fine proportion; thus possessing the lightness of the Sylph and the luxuriant fullness of the Hebe.

Her countenance was alike expressive of intellectuality and strong passions. Her large black eyes were full of fire, and their glances seemed to penetrate the soul. Her nose, of the finest aquiline development,—her lips, narrow, but red and pouting, with the upper one short and slightly projecting over the lower,—and her small, delicately rounded chin, indicated both decision and sensuality: but the insolent gaze of the libertine would have quailed beneath the look of sovereign hauteur which flashed from those brilliant eagle eyes. In a word, she appeared to be a woman well adapted to command the admiration—receive the homage—excite the passions—and yet repel the insolence of the opposite sex. But those appearances were to some degree deceitful; for never was homage offered to her—never was she courted nor flattered.

Ten years previously to the time of which we are writing—and when she was only fifteen—the death of her mother, under strange and mysterious circumstances, as it was generally reported, made such a terrible impression on her mind, that she hovered for months on the verge of dissolution; and when the physician who attended upon her communicated to her father the fact that her life was at length beyond danger, that assurance was followed by the sad and startling declaration, that she had forever lost the sense of hearing and the power of speech. No wonder, then, that homage was never paid nor adulation offered to Nisida—the deaf and dumb daughter of the proud Count of Riverola!

Those who were intimate with this family ere the occurrence of that sad event—especially the physician, Dr. Duras, who had attended upon the mother in her last moments, and on the daughter during her illness— declared that, up to the period when the malady assailed her, Nisida was a sweet, amiable and retiring girl; but she had evidently been fearfully changed by the terrible affliction which that malady had left behind. For if she could no longer express herself in words, her eyes darted lightnings upon the unhappy menials who had the misfortune to incur her displeasure; and her lips would quiver with the violence of concentrated passion, at the most trifling neglect or error of which the female dependants immediately attached to her own person might happen to be guilty.

Toward her father she often manifested a strange ebullition of anger—bordering even on inveterate spite, when he offended her: and yet, singular though it were, the count was devotedly attached to his daughter. He frequently declared that, afflicted as she was, he was proud of her: for he was wont to behold in her flashing eyes—her curling lip—and her haughty air, the reflection of his own proud—his own inexorable spirit.

The youth of nineteen to whom we have alluded was Nisida's brother; and much as the father appeared to dote upon the daughter, was the son proportionately disliked by that stern and despotic man.

Such were the three persons whom we have thus minutely described to our readers.

The count had been ill for some weeks at the time when this chapter opens; but on the night which marks that commencement, Dr. Duras had deemed it his duty to warn the nobleman that he had not many hours to live.

The count had fallen into a lethargic stupor, which lasted until four in the morning, when his spirit passed gently away.

The moment Francisco and Nisida became aware that they were orphans, they threw themselves into each other's arms, and renewed by that tender embrace the tacit compact of sincere affection which had ever existed between them. Francisco's tears flowed freely; but Nisida did not weep!

A strange—an almost portentous light shone in her brilliant black eyes; and though that wild gleaming denoted powerful emotions, yet it shed no lustre upon the depths of her soul—afforded no clew to the real nature of these agitated feelings.

Suddenly withdrawing himself from his sister's arms, Francisco conveyed to her by the language of the fingers the following tender sentiment:—"You have lost a father, beloved Nisida, but you have a devoted and affectionate brother left to you!"

And Nisida replied through the same medium, "Your happiness, dearest brother, has ever been my only study, and shall continue so."

The physician and Father Marco, the priest, now advanced, and taking the brother and sister by the hands, led them from the chamber of death.

The orphans embraced each other, and retired to their respective apartments.

Eight days after the death of the Count of Riverola, the funeral took place.

The obsequies were celebrated at night, with all the pomp observed amongst noble families on such occasions. The church in which the corpse was buried, was hung with black cloth; and even the innumerable wax tapers which burned upon the altar and around the coffin failed to diminish the lugubrious aspect of the scene.

Around the coffin stood Dr. Duras and other male friends of the deceased: for the females of the family were not permitted, by the custom of the age and the religion, to be present on occasions of this kind.

It was eleven o'clock at night: and the weather without was stormy and tempestuous.

The wind moaned through the long aisles, raising strange and ominous echoes, and making the vast folds of sable drapery wave slowly backward and forward, as if agitated by unseen hands. A few spectators, standing in the background, appeared like grim figures on a black tapestry; and the gleam of the wax tapers, oscillating on their countenances, made them seem deathlike and ghastly.

From time to time the shrill wail of the shriek-owl, and the flapping of its wings against the diamond-paned windows of the church, added to the awful gloom of the funeral scene.

And now suddenly arose the chant of the priests—the parting hymn for the dead!

The priests were in the midst of their solemn chant—a deathlike silence and complete immovability prevailed among the mourners and the spectators—and the wind was moaning beneath the vaulted roofs, awaking those strange and tomb-like sounds which are only heard in large churches,—when light but rushing footsteps were heard on the marble pavement; and in another minute a female, not clothed in a mourning garb, but splendidly as for a festival, precipitated herself toward the bier.

There her strength suddenly seemed to be exhausted; and, with a piercing scream, she sank senseless on the cold stones.

The chant of the priest was immediately stilled; and Francisco hurrying forward, raised the female in his arms, while Dr. Duras asked for water to sprinkle on her countenance.

Over her head the stranger wore a white veil of rich material, which was fastened above her brow by a single diamond of unusual size and brilliant lustre. When the veil was drawn aside, shining auburn tresses were seen depending in wanton luxuriance over shoulders of alabaster whiteness: a beautiful but deadly pale countenance was revealed; and a splendid purple velvet dress delineated the soft and flowing outlines of a form modelled to the most perfect symmetry.

She seemed to be about twenty years of age,—in the full splendour of loveliness, and endowed with charms which presented to the gaze of those around a very incarnation of the ideal beauty which forms the theme of raptured poets.

And now, as the vacillating and uncertain light of the wax-candles beamed upon her, as she lay senseless in the arms of the Count Riverola, her pale, placid face appeared that of a classic marble statue; but nothing could surpass the splendid effects which the funeral tapers produced on the rich redundancy of her hair, which seemed dark where the shadows rested on it, but glittering as with a bright glory where the lustre played on its shining masses.

In spite of the solemnity of the place and the occasion, the mourners were struck by the dazzling beauty of that young female, who had thus appeared so strangely amongst them; but respect still retained at a distance those persons who were merely present from curiosity to witness the obsequies of one of the proudest nobles of Florence.

At length the lady opened her large hazel eyes, and glanced wildly around, a quick spasm passing like an electric shock over her frame at the same instant; for the funeral scene burst upon her view, and reminded her where she was, and why she was there.

Recovering herself almost as rapidly as she had succumbed beneath physical and mental exhaustion, she started from Francisco's arms; and turning upon him a beseeching, inquiring glance, exclaimed in a voice which ineffable anguish could not rob of its melody: "Is it true—oh, tell me is it true that the Count Riverola is no more?"

"It is, alas! too true, lady," answered Francisco, in a tone of the deepest melancholy.

The heart of the fair stranger rebounded at the words which thus seemed to destroy a last hope that lingered in her soul; and a hysterical shriek burst from her lips as she threw her snow-white arms, bare to the shoulders, around the head of the pall-covered coffin.

"Oh! my much-loved—my noble Andrea!" she exclaimed, a torrent of tears now gushing from her eyes.

"That voice!—is it possible?" cried one of the spectators who had been hitherto standing, as before said, at a respectful distance: and the speaker—a man of tall, commanding form, graceful demeanour, wondrously handsome countenance, and rich attire—immediately hurried toward the spot where the young female still clung to the coffin, no one having the heart to remove her.

The individual who had thus stepped forward, gave one rapid but searching glance at the lady's countenance; and, yielding to the surprise and joy which suddenly animated him, he exclaimed: "Yes—it is, indeed, the lost Agnes!"

The young female started when she heard her name thus pronounced in a place where she believed herself to be entirely unknown; and astonishment for an instant triumphed over the anguish of her heart.

Hastily withdrawing her snow-white arms from the head of the coffin, she turned toward the individual who had uttered her name, and he instantly clasped her in his arms, murmuring, "Dearest—dearest Agnes, art thou restored—"

But the lady shrieked, and struggled to escape from that tender embrace, exclaiming, "What means this insolence? will no one protect me?"

"That will I," said Francisco, darting forward, and tearing her away from the stranger's arms. "But, in the name of Heaven! let this misunderstanding be cleared up elsewhere. Lady—and you, signor—I call on you to remember where you are, and how solemn a ceremony you have both aided to interrupt."

"I know not that man!" ejaculated Agnes, indicating the stranger. "I come hither, because I heard—but an hour ago—that my noble Andrea was no more. And I would not believe those who told me. Oh! no—I could not think that Heaven had thus deprived me of all I loved on earth!"

"Lady, you are speaking of my father," said Francisco, in a somewhat severe tone.

"Your father!" cried Agnes, now surveying the young count with interest and curiosity. "Oh! then, my lord, you can pity—you can feel for me, who in losing your father have lost all that could render existence sweet!"

"No—you have not lost all!" exclaimed the handsome stranger, advancing toward Agnes, and speaking in a profoundly impressive tone. "Have you not one single relative left in the world? Consider, lady—an old, old man—a shepherd in the Black Forest of Germany—"

"Speak not of him!" cried Agnes, wildly. "Did he know all, he would curse me—he would spurn me from him—he would discard me forever! Oh! when I think of that poor old man, with his venerable white hair,— that aged, helpless man, who was so kind to me, who loved me so well, and whom I so cruelly abandoned. But tell me, signor," she exclaimed, in suddenly altered tone, while her breath came with the difficulty of acute suspense,—"tell me, signor, does that old man still live?"

"He lives, Agnes," was the reply. "I know him well; at this moment he is in Florence!"

"In Florence!" repeated Agnes; and so unexpectedly came this announcement, that her limbs seemed to give way under her, and she would have fallen on the marble pavement, had not the stranger caught her in his arms.

"I will bear her away," he said; "she has a true friend in me."

And he was moving off with his senseless burden, when Francisco, struck by a sudden idea, caught him by the elegantly slashed sleeve of his doublet, and whispered thus, in a rapid tone: "From the few, but significant words which fell from that lady's lips, and from her still more impressive conduct, it would appear, alas! that my deceased father had wronged her. If so, signor, it will be my duty to make her all the reparation that can be afforded in such a case."

"'Tis well, my lord," answered the stranger, in a cold and haughty tone. "To-morrow evening I will call upon you at your palace."

He then hurried on with the still senseless Agnes in his arms; and the Count of Riverola retraced his steps to the immediate vicinity of the coffin.

When Agnes awoke from the state of stupor in which she had been conveyed from the church, she found herself lying upon an ottoman, in a large and elegantly furnished apartment.

As she slowly and languidly opened her large hazel eyes, her thoughts collected themselves in the gradient manner; and when her glance encountered that of her unknown friend, who was bending over her with an expression of deep interest on his features, there flashed upon her mind a recollection of all that had so recently taken place.

"Where am I?" she demanded, starting up, and casting her eyes wildly around her.

"In the abode of one who will not injure you," answered the stranger, in a kind and melodious tone.

"But who are you? and wherefore have you brought me hither?" exclaimed Agnes. "Oh! remember—you spoke of that old man—my grandfather—the shepherd of the Black Forest—"

"I am Fernand Wagner!" he exclaimed, folding her in his embrace.

"The mansion to which I have brought you is mine. It is in a somewhat secluded spot on the banks of the Arno, and is surrounded by gardens. My household consists of but few retainers; and they are elderly persons—docile and obedient. Here, henceforth, Agnes, shalt thou dwell; and let the past be forgotten. But there are three conditions which I must impose upon thee."

"Name them," said Agnes; "I promise obedience beforehand."

"The first," returned Fernand, "is that you henceforth look upon me as your brother, and call me such when we are alone together or in the presence of strangers. The second is that you never seek to remove the black cloth which covers yon place—"

Agnes glanced toward the object alluded to and shuddered—as if the veil concealed some new mystery.

"And the third condition is that you revive not on any future occasion the subject of our present conversation, nor even question me in respect to those secrets which it may suit me to retain within my own breast."

Agnes promised obedience, and, embracing Wagner, said,

"Heaven has been merciful to me, in my present affliction, in that it has given me a brother!"

At this moment, Agnes' narrative was interrupted by a piercing shriek which burst from her lips; and extending her arms toward the window of the apartment, she screamed hysterically, "Again that countenance!" and fell back on the ottoman.

Agnes and Wagner were, moreover, placed near the window which looked into a large garden attached to the mansion; and thus it was easy for the lady, whose eyes happened to be fixed upon the casement in the earnest interest with which she was relating her narrative, to perceive the human countenance that appeared at one of the panes.

The moment her history was interrupted by the ejaculation of alarm that broke from her lips, Wagner started up and hastened to the window; but he could see nothing save the waving evergreens in his garden, and the light of a mansion which stood at a distance of about two hundred yards from his own abode.

He was about to open the casement and step into the garden, when Agnes caught him by the arm, exclaiming wildly, "Leave me not—I could not—I could not bear to remain alone!"

"No, I will not quit you, Agnes," replied Wagner, conducting her back to the sofa and resuming his seat by her side. "But wherefore that ejaculation of alarm? Whose countenance did you behold? Speak, dearest Agnes!"

"I will hasten to explain the cause of my terror," retorted Agnes, becoming more composed. "Ere now I was about to detail the particulars of my journey to Florence, in company with the Count of Riverola, and attended by Antonio; but as those particulars are of no material interest, I will at once pass on to the period when we arrived in this city."

"But the countenance at the window?" said Wagner, somewhat impatiently.

"Listen—and you will soon know all," replied Agnes. "It was in the evening when I entered Florence for the first time. Antonio had proceeded in advance to inform his mother—a widow who resided in a decent house, but in an obscure street near the cathedral—that she was speedily to receive a young lady as a guest. Having seen me comfortably installed in Dame Margaretha's best apartment, he quitted me, with a promise to return on the morrow."

Agnes paused for a few moments, sighed, and continued her narrative in the following manner:

"In the course of the morning rich furniture was brought to the house, and in a few hours the apartments allotted to me were converted, in my estimation, into a little paradise. The count arrived soon afterward, and I now—pardon me the neglect and ingratitude which my words confess—I now felt very happy. The noble Andrea enjoined me to go abroad but seldom, and never without being accompanied by Dame Margaretha; he also besought me not to appear to recognise him should I chance to meet him in public at any time, nor to form acquaintances; in a word, to live retired and secluded as possible, alike for his sake and my own. I promised compliance with all he suggested, and he declared in return that he would never cease to love me."

"He generally spent two hours with me every day, and frequently visited me again in the evening. Thus did time pass; and at length I come to that incident which will explain the terror I ere now experienced."

Agnes cast a hasty glance toward the window, as if to assure herself that the object of her fears was no longer there; and, satisfied on this head, she proceeded in the following manner:

"It was about six months ago that I repaired as usual on the Sabbath morning to mass, accompanied by Dame Margaretha, when I found myself the object of some attention on the part of a lady, who was kneeling at a short distance from the place which I occupied in the church. The lady was enveloped in a dark, thick veil, the ample folds of which concealed her countenance, and meandered over her whole body's splendidly symmetrical length of limb in such a manner as to aid her rich attire in shaping, rather than hiding, the contours of that matchless form. I was struck by her fine proportions, which gave her, even in her kneeling attitude, a queen-like and majestic air; and I longed to obtain a glimpse of her countenance—the more so as I could perceive by her manner and the position of her head that from beneath her dark veil her eyes were intently fixed upon myself. At length the scrutiny to which I was thus subjected began to grow so irksome—nay, even alarming, that I hurriedly drew down my own veil, which I had raised through respect for the sacred altar whereat I was kneeling. Still I knew that the stranger lady was gazing on me; I felt that she was. A certain uneasy sensation—amounting almost to a superstitious awe—convinced me that I was the object of her undivided attention. Suddenly the priests, in procession, came down from the altar; and as they passed us, I instinctively raised my veil again, through motives of deferential respect. At the same instant I glanced toward the stranger lady; she also drew back the dark covering from her face. Oh! what a countenance was then revealed to me—a countenance of such sovereign beauty that, though of the same sex, I was struck with admiration; but, in the next moment, a thrill of terror shot through my heart—for the fascination of the basilisk could scarcely paralyse its victim with more appalling effect than did the eyes of that lady. It might be conscience qualms, excited by some unknown influence—it might even have been imagination; but it nevertheless appeared as if those large, black, burning orbs shot forth lightnings which seared and scorched my very soul! For that splendid countenance, of almost unearthly beauty, was suddenly marked by an expression of such vindictive rage, such ineffable hatred, such ferocious menace, that I should have screamed had I not been as it were stunned—stupefied!

"The procession of priests swept past. I averted my head from the stranger lady. In a few moments I again glanced hurriedly at the place which she had occupied—but she was gone. Then I felt relieved! On quitting the church, I frankly narrated to old Margaretha these particulars as I have now unfolded them to you; and methought that she was for a moment troubled as I spoke! But if she were, she speedily recovered her composure—endeavoured to soothe me by attributing it all to my imagination, and earnestly advised me not to cause any uneasiness to the count by mentioning the subject to him. I readily promised compliance with this injunction; and in the course of a few days ceased to think upon the incident which has made so strange but evanescent an impression on my mind."

"Doubtless Dame Margaretha was right in her conjecture," said Wagner; "and your imagination—"

"Oh, no—no! It was not fancy!" interrupted Agnes, hastily. "But listen, and then judge for yourself. I informed you ere now that it was about six months ago when the event which I have just related took place. At that period, also, my noble lover—the ever-to be lamented Andrea—first experienced the symptoms of that internal disease which has, alas! carried him to the tomb."

Agnes paused, wiped away her tears, and continued thus:

"His visits to me consequently became less frequent;—I was more alone—for Margaretha was not always a companion who could solace me for the absence of one so dearly loved as my Andrea; and repeated fits of deep despondency seized upon my soul. At those times I felt as if some evil—vague and undefinable, but still terrible—were impending over me.

Was it my lord's approaching death of which I had a presentiment? I know not! Weeks passed away; the count's visits occurred at intervals growing longer and longer—but his affection toward me had not abated. No: a malady that preyed upon his vitals retained him much at home;—and at last, about two months ago, I received through Antonio the afflicting intelligence that he was confined to his bed. My anguish now knew no bounds. I would fly to him—oh! I would fly to him:—who was more worthy to watch by his couch than I, who so dearly loved him! Dame Margaretha represented to me how painful it would be to his lordship were our amour to transpire through any rash proceeding on my part—the more so, as I knew that he had a daughter and a son! I accordingly restrained my impetuous longing to hasten to his bedside:—I could not so easily subdue my grief!

"One night I sat up late in my lonely chamber—pondering on the melancholy position in which I was placed,—loving so tenderly, yet not daring to fly to him whom I loved,—and giving way to all the mournful ideas which presented themselves to my imagination. At length my mind grew bewildered by those sad reflections; vague terrors gathered around me—multiplying in number and augmenting in intensity,—until at length the very figures on the tapestry with which the room was hung appeared animated with power to scare and affright me. The wind moaned ominously without, and raised strange echoes within; oppressive feelings crowded on my soul. At length the gale swelled to a hurricane—a whirlwind, seldom experienced in this delicious clime. Howlings in a thousand tones appeared to flit through the air; and piercing lamentations seemed to sound down the black clouds that rolled their mighty volumes together, veiling the moon and stars in thickest gloom. Overcome with terror, I retired to rest—and I slept. But troubled dreams haunted me throughout the night, and I awoke at an early hour in the morning. But—holy angels protect me!—what did I behold? Bending over me, as I lay, was that same countenance which I had seen four months before in the church,—and now, as it was then, darting upon me lightning from large black eyes that seemed to send shafts of flame and fire to the inmost recesses of my soul! Yet—distorted as it was with demoniac rage—that face was still endowed with the queen-like beauty—the majesty of loveliness, which had before struck me, and which even lent force to those looks of dreadful menace that were fixed upon me. There were the high forehead—the proud lip, curled in scorn,—the brilliant teeth, glistening between the quivering vermilion,—and the swan-like arching of the dazzling neck; there also was the dark glory of the luxuriant hair!

"For a few moments I was spell-bound—motionless—speechless. Clothed with terror and sublimity, yet in all the flush of the most perfect beauty, a strange—mysterious being stood over me: and I knew not whether she were a denizen of this world, or a spirit risen from another. Perhaps the transcendent loveliness of that countenance was but a mask and the wondrous symmetry of that form but a disguise, beneath which all the passions of hell were raging in the brain and in the heart of a fiend. Such were the ideas that flashed through my imagination; and I involuntarily closed my eyes, as if this action could avert the malignity that appeared to menace me. But dreadful thoughts still pursued me—enveloping me, as it were, in an oppressive mist wherein appalling though dimly seen images and forms were agitating; and I again opened my eyes. The lady—if an earthly being she really were—was gone. I rose from my couch and glanced nervously around—expecting almost to behold an apparition come forth from behind the tapestry, or the folds of the curtains. But my attention was suddenly arrested by a fact more germane to worldly occurrences. The casket wherein I kept the rich presents made to me at different times by my Andrea had been forced open and the most valuable portion of its contents were gone. On a closer investigation I observed that the articles which were left were those that were purchased new; whereas the jewels that had been abstracted were old ones, which, as the count had informed me, had belonged to his deceased wife.

"On discovering this robbery, I began to suspect that my mysterious visitress, who had caused me so much alarm, was the thief of my property; and I immediately summoned old Margaretha. She was of course astounded at the occurrence which I related; and, after some reflection, she suddenly remembered that she had forgotten to fasten the house-door ere she retired to rest on the preceding evening. I chided her for a neglect which had enabled some evil-disposed woman to penetrate into my chamber, and not only terrify but also plunder me. She implored my forgiveness, and besought me not to mention the incident to the count when next we met. Alas! my noble Andrea and I never met again.

"I was sorely perplexed by the event which I have just related. If the mysterious visitress were a common thief, why did she leave any of the jewels in the casket? and wherefore had she on two occasions contemplated me with looks of such dark rage and infernal menace? A thought struck me. Could the count's daughter have discovered our amour? and was it she who had come to gain possession of jewels belonging to the family? I hinted my suspicions to Margaretha; but she speedily convinced me that they were unfounded.

"'The Lady Nisida is deaf and dumb,' she said, 'and cannot possibly exercise such faculties of observation, nor adopt such means of obtaining information as would make her acquainted with all that has occurred between her father and yourself. Besides—she is constantly in attendance on her sire, who is very, very ill.'

"I now perceived the improbability of a deaf and dumb female discovering an amour so carefully concealed; but to assure myself more fully on that head, I desired Margaretha to describe the Lady Nisida. This she readily did, and I learnt from her that the count's daughter was of a beauty quite different from the lady whom I had seen in the church and in my own chamber. In a word, it appears that Nisida has light hair, blue eyes and a delicate form: whereas, the object of my interest, curiosity, and fear, is a woman of dark Italian loveliness.

"I have little more now to say. The loss of the jewels and the recollection of the mysterious lady were soon absorbed in the distressing thoughts which the serious illness of the count forced upon my mind. Weeks passed away, and he came not; but he sent repeated messages by Antonio, imploring me to console myself, as he should soon recover, and urging me not to take any step that might betray the existence of our amour. Need I say how religiously I obeyed him in the latter respect? Day after day did I hope to see him again, for I knew not that he was dying: and I used to dress myself in my gayest attire—even as now I am apparelled—to welcome his expected visit. Alas! he never came; and his death was concealed from me, doubtless that the sad event might not be communicated until after the funeral, lest in the first frenzy of anguish I should rush to the Riverola palace to imprint a last kiss upon the cheek of the corpse. But a few hours ago, I learned the whole truth from two female friends of Dame Margaretha who called to visit her, and whom I had hastened to inform that she was temporarily absent. My noble Andrea was dead, and at that very moment his funeral obsequies were being celebrated in the neighbouring church—the very church in which I had first beheld the mysterious lady! Frantic with grief— unmindful of the exposure that would ensue—reckless of the consequences, I left the house—I hastened to the church—I intruded my presence amidst the mourners. You know the rest, Fernand. It only remains for me to say that the countenance which I beheld ere now at the window—strongly delineated and darkly conspicuous amidst the blaze of light outside the casement—was that of the lady whom I have thus seen for the third time! But, tell me, Fernand, how could a stranger thus obtain admission to the gardens of your mansion?"

"You see yon lights, Agnes!" said Wagner, pointing toward the mansion which, as we stated at the commencement of that chapter, was situated at a distance of about two hundred yards from Fernand's dwelling, the backs of the two houses thus looking toward each other. "Those lights," he continued, "are shining in a mansion the gardens of which are separated from my own by a simple hedge of evergreens, that would not bar even the passage of a child. Should any inmate of that mansion possess curiosity sufficient to induce him or her to cross the boundary, traverse my gardens, and approach the casements of my residence, that curiosity may be easily gratified."

"And to whom does yon mansion belong?" asked Agnes.

"To Dr. Duras, an eminent physician," was the reply.

"Dr. Duras, the physician who attended my noble Andrea in his illness!" exclaimed Agnes. "Then the mysterious lady of whom I have spoken so much, and whose countenance ere now appeared at the casement, must be an inmate of the house of Dr. Duras; or at all events, a visitor there! Ah! surely there is some connection between that lady and the family at Riverola?"

"Time will solve the mystery, dearest sister, for so I am henceforth to call you," said Fernand. "But beneath this roof, no harm can menace you. And now let me summon good Dame Paula, my housekeeper, to conduct you to the apartments which have been prepared for your reception. The morning is far advanced, and we both stand in need of rest."

On the ensuing evening, Francisco, Count of Riverola, was seated in one of the splendid saloons of his palace, pondering upon the strange injunction which he had received from his deceased father, relative to the mysterious closet, when Wagner was announced.

Francisco rose to receive him, saying in a cordial though melancholy tone, "Signor, I expected you."

"And let me hasten to express the regret which I experienced at having addressed your lordship coldly and haughtily last night," exclaimed Wagner. "But, at the moment, I only beheld in you the son of him who had dishonoured a being very dear to my heart."

"I can well understand your feelings on that occasion, signor," replied Francisco. "Alas! the sins of the fathers are too often visited upon the children in this world. But, in whatever direction our present conversation may turn, I implore you to spare as much as possible the memory of my sire."

"Think not, my lord," said Wagner, "that I should be so ungenerous as to reproach you for a deed in which you had no concern, and over which you exercised no control. Nor should I inflict so deep an injury upon you, as to speak in disrespectful terms of him who was the author of your being, but who is now no more."

"Your kind language has already made me your friend," exclaimed Francisco. "And now point out to me in what manner I can in any way repair—or mitigate—the wrong done to that fair creature in whom you express yourself interested."

"That young lady is my sister," said Wagner, emphatically.

"Your sister, signor! And yet, meseems, she recognised you not—"

"Long years have passed since we saw each other," interrupted Fernand; "for we were separated in our childhood."

"And did you not both speak of some relative—an old man who once dwelt on the confines of the Black Forest of Germany, but who is now in Florence?" asked Francisco.

"Alas! that old man is no more," returned Wagner. "I did but use his name to induce Agnes to place confidence in me, and allow me to withdraw her from a scene which her wild grief so unpleasantly interrupted; for I thought that were I then and there to announce myself as her brother, she might not believe me—she might suspect some treachery or snare in a city so notoriously profligate as Florence. But the subsequent explanations which took place between us cleared up all doubts on that subject."

"I am well pleased to hear that the poor girl has found so near a relative and so dear a friend, signor," said Francisco. "And now acquaint me, I pray thee, with the means whereby I may, to some extent, repair the injury your sister has sustained at the hands of him whose memory I implore you to spare!"

"Wealth I possess in abundance—oh! far greater abundance than is necessary to satisfy all my wants!" exclaimed Wagner, with something of bitterness and regret in his tone; "but, even were I poor, gold would not restore my sister's honour. No—let that subject, however, pass. I would only ask you, count, whether there be any scion of your family—any lady connected with you—who answers this description?"

And Wagner proceeded to delineate, in minute terms, the portraiture of the mysterious lady who had inspired Agnes on three occasions with so much terror, and whom Agnes herself had depicted in such glowing language.

"Signor! you are describing the Lady Nisida, my sister!" exclaimed Francisco, struck with astonishment at the fidelity of the portrait thus verbally drawn.

"Your sister, my lord!" cried Wagner. "Then has Dame Margaretha deceived Agnes in representing the Lady Nisida to be rather a beauty of the cold north than of the sunny south."

"Dame Margaretha!" said Francisco; "do you allude, signor, to the mother of my late father's confidential dependent, Antonio?"

"The same," was the answer. "It was at Dame Margaretha's house that your father placed my sister Agnes, who has resided there nearly four years."

"But wherefore have you made those inquiries relative to the Lady Nisida?" inquired Francisco.

"I will explain the motive with frankness," responded Wagner.

He then related to the young count all those particulars relative to the mysterious lady and Agnes, with which the reader is already acquainted.

"There must be some extraordinary mistake—some strange error, signor, in all this," observed Francisco. "My poor sister is, as you seem to be aware, so deeply afflicted that she possesses not faculties calculated to make her aware of that amour which even I, who possess those faculties in which she is deficient, never suspected, and concerning which no hint ever reached me, until the whole truth burst suddenly upon me last night at the funeral of my sire. Moreover, had accident revealed to Nisida the existence of the connection between my father and your sister, signor, she would have imparted the discovery to me, such is the confidence and so great is the love that exists between us. For habit has rendered us so skilful and quick in conversing with the language of the deaf and dumb, that no impediment ever exists to the free interchange of our thoughts."

"And yet, if the Lady Nisida had made such a discovery, her hatred of Agnes may be well understood," said Wagner; "for her ladyship must naturally look upon my sister as the partner of her father's weakness—the dishonoured slave of his passions."

"Nisida has no secret from me," observed the young count, firmly.

"But wherefore did Dame Margaretha deceive my sister in respect to the personal appearance of the Lady Nisida?" inquired Wagner.

"I know not. At the same time—"

The door opened, and Nisida entered the apartment.

She was attired in deep black; her luxuriant raven hair, no longer depending in shining curls, was gathered up in massy bands at the sides, and a knot behind, whence hung a rich veil that meandered over her body's splendidly symmetrical length of limb in such a manner as to aid her attire in shaping rather than hiding the contours of that matchless form. The voluptuous development of her bust was shrouded, not concealed, by the stomacher of black velvet which she wore, and which set off in strong relief the dazzling whiteness of her neck.

The moment her lustrous dark eyes fell upon Fernand Wagner, she started slightly; but this movement was imperceptible alike to him whose presence caused it, and to her brother.

Francisco conveyed to her, by the rapid language of the fingers, the name of their visitor, and at the same time intimated to her that he was the brother of Agnes, the young and lovely female whose strange appearance at the funeral, and avowed connection with the late noble, had not been concealed from the haughty lady.

Nisida's eyes seemed to gleam with pleasure when she understood in what degree of relationship Wagner stood toward Agnes; and she bowed to him with a degree of courtesy seldom displayed by her to strangers.

Francisco then conveyed to her in the language of the dumb, all those details already related in respect to the "mysterious lady" who had so haunted the unfortunate Agnes.

A glow of indignation mounted to the cheeks of Nisida; and more than usually rapid was the reply she made through the medium of the alphabet of the fingers.

"My sister desires me to express to you, signor," said Francisco, turning toward Wagner, "that she is not the person whom the Lady Agnes has to complain against. My sister," he continued, "has never to her knowledge seen the Lady Agnes; much less has she ever penetrated into her chamber; and indignantly does she repel the accusation relative to the abstraction of the jewels. She also desires me to inform you that last night after reading of our father's last testament, she retired to her chamber, which she did not quit until this morning at the usual hour; and that therefore it was not her countenance which the Lady Agnes beheld at the casement of your saloon."

"I pray you, my lord, to let the subject drop now, and forever!" said Wagner, who was struck with profound admiration—almost amounting to love—for the Lady Nisida: "there is some strange mystery in all this, which time alone can clear up. Will your lordship express to your sister how grieved I am that any suspicion should have originated against her in respect to Agnes?"

Francisco signalled these remarks to Nisida; and the latter, rising from her seat, advanced toward Wagner, and presented him her hand in token of her readiness to forget the injurious imputations thrown out against her.

Fernand raised that fair hand to his lips, and respectfully kissed it; but the hand seemed to burn as he held it, and when he raised his eyes toward the lady's countenance, she darted on him a look so ardent and impassioned that it penetrated into his very soul.

That rapid interchange of glances seemed immediately to establish a kind of understanding—a species of intimacy between those extraordinary beings; for on the one side, Nisida read in the fine eyes of the handsome Fernand all the admiration expressed there, and he, on his part, instinctively understood that he was far from disagreeable to the proud sister of the young Count of Riverola. While he was ready to fall at her feet and do homage to her beauty, she experienced the kindling of all the fierce fires of sensuality in her breast.

But the unsophisticated and innocent-minded Francisco observed not the expression of these emotions on either side, for their manifestation occupied not a moment. The interchange of such feelings is ever too vivid and electric to attract the notice of the unsuspecting observer.

When Wagner was about to retire, Nisida made the following signal to her brother:—"Express to the signor that he will ever be a welcome guest at the palace of Riverola; for we owe kindness and friendship to the brother of her whom our father dishonoured."

But, to the astonishment of both the count and the Lady Nisida, Wagner raised his hands, and displayed as perfect a knowledge of the language of the dumb as they themselves possessed.

"I thank your ladyship for this unexpected condescension," he signalled by the rapid play of his fingers; "and I shall not forget to avail myself of this most courteous invitation."

It were impossible to describe the sudden glow of pleasure and delight which animated Nisida's splendid countenance, when she thus discovered that Wagner was able to hold converse with her, and she hastened to reply thus: "We shall expect you to revisit us soon."

Wagner bowed low and took his departure, his mind full of the beautiful Nisida.

Upward of two months had passed away since the occurrences related in the preceding chapter, and it was now the 31st of January, 1521.

The sun was verging toward the western hemisphere, but the rapid flight of the hours was unnoticed by Nisida and Fernand Wagner, as they were seated together in one of the splendid saloons of the Riverola mansion.

Their looks were fixed on each other's countenance; the eyes of Fernand expressing tenderness and admiration, those of Nisida beaming with all the passions of her ardent and sensual soul.

Suddenly the lady raised her hands, and by the rapid play of the fingers, asked, "Fernand, do you indeed love me as much as you would have me believe I am beloved?"

"Never in this world was woman so loved as you," he replied, by the aid of the same language.

"And yet I am an unfortunate being—deprived of those qualities which give the greatest charm to the companionship of those who love."

"But you are eminently beautiful, my Nisida; and I can fancy how sweet, how rich-toned would be your voice, could your lips frame the words, 'I love thee!'"

A profound sigh agitated the breast of the lady; and at the same time her lips quivered strangely, as if she were essaying to speak.

Wagner caught her to his breast; and she wept long and plenteously. Those tears relieved her; and she returned his warm, impassioned kisses with an ardour that convinced him how dear he had become to that afflicted, but transcendently beautiful being. On her side, the blood in her veins appeared to circulate like molten lead; and her face, her neck, her bosom were suffused with burning blushes.

At length, raising her head, she conveyed this wish to her companion: "Thou hast given me an idea which may render me ridiculous in your estimation; but it is a whim, a fancy, a caprice, engendered only by the profound affection I entertain for thee. I would that thou shouldst say, in thy softest, tenderest tones, the words 'I love thee!' and, by the wreathing of thy lips, I shall see enough to enable my imagination to persuade itself that those words have really fallen upon my ears."

Fernand smiled assent; and, while Nisida's eyes were fixed upon him with the most enthusiastic interest, he said, "I love thee!"

The sovereign beauty of her countenance was suddenly lighted up with an expression of ineffable joy, of indescribable delight; and, signalling the assurance, "I love thee, dearest, dearest Fernand!" she threw herself into his arms.

But almost at the same moment voices were heard in the adjacent room: and Wagner, gently disengaging himself from Nisida's embrace, hastily conveyed to her an intimation of the vicinity of others.

The lady gave him to understand by a glance that she comprehended him; and they remained motionless, fondly gazing upon each other.

Nisida's countenance assumed an expression of the deepest solicitude, and her eloquent, sparkling eyes, implored him to intimate to her what ailed him.

But, starting wildly from his seat, and casting on her a look of such bitter, bitter anguish, that the appalling emotions thus expressed struck terror to her soul—Fernand rushed from the room.

Nisida sprung to the window; and, though the obscurity of the evening now announced the last flickerings of the setting sunbeams in the west, she could perceive her lover dashing furiously on through the spacious gardens that surrounded the Riverola Palace.

On—on he went toward the River Arno; and in a few minutes was out of sight.

We must now return to Nisida, whom we left gazing from the window of the Riverola mansion, at the moment when Wagner rushed away from the vicinity of his lady-love on the approach of sunset.

The singularity of his conduct—the look of ineffable horror and anguish which he cast upon her, ere he parted from her presence—and the abruptness of his departure, filled her mind with the most torturing misgivings, and with a thousand wild fears.

Had his senses suddenly left him? was he the prey to fits of mental aberration which would produce so extraordinary an effect upon him? had he taken a sudden loathing and disgust to herself? or had he discovered anything in respect to her which had converted his love into hatred?

She knew not—and conjecture was vain! To a woman of her excitable temperament, the occurrence was particularly painful. She had never known the passion of love until she had seen Wagner; and the moment she did see him, she loved him. The sentiment on her part originated altogether in the natural sensuality of her disposition; there was nothing pure—nothing holy—nothing refined in her affection for him; it was his wonderful personal beauty that had made so immediate and profound an impression upon her heart.

There was consequently something furious and raging in that passion which she experienced for Fernand Wagner—a passion capable of every extreme—the largest sacrifices, or infuriate jealousies—the most implicit confidence, or the maddest suspicion! It was a passion which would induce her to ascend the scaffold to save him; or to plunge the vengeful dagger into his heart did she fancy that he deceived her!

To one, then, whose soul was animated by such a love, the conduct of Fernand was well adapted to wear even an exaggerated appearance of singularity; and as each different conjecture swept through her imagination, her emotions were excited to an extent which caused her countenance to vary its expressions a hundred times in a minute.

The fury of the desolating torrent, the rage of the terrific volcano, the sky cradled in the blackest clouds, the ocean heaving tempestuously in its mighty bed, the chafing of a tremendous flood against an embankment which seems ready every moment to give way, and allow the collected waters to burst forth upon the broad plains and into the peaceful valleys—all these occurrences in the physical world were imagined by the emotions that now agitated within the breast of the Italian lady.

Her mind was like the sea put in motion by the wind; and her eyes flashed fire, her lips quivered, her bosom heaved convulsively, her neck arched proudly, as if she were struggling against ideas that forced themselves upon her and painfully wounded her boundless patrician pride.

For the thought that rose uppermost amidst all the conjectures which rushed to her imagination, was that Fernand had conceived an invincible dislike toward her.

Wherefore did he fly thus—as if eager to place the greatest possible distance between herself and him?

Then did she recall to mind every interchange of thought that had passed between them through the language of the fingers; and she could fix upon nothing which, emanating from herself, had given him offence.

Had he then really lost his senses?

Madly did he seem to be rushing toward the Arno, on whose dark tide the departing rays of the setting sun glinted with oscillating and dying power.

She still continued to gaze from the window long after he had disappeared; obscurity was gathering rapidly around; but, even had it been noonday, she would have seen nothing. Her ideas grew bewildered: mortification, grief, anger, suspicion, burning desire, all mingled together and at length produced a species of stunning effect upon her, so that the past appeared to be a dream, and the future was wrapt in the darkest gloom and uncertainty.

This strange condition of her mind did not, however, last long; the natural energy of her character speedily asserted its empire over the intellectual lethargy which had seized upon her, and, awakening from her stupor, she resolved to waste not another instant in useless conjecture as to the cause of her lover's conduct.

Hastening to her own apartments, Nisida secured the outer door of her own suit of apartments, and hurried to her bedchamber. There she threw aside the garb belonging to her sex, and assumed that of a cavalier, which she took from a press opening with a secret spring. Then, having arranged her hair beneath a velvet tocque shaded with waving black plumes, in such a manner that the disguise was as complete as she could render it, she girt on a long rapier of finest Milan steel, and throwing the short cloak edged with costly fur, gracefully over her left shoulder, she quitted her chamber by a private door opening behind the folds of the bed curtains.

A narrow and dark staircase admitted her into the gardens of the Riverola mansion. These she crossed with a step so light and free, that had it been possible to observe her in the darkness of the evening, she would have been taken for the most elegant and charming cavalier that ever honoured the Florentine Republic with his presence.

In about a quarter of an hour she reached the abode of Dr. Duras; but instead of entering it, she passed round one of its angles, and opening a wicket by means of a key which she had about her, gained access to the gardens in the rear of the mansion.

She traversed these grounds with hasty steps, passing the boundary which separated them from the gardens of Wagner's dwelling, and then relaxing her pace, advanced with more caution to the windows of this very apartment where Agnes had been so alarmed two months previously, by observing the countenance at the casement.

But all was now dark within. Wagner was not in his favourite room—for Nisida knew that this was her lover's favourite apartment.

Perhaps he had not yet returned?

Thus thought the lady; and she walked slowly round the spacious dwelling, which, like the generality of the patrician mansions of Florence in those times—as indeed is now the case to a considerable extent—stood in the midst of extensive gardens.

There were lights in the servants' offices; but every other room seemed dark. No; one window in the front, on the ground-floor, shone with the lustre of a lamp.

Nisida approached it, and beheld Agnes reclining in a pensive manner on a sofa in a small but elegantly-furnished apartment. Her countenance was immediately overclouded; and for an instant she lingered to gaze upon the sylph-like form that was stretched upon that ottoman. Then she hastily pursued her way; and, having perfected the round of the building, once more reached the windows of her lover's favourite room.

Convinced that he had not returned, and fearful of being observed by any of the domestics who might happen to pass through the gardens, Nisida retraced her way toward the dwelling of Dr. Duras. But her heart was now heavy, for she knew not how to act.

Her original object was to obtain an interview with Wagner that very night, and learn, if possible, the reason of his extraordinary conduct toward her: for the idea of remaining in suspense for many long, long hours, was painful in the extreme to a woman of her excitable nature.

While all nature was wrapped in the listening stillness of admiration at the rising sun, Fernand Wagner dragged himself painfully toward his home.

His garments were besmeared with mud and dirt; they were torn, too, in many places; and here and there were stains of blood, still wet, upon them.

In fact, had he been dragged by a wild horse through a thicket of brambles, he could scarcely have appeared in a more wretched plight.

His countenance was ghastly pale; terror still flashed from his eyes, and despair sat on his lofty brow.

Stealing through the most concealed part of his garden, he was approaching his own mansion with the air of a man who returns home in the morning after having perpetrated some dreadful deed of turpitude under cover of the night.

But the watchful eyes of a woman have marked his coming from the lattice of her window; and in a few minutes Agnes, light as a fawn, came bounding toward him, exclaiming, "Oh! what a night of uneasiness have I passed, Fernand! But at length thou art restored to me—thou whom I have ever loved so fondly; although," she added, mournfully, "I abandoned thee for so long a time!"

And she embraced him tenderly.

"Agnes!" cried Fernand, repulsing her with an impatience which she had never experienced at his hands before: "wherefore thus act the spy upon me? Believe me, that although we pass ourselves off as brother and sister, yet I do not renounce that authority which the real nature of those ties that bind us together—"

"Fernand! Fernand! this to me!" exclaimed Agnes, bursting into tears. "Oh! how have I deserved such reproaches?"

"My dearest girl, pardon me, forgive me!" cried Wagner, in a tone of bitter anguish. "My God! I ought not to upbraid thee for that watchfulness during my absence, and that joy at my return, which prove that you love me! Again I say, pardon me, dearest Agnes."

"You need not ask me, Fernand," was the reply. "Only speak kindly to me—"

"I do, I will, Agnes," interrupted Wagner. "But leave me now! Let me regain my own chamber alone; I have reasons, urgent reasons for so doing; and this afternoon, Agnes, I shall be composed—collected again. Do you proceed by that path; I will take this."

And, hastily pressing her hand, Wagner broke abruptly away.

For a few moments Agnes stood looking after him in vacant astonishment at his extraordinary manner, and also at his alarming appearance, but concerning which latter she had not dared to question him.

When he had entered the mansion by a private door, Agnes turned and pursued her way along a circuitous path shaded on each side by dark evergreens, and which was the one he had directed her to take so as to regain the front gate of the dwelling.

But scarcely had she advanced a dozen paces, when a sudden rustling among the trees alarmed her; and in an instant a female form—tall, majestic, and with a dark veil thrown over her head, stood before her.

Agnes uttered a faint shriek: for, although the lady's countenance was concealed by the veil, she had no difficulty in recognising the stranger who had already terrified her on three previous occasions, and who seemed to haunt her.

And, as if to dispel all doubt as to the identity, the majestic lady suddenly tore aside her veil, and disclosed to the trembling, shrinking Agnes, features already too well known.

But, if the lightning of those brilliant, burning, black eyes had seemed terrible on former occasions, they were now absolutely blasting, and Agnes fell upon her knees, exclaiming, "Mercy! mercy! how have I offended you?"

For a few moments those basilisk-eyes darted forth shafts of fire and flame, and the red lips quivered violently, and the haughty brow contracted menacingly, and Agnes was stupefied, stunned, fascinated, terribly fascinated by that tremendous rage, the vengeance of which seemed ready to explode against her.

But only a few moments lasted that dreadful scene; for the lady, whose entire appearance was that of an avenging fiend in the guise of a beauteous woman, suddenly drew a sharp poniard from its sheath in her bodice, and plunged it into the bosom of the hapless Agnes.

The victim fell back; but not a shriek—not a sound escaped her lips. The blow was well aimed, the poniard was sharp and went deep, and death followed instantaneously.

For nearly a minute did the murderess stand gazing on the corpse—the corpse of one erst so beautiful; and her countenance, gradually relaxing from its stern, implacable expression, assumed an air of deep remorse—of bitter, bitter compunction.

But probably yielding to the sudden thought that she must provide for her own safety, the murderess drew forth the dagger from the white bosom in which it was buried: hastily wiped it upon a leaf; returned it to the sheath; and, replacing the veil over her countenance, hurried rapidly away from the scene of her fearful crime.

THE DARK WOMAN; OR, DAYS OF THE PRINCE REGENT

Malcolm J. Errym

Written by Malcolm J. Errym, one of the many pseudonyms for James Malcolm Rymer, *The Dark Woman* is a considerable penny blood that tells the venomous relationship of Linda Mowbray and George IV. Initially published in serial format, this episodic narrative of corruption and vengeance ran weekly from 13 August 1860 to 1 August 1862 in 104 parts, until published in a two-volume set edition by John Dicks.

Set in the early-nineteenth century during the reign of His Royal Highness the Prince Regent, George IV, *The Dark Woman* is a tale of Gothic sensationalism about a woman manipulated by the promises of a licentious royal. The eponymous Dark Woman, also known as Linda de Chevenaux, is the leader of the subterranean criminal gang, Paul's Chickens, and *femme fatale* mastermind of deception, adaptive identities, and social assimilation. Once known as the innocent, angelic, and charming daughter of an aristocrat, Linda is tricked into a falsified marriage by the Prince, one that ultimately resulted in childbirth. Unbeknownst to Linda, she is forced into the role of the fallen woman and declared as a hysterical by George IV, who then takes the child and imprisons her within an asylum. The tale begins after Linda escapes isolation and is in the ferocious role of the criminal Dark Woman who searches for her lost child and seeks vengeance against the Prince and a rejective society.

A perfect example of how dangerous women in the Gothic are figurations of social abuse and rejection, *The Dark Woman*, albeit extensive in its content, is exemplary in its exhibition of the so-called monstrosity of women. As the initial text is considerable and branches into a multitude of side-plots, the following content is only a focused excerpt about the struggles of Linda de Chevenaux.

T the Italian Opera House, now named Her Majesty's Theatre, there was, on the night of February the 1st, in the year 1814, a masquerade; and notwithstanding the intense cold of the season, for the snow was heaped up in the streets, and the Thames was frozen completely from bank to bank, never had the vast area of the magnificent building been more entirely filled by a madly-excited throng, and never before had there seemed that utter abandonment to the pleasure of the scene which characterised the maskers.

Laughter loud, shrill, hysterical in its vehemence—prolonged beyond all power of cessation—a Babel of voices that rang through the house with a million of echoes; music that, with its clashing sounds, only now and then made itself heard above the wild rout of noises; now and then the angry tones of quarrel, the screams of those entangled in some brawl; those of the softer sex, who were as well represented, so far as numbers went, in the busy scene; whirling, dancing figures, half-mad with excitement; the blaze of lights; the aroma of rich wines; the sparkle of jewels; the clash of swords; all made up a confusion and riot, that up to the hour of three o'clock on the morning of the 2nd of February, showed no signs of flagging or abating.

The wine, fiery as it was, and indiscriminately indulged in, did its demoniac duty, and by the time we mention—three o'clock—intoxication began to add its vague terrors to the scene of mental excitement.

Then arose still wilder laughter from the whirling throng; still louder shouts—still fiercer brawls and quarrels.

Swords were drawn, and more than one sudden quarrel was as suddenly ended in bloodshed.

The shrieks of dismay that would then arise rang high above the music. All order was lost. The throng became a mob; the dancing ceased; the music was hushed.

Officers, Turks, Indians, fiends, grotesque animals, dominoes,—all were mingled up together in one dense mass with an army of dancing-girls, flower-sellers, ballet posturers, mythological divinities, and, in fact, every possible and impossible representation of real or supposed existences in and above or below the world.

Roaring, shouting, screaming, and yelling—crying for more wine, crying for more music, for more dancing, in a place now so full, that not a square yard could have been found unoccupied in even the remotest corner.

It was something dreadful to look down from the tier of boxes upon the whirling, roaring, excited mass, in the boarded-over area of pit and stage.

Then there were fights for places—fights almost for life.

Several maskers fell headlong into the midst of the toiling mob below, from the boxes.

Cries arose for constables—cries for the guards—summonses for help of any shape.

And then—then at half-past three o'clock exactly, one voice raised a shriek so intense in its terror and distraction, that for a moment it had the effect of stilling all other sounds; and the motley throng was still.

Still, perhaps, while you could have counted five moderately quick—still in voice, still in gestures; and during that brief period the same voice that had uttered the high and terrible scream, cried out, "The chandelier!"

A magnificent chandelier of heavy cut glass, carrying a thousand wax candles, descended from the ceiling.

The chandelier was seen coming down.

A massive chain with broad links appeared to be its principal support. These broad links were seen to collapse, and become narrow ones.

The chandelier moved bodily down about two feet.

Then a yell so awful, that it might be supposed the concussion of the air above aided the catastrophe, arose from the throng below.

There was a wild, terrific fight to get out of the way of the falling mass.

It was perfectly unsuccessful that fight to escape; not a soul could get out of the way. Those outside the entrance of the pit fought them back into their places.

Then down came the chandelier!

It seemed to grow larger as it came with an awful swing through the hot air!

Crash!

It was with a dull, heavy crash it reached the masses of heads beneath it!

A roar of pain—a terrible cry arose from the killed and maimed people!

The house was suddenly darkened! Those thousand lights had, at one blow, shorn it of its refulgent splendour!

There only remained a few side lights in and about the stage, and in the corridors!

And there, upon that arena which had glittered with youth, with beauty, and with mad delight, lay a writhing, shrieking mass—a mass of bright colours—of broken glass—of blood!

Close the eyes, that they may not see those poor glittering worms of fantastic pleasure, in their gay and sparkling habiliments, seeking to writhe their way with broken limbs from the catastrophe!

Shut the ears against the groans—the shrieks—the prayers—there were prayers then—of the wounded and of the dying!

Then arose a new cry!

"Fire!"

"Fire! fire! fire!" shouted a thousand voices. "Fire! fire! fire!"

The dresses, light and gauzy, of some of those who had not been within the actual circle of death comprehended by the falling chandelier, had been set fire to!

The wax candles had been scattered far and wide by the concussion of the huge mass of glass that covered them, and had fallen, still ignited, on many an inflammable costume!

It was dreadful to see these poor creatures shrieking in flames!

Those flames caught the light hangings with which the house was adorned for the occasion! Long wreathes of artificial roses caught light, and the bright flames ran along them with a rapidity that the eye could scarcely follow!

The whole interior of the Opera House appeared to be in flames!

The heat was now suffocating!

"Fire! fire! fire!"

That was not the cry that stifled all others—the cry that came from all throats, and which struck like a death-knell upon all ears!

Panting, bleeding, and with their gay dresses torn to shreds, and hanging about them in fluttering fragments, some of the maskers now began to show themselves in the open street! They were of those nearest to the doors, and who had managed to escape!

They lifted up their arms, and raised cries of joy as they felt the keen night air; some flung themselves upon the great heaps of snow, and rolled in the frigid mass.

But within the house the scene of horror and dismay continued.

And now, amid the scene of confusion, of semi-darkness and dismay, there began to come out into relief from the general throng, episodes compounded of suffering and of heroism.

At this grand and attractive masquerade at the Italian Opera House on the first day of February, in the year 1814, were present the Royal Princes.

His Royal Highness George Prince of Wales, then Regent of this kingdom, in consequence of the more noticeable insanity of George the Third, was present.

Some few moments before the fall of the great chandelier, the Regent, who was masked and attired in a Persian costume, which was made all in one piece, and under which he had an ordinary evening dress, spoke rather impatiently to his then "Master of the Pleasures," Sir Hinckton Moys.

It was at this moment that that awful cry, which stilled all the other sounds, arose, and in three seconds more the chandelier had fallen.

The moment it fell, the Regent heard, or fancied he heard, a voice close to him say, "Secure!"

A couple of hands were then laid violently upon him, and he was forced backward through a small doorway at the side of the pit, close to the royal box, and the door closed.

The Regent was in utter darkness.

The fear that came over him was at once intense and ludicrous.

He raved—he shouted—he called for help—he swore!

But the cries, groans, shrieks, and yells without the place in which he was, and which he thought was a cupboard or closet of some kind, effectively drowned his voice; for all that terrible uproar, of which we have endeavoured to give some idea, and which followed the fall of the chandelier, was at its height.

"Hilloa! Help, here! I am the Regent! Hoy! I say, the Regent! Guard—guard! Let me out of this place! Hoy! hoy! Moys, I say! What the—a—deuce—Hoy! Murder! murder!"

No one paid any attention; but the wild cries in the pit of the house were beginning to subside, and then a deep-toned voice apparently close to him, said, "George, Prince of Wales and Regent of England, your cries are vain: you are at the mercy of one who has already shown that feeling."

"Eh, who is that? At mercy? Murder!"

"Are you dead?"

"Dead? dead? No! Don't speak to me of being dead! Open the door! There is a door! there was a door!"

"Then you are spared!"

"What do you mean?"

"You live!"

"Of course, I live. By Jove! Open the door at once! I command it—open the door!"

"No! Beyond that door is death—death in such terrors, that you may well fancy you are specially watched over, to find yourself where you are."

"But I don't comprehend?"

"Follow!"

"Ah, then," he said, "this is not a cupboard?"

"No," replied the voice. "Follow!"

"But I think I would rather go out by the way I came in."

"There is death, I tell you, there. By the accident that has happened, many a poor wretch who came to this place for pleasure has found agony and death!"

"But I don't see what this is to me, so long as I get away in safety."

"There spoke George, Prince of Wales!" said the voice.

"What?"

"Self! self! self!"

"Well, I fancy I am not peculiar in that; but if by following you, whoever you are, I can be safely led out of this house, you may count upon a reward."

"Follow!"

The little star-like light slowly receded, and the Regent, holding his arms out as far as he could, slowly followed.

That he was in one of the numerous passages that abounded at the back of the boxes and stage of the theatre he had now no doubt; and well he knew that without a guide who was acquainted with their intricacies it would be impossible to find his way.

"Recollect," he said, in a voice that betrayed some flurry and fear—"recollect, that you will get a reward if you conduct me in perfect safety out of this place. Always recollect that."

"Follow!" was the only reply that the voice vouchsafed to make to this speech.

The Regent thought that he saw, now that his eyes were getting accustomed to the darkness, a dark shadowy figure walking before him, and holding aloft above its head the small star-like light which he was told to follow.

To say that he felt at ease, or that he had full confidence in his conductor, would be far from the truth; and yet he had, perhaps, fewer apprehensions than many an ordinary person with more courage than he possessed would have had.

This arose from the sort of education and culture he had had.

From earliest childhood, he had always found that everybody about him was intent upon performing some service for him; and, therefore, he concluded that this shadowy form with the light, enigmatical as was the language it used, would end by humbly showing him out of the Opera House.

He was mistaken.

The passage through which the Regent followed the mysterious figure with the star-like light was long and tortuous, and took so many windings, that it seemed as though it must have gone half-way round the entire building.

Suddenly, then, the light stopped.

"Halt!" said the figure.

"Well, but I don't see the way out!"

Even as he spoke, the Regent saw a tall, narrow door opened; and there issued through the opening a faint light. The dark figure appeared now much more distinctly; and the Regent saw that it wore a cloak of some black-looking material that trailed on the floor, and that a half-mask of black lace reached from the lower rim of the mask to the chin, and so completely disguised the features.

This person, too, wore a black hat of a peculiar, conical-looking shape from which one long, drooping feather, which was either black, the Regent thought, or a very dark blood-red, depended.

"Enter!" said the voice.

"In there?"

"Enter!"

"Well, you will find that I am armed."

"Enter!"

The voice was so calm in its tones that the Regent said not another word, but passed through the doorway, and entered a small room, dimly lighted by some apparently reflected light that came through a curtain that was drawn over one side of the room.

This reflected light was of a reddish colour, which it borrowed of the curtain, which was of crimson silk, through which it passed.

"Ah!" said the Regent, "I know where I am!"

"You do?" said the voice.

"This is the ante-room to the King's box."

"It is."

"And beyond that curtain is the box."

"It is so."

"I will—"

"Hold, for your life's sake!"

The Regent had been about to push aside the crimson silk curtain that divided the ante-room he was in from the royal box, by which he would at once have seen into the house; but he paused at the sound of that warning voice, and drew back.

"Why should there be danger?" he said.

"There is!"

"Ah, I hear! I am safe!"

From the pit of the theatre below some sounds met his ears.

"The fire is out!" said one.

"Quite," replied another voice. "Hold your flambeaux high."

"Yes, sir."

"Now remove the bodies carefully."

"Halt!" then said another voice, in a decidedly military tone. "Pile arms!"

There was a rattle of muskets.

"Mr. High Constable," added the voice that had given the military orders, "my men will help you now in your work."

"I am much obliged to you, Captain."

"Ah," said the Regent, "I have nothing not to do but to go into the royal box, and they will help me from it into the pit; and I can leave the house with an escort."

"And so expose your presence here," said the voice of the cloaked and masked figure.

The Regent again advanced to the curtain, and drew it aside a few inches. He recoiled in terror.

Two men faced him, and the gleam of two dagger-like weapons glittered before his eyes, as their points touched his breast.

"Assassins!"

"You see them?" said the voice.

The Regent was as pale as death.

"Take all I have, and spare my life!" he said. "I will give a thousand pounds for my life! Two thousand pounds for my life!"

"Peace!"

"Yes. I—a—I will say no more; only—"

"Peace, I say! Is there anything, however distant, in my voice which awakens a memory?"

"Awakens a memory? I—a—Well, I fancy I have heard it before."

"You fancy so?"

"I do, certainly. But you know, if I call out, you will be taken into custody."

"Yes."

"Well, then—"

"One moment! Your dead body will be found here at the same time!"

These last words of the mysterious person in the cloak and the mask appeared thoroughly to break down the last effort at resistance which the Regent could muster courage to make.

The figure in the cloak and mask then slowly permitted the cloak to fall to its feet. Then removing the singular-shaped hat, the contour of the head at once showed that it was a female who had been so disguised. The mask still, however, remained.

"Do you know me now?" she said.

"I seem to know the voice."

"Oh, heart!—oh, human heart!"

There was a world of agony in the tones in which these words were uttered.

They had hardly been spoken when, by a touch, the mask was pushed upwards to the top of the head, and the features of its wearer were exposed to view in the strange, dim light of that apartment.

"Behold!" she said.

Then the Regent seemed as if he shrunk within himself, while his eyes only increased in size until he absolutely glared in the countenance of the mysterious person before him.

"You know me now!" she said, in a fearfully strange, gasping manner.

"Linda!" said the Regent. "Lin—"

He would have repeated the name, but his tongue refused its office. He felt parched and hit in such mortal fear that his knees smote each other, and he could scarcely keep his feet.

"Yes, I am Linda! I am more, too!"

"Oh, no! no!"

"Yes, I am!"

"Don't! don't! I thought you were dead—dead—dead!"

The word "dead" seemed to him easy to pronounce, or he felt a pleasure in repeating it, as if by doing so it would go somewhat towards accomplishing a death he would have been so glad of.

"No, I live!"

"Let—let—me—go! I thought—the poison—they told me—you had taken it."

"I did!"

"And—"

"It did not kill me. I am here!"

"You—are—here! You—you want—you wanted to live—to vex me."

"No; to question you. I am—"

"Oh, don't—oh, don't! Somebody may hear."

"Your—"

"Hush! hush! you are mad!"

"Wife!"

"There, now—you go on in that way, but you don't know what you say, Linda. It was so long ago. Nineteen years now."

"This day!"

"This—Eh?"

"This day nineteen years ago."

"Oh, was it? Well—I—a—well—you know that a marriage contracted by me is null and void, because the—a—Royal Marriage Act requires the consent of the Crown to my marriage."

"You brought me the written consent of the King, your father."

"Yes, but that was a—little ruse."

"A forgery! I know it now; but you will perhaps not like to admit so much, in order to get rid of my claims, should I make them."

"Come, come, Linda; you know you used to be sensible. Come, come! I will settle something on you, and you can go home—to Dover Court—to your friends, you know.

"But—but what is the use, now of plaguing me? I have, as you are well aware, contracted a royal marriage, and a nice one it is, too!"

"George!"

"Hem! You are familiar."

"George, there is one condition on which I will not only release you from all persecution, but bless you—yes, I will still bless you!"

"Indeed, Linda!"

"Yes! yes! I need not, surely, remind you that I had a son?"

The voice of this strange female shook and melted into sobs as she uttered these words, and the Prince Regent at once felt his advantage, or fancied he did so, for he said, "And what then? What then?—eh?"

"If you George—if you will but tell me what had become of him—if he be alive or dead;—if you will, in some solemn way, so that I may believe you, tell me what became of that dear, dear, little one, whom I held to my heart once—only once—before it was torn from me! Oh, heaven! Oh, heaven!"

"Ah! Hem! Well, my good woman, I don't know! So there is an end of that!"

"Oh, yes!—yes! I implore you! I will pray to heaven to soften your heart! Steeped in selfishness and indulgence as you are, I will pray for you, if you will tell me what became of my son—my child! I was so very near death; but I heard someone say, 'It is a boy;' and then the whole air was red as blood about me; and when I recovered I was in a cell—the cell of a madhouse; and they said I had been there for ten long years!"

"Why, they told me you were dead!"

"That was to conceal that I escaped!"

"Ah!"

"One year since, I escaped! From that time to this I have followed you—I have dogged your footsteps—I have been as a shadow to you—because I resolved upon asking you this question: 'Where is my son?' I ask you now!"

"Then I don't know anything about him!"

"Then you die!"

"Die? die? Linda!"

"Vengeance long delayed cometh at last! I say that you die! When your desertion of me was manifest, I took poison. It did not kill. You see I am here, and I ask you where is my son? You do not know—you, the father—or you will not know—you the careless sybarite, who cares for nothing, loves nothing!"

"Stop! stop! I think I can find out what you want to know. In fact, I know I can. But if I am murdered, you will never know."

"You shall live then!"

"Ah! yes!"

The Regent drew a long breath of relief.

"You shall live then, George, Prince of Wales; but until you give me this information, and I am convinced that it is truthful, I will haunt you!"

"Haunt me?"

"Yes! At bed and board, sleeping and waking; in the inmost recesses of your palace; when you are at the revel with your associates—when least you expect me, I will rise up before your eyes, and I will say to you, 'Where is my son?' One year I will give you to answer me."

"One year?"

"And what then?"

"We will conclude he is no more!"

"Conclude that now?"

"Do you assure me of it?"

"Well, I—I suppose if I do, you and I are done with each other?"

"No! We will go together!"

"Together? Where?"

"To another and a better world than this, to seek him!"

"Mad! mad!"

"It may be so, but that is my determination. Find him for me, and I forgive you; and he and I will never cross your path again. Otherwise I am the enemy of you, and all belonging to you."

"Stop, stop—Linda, you were once so different—so very mild and gentle!"

"I was, until you stole the sunshine from this poor heart, and placed there in its stead strange fires. Find me my son, and you are free! Find him not, and I am your shadow—your destiny! Farewell! We shall soon meet again. I will give you some time to find the answer to the question I ask of you."

"Stop! stop, Linda! I—a—stay—I think I have a clue to what became of the boy."

"Ah!"

"Which I will investigate, and if he yet live—"

"Oh, heaven!"

"If he yet live, I will, on condition of your silence, provide for him."

"No! no! To me—to me! He must come to me. To me, ever and ever—my compensation!"

"Well, be it so. But you must let me know where to find you?"

"In the air!"

"The air?"

"Yes, go forth into the air and speak a message to me: I shall hear it."

"To you, as Linda Mowbray?"

"No, I am called something else now."

"What, what?"

"THE DARK WOMAN!"

No sooner had Linda uttered the name with which she concluded her interview with the Regent, than she left the royal box with an abruptness that almost looked like a magical disappearance.

The Regent cried out after her, "Stop! Stop! I don't comprehend. I don't at all understand what you mean? Oh, you won't stop! You will be off, will you? Well, we shall soon see! Ha! Yes, we shall soon see!"

And now we must elucidate one of the mysterious actions of the Dark Woman.

During that part of the evening which commenced at half-past eleven o'clock and terminated at one, a handsome coach, with richly-emblazoned arms on its panels, stood at the door of a lapidary's shop in St. Paul's Churchyard, a few doors from the principal entrance to Doctors' Commons.

The noble-looking horses champed their bits, and pawed the pavement, but not very impatiently; for coachman, footmen, and horses were all well accustomed to waiting many an hour at the routs and balls of the Court and the aristocracy.

That equipage belonged to the Countess de Launy, the widow of one of the old French noblesse, who had perished amid the horrors and massacres of the great revolution.

So it was reported.

And she was immensely rich.

That was reported, too.

Another moment, and there emerged from the small opening in the floor the head of the Dark Woman.

There must have been some flight of steps nearly perpendicular, up which she came, for her appearance was spectral-like, and appeared to rise out of the floor, as if impelled by some power that required not the aid of ordinary means of ascent.

That she had a secret passage from the vaults of St. Paul's to that house of the lapidary was evident; and that it was the route which she took in order to meet Paul's Chickens, and to leave the meetings, there could be no doubt; but the most remarkable change that ever pantomimic presentation knew was taking place in the Dark Woman as she preceded to the upper part of the house.

With nimble fingers, she loosened from round her neck the outer robe, or dress, that she wore, and she let it roll off her, and fall to her feet.

Beneath, she appeared in a splendid dress of pearly satin, richly embroidered with roses.

A touch brought then away from her head the peculiar hat she had worn, and the mask was removed from her face. A mass of beautiful ringlets of light brown hair, with just sufficient warmth of colour in it to redeem it from the commonplace, fell about her neck and shoulders.

Costly jewels sparkled on her fingers, as she disclosed them by casting aside dark-coloured gloves that she had worn. Her neck was encircled by a row of costly pearls, each one of which must have been worth a thousand pounds. Diamonds glittered in her hair; and, take her for all in all, as she stood in the little shop of the lapidary, a more brilliant and beautiful being than this mysterious personage could not have been found.

The fair and beautiful Countess de Launy, otherwise Linda, otherwise the Dark Woman sat in her splendid boudoir in her town house.

An elegant robe of quilted satin, on which were embroidered roses, was the costly morning dress of the Countess, for she was in the habit of receiving calls in that boudoir with almost the state of a crowned queen.

The atmosphere was full of the delicate fragrance of the Turkish coffee, of which she was so fond, and a bright fire, partly of coal and partly of cedar wood, blazed in the grate, and imparted an agreeable warmth to the apartment.

The door was very gently opened, and a young boy, not above ten years of age, but remarkable for the elegance of his form, and attired in a fanciful page's costume, made his appearance.

"Well, Felix, what is it?"

"A man, my lady, who calls himself Willes, humbly requests to see you."

"It is well."

A meaning smile played for a moment over the beautiful lips of the Countess, and then she added, "You will admit him, Felix. Be within call, and let him out by the stables at the back."

"Yes, madam."

In a few moments, the Regent's valet, Willes, looking pale and half-scared, was shown into the boudoir of the Countess.

Her ladyship put on a look of well-acted surprise, as she saw Willes, and he, after a low bow, spoke hesitatingly, "Madam—my lady—I don't know what to say; but—but that I am here."

"And what are you here for?"

"To be the humble servant of your ladyship, and to say that if there is anything at any time which your ladyship would like to know as taking place at the Palace, I shall only be too happy to bring you the information."

The Countess regarded him for a few moments in silence; then, in a voice which was at once firm and re-assuring, she said, "Richard Willes, I know you well. I have means, too, of knowing whatever I want to know, without being beholden to any being of this earth for the intelligence."

"Oh, my lady!"

"Peace! Hear me out! Spirits of the air are beings of so subtle a nature that it requires a process, even with all my power, to command their presence and their services. That process involves trouble, so that the information I require, if it come through human agency, will me as well."

"Yes, my lady."

"Now, you will incur no danger whatever in bringing me, once a day, or once on every alternate day, news of the events taking place in the Palace."

"I am quite willing to do so."

"You shall not be without your reward. You are now in distress about some jewels that have disappeared from the Regent's toilette?"

"I am—I am indeed! I took—that is, I wanted—"

"You wanted money, and you took the jewels to procure it! Now, listen to me! Money is to me no object whatever."

"Oh, my lady!"

"And whatever you want you can have of me, provided I find you faithful, and willing to obey me in all things."

"Command my life!"

"I do not want that! You are useful to me living, but not at all dead! In this small pocket you will find the trinkets and jewels which you have taken from the Regent's toilette, and which you are afraid, when their loss should be discovered, would arm your enemy, Sir Hinckton Moys, against you."

"Oh, how can I thank you? And yet you terrify me, madam, for how is it that you could become possessed of these things."

"That is my secret! I have power of which you, who are merely human, know nothing! Now, tell me what is going on at the Palace?"

"Why, madam, Sir Hinckton Moys, has brought to the private suite of rooms that look into the Colour Court, one of the young girls who was dressed as 'Follies' at the masquerade. He intends to-night to affect to marry her, which has been the pretence that brought her to the Palace."

"Ah! and then?"

"And then he will abandon her!"

"To another?"

"Yes; to the Regent!"

The Dark Woman rose and paced the room for a few seconds, and she opened and shut her hands in the manner usual with her when her passions were strongly stirred by anything.

"Well, well!" she said then. "I fancy such things have happened before!"

As the Countess spoke, she pretended that too much light came in by the window that was nearest to her, and she pulled a silken cord, which brought down a silk blind of a pale green colour, that shed some of its reflection upon her face.

"I listen to you, my lady, with the greatest attention and respect," said Willes.

"Perhaps, then, you are aware that only about one or two months before his marriage with Caroline of Brunswick, the Regent was attached to a lady, whom he had privately wedded?"

"I have heard something of it, madam."

"She was a dear friend of mine. Her name was Linda."

"Ah, madam, I have heard the Prince and Sir Hinckton Moys mention that name."

"In what way?"

"I only heard the name."

"If on other occasions you hear as much, you will oblige me by listening to all."

"I will, your ladyship may be assured."

"This lady, then, was the daughter of an Englishman, but her mother was Italian. The Prince Regent married her; and at the time he did so, he produced, in writing, the consent of the King, his father, which made the marriage legal."

"Did he, my lady?"

"He assuredly did. But there is reason to think that he will now rather say that that was a forgery than admit it."

"But the King—"

"Is mad, and his admission or rejection of the document would be equally of no moment as regards its validity."

Willes bowed.

The Countess de Launy proceeded in a lower tone, and, as Willes thought, with a struggle to speak quite calmly and without emotion.

"As usual, with George, Prince of Wales, this lady was deserted soon after the marriage."

"Ah, yes; he always does!"

"But she kept him disagreeably aware of her existence by what he called persecuting him, for she expected that to her other troubles would be added that of a mother."

"Oh!"

"The fact she impressed upon the mind of the Regent—not then a Regent, though, but only Prince of Wales—and he suddenly pretended to be pleased, and paid her much attention, placing her in one of the royal lodges at Hampton Court. In fact, in the old palace of Wolsey, nineteen years ago, this real wife of the Prince of Wales was delivered of a son."

The Dark Woman was now silent for a few minutes. Memory seemed to carry her back to scenes and events which choked her utterance.

Twice did Willes say, "Yes, madam," and was in a still lower voice that she added, "The Prince was in the house on the occasion, and the Princess of Wales only had strength to hear someone say, 'It is a boy,' when she fell into a deep faint, which lasted many hours."

"The Princess of Wales, madam?"

"Yes."

"But—"

"Who else," cried the Dark Woman, with sudden vehemence,—"who else is the Princess of Wales but the first wife of George, Prince of Wales?"

"Oh, of course! Certainly! That is—a—yes! Oh, dear, yes! Of course, madam, if you say so!"

"I do say so!"

"Then that's settled. May I ask what became of the affair?"

"The child!"

"Yes, madam."

"That is unknown, except to the Regent, and a woman of the name of Adams, who was in his employment."

"It's dead, I suppose?"

"Dead? Dead? How dare you tell me the boy is dead?"

The anger with which the Dark Woman uttered these words terrified Willes, and he hastened to qualify what he had said.

"I did not mean, my lady, to say that the child was dead, only I thought you meant to say it."

"Never! Never!"

"Yes, madam,—just do. As you say—never! never!"

"From that day to this, the mother had not seen her child."

"And—and the mother?"

"Ah! She has suffered much."

"Poor woman!"

"She has suffered so much that she cannot look back without horror. Would you like to see her?"

Willes started, for he had been rapidly making up his mind that the so-called Countess de Launy was not other than the person she spoke of,— and she, too, had begun to be fearful that the intense interest she manifested in the story she was telling would have just that effect upon the mind of Willes, so she wished to do or to say something that would have a tendency to dislodge from his brain such a notion.

Hence was it, therefore, that she suddenly asked him if he would like to see the Princess of Wales, as she chose to name the unfortunate victim of the Regent.

"Well, madam," replied Willes, "if you think that I could do any good?"

"I do not know. She is somewhat dangerous, and has taken several lives; but you shall see her."

"Not for the world, madam, if you please. I am not afraid,—oh dear, no! not in the least! The fact is, I am quite a lion when men are in the case; but my heart is so tender, that if I were to be attacked by a woman, I should just have to let her kill me out of hand."

"Be it so. It might irritate her to see a stranger."

"Oh! no doubt it would, poor lady!"

"Well, you now know all. From that time to this she has not seen her child; and she believes that the Regent could, if he chose, give her such information as would enable her to discover him—or, at all events, thoroughly satisfy herself if he were alive or dead. It will be for you to keep this object in your mind, and to bring me any news, let it be however slight, which in any way bears upon the subject."

"I will, indeed, madam! You may depend upon my services!"

"I know I can! Good day! You will always find me at this hour here; but beware!"

"Beware?"

"Yes! Beware of the slightest indiscretion; for should you allow yourself to utter to any one the secret of our conversations, you would bring upon yourself such unheard-of horrors, that although I have some imperfect knowledge of what your sufferings would be, I do not wish to burden your imagination with so much terror as a mere hint of them would produce."

Willes was thoroughly terrified.

The denunciations of the Countess de Launy tallied so completely with what had been said to him at the house of the astrologer, that he could no longer doubt his extreme peril if he should commit any breach of faith in respect to his instructions and arrangements with her.

He left the splendid mansion with many protestations of fidelity.

While all these circumstances in connexion with those in whose fortunes we feel interested were in course of procedure, his Royal Highness the Prince Regent began to be a prey to great anxiety.

The persecutions of the Dark Woman began to have an effect upon his mind.

As Sir Hinckton Moys, then, went out of favour with the Regent, a certain Colonel Hanger, whom we have incidentally mentioned, came in.

The Regent lay at length upon a crimson velvet couch sipping tokay, which, for the last few weeks, he had taken a fancy to.

Colonel Hanger was sitting in a high-backed chair opposite to the fire, looking so insolent, so bloated, and so vicious, that one might well wonder how even the Regent, who had about him some of the tastes and instincts of a gentleman, could endure him.

But probably it was because Hanger was so thorough a scoundrel that the Regent esteemed his company; for with him there need be no scruples about anything, and his suggestions of dissipation and wickedness were of the most awful character.

"I am honoured by your Royal Highness's offered confidence," drawled Colonel Hanger, as he sipped his wine, "and I don't doubt for a moment, but I shall see my way."

"I hope you may. I mean to tell you all, Hanger."

"Well, Prince, out with it."

"Then I will tell you. A long time ago, I suppose I may say that I fell in love?"

"Oh, dear!"

"Don't interrupt me, Hanger."

"I am all attention."

"Well, when I say I fell in love, it is, perhaps, too strong a term; but I can say that I took a fancy to a woman."

"I thought it was a woman!"

"She was then exceedingly lovely. Indeed, I have her portrait now by me."

The Colonel brought a rather large-sized miniature to the Prince, who, still reclining on the velvet couch, touched the spring that opened the case, and took the miniature out from it.

It represented a very charming young woman, with a hat, in which were entwined some wildflowers. She was attired in a very simple country costume, and looked innocent, and serene, and thoughtful.

"She was, then, the only daughter of old John de Chevenaux, who had an estate in Berkshire, called Dover Court.

"And her name was Linda.

"I became madly enamoured of her, I admit, and would have done anything in the world to get possession of her; but she was inflexible.

"Yes, I tried flattery—presents—tears—everything; but she made but one reply—and that was, which she could accept would be an offer of marriage. I made, at last, that offer to her."

"A mock one?"

"No! By heaven, a real marriage!"

"But the whole affair would be illegal without the consent of the Crown."

"She knew that."

"Then she was not so scrupulous, after all?"

"By Jove, she was, for she demanded of me the consent of the Crown."

"The deuce she did!"

"And I produced it."

"You, Prince?"

"Yes; under the sign manual of the King. But I did not trouble him about it; and it is no small portion of my perplexities, that I don't know now if that document be in existence or not.

"We were married.

"A real marriage by a clergyman, who luckily since then is dead; and oddly enough the church was burnt down, and the register of the transaction perished in the flames.

"Well, in about a year, I found that Linda de Chevenaux had some faults."

"Of course."

"And that I was rather mistaken in her beauty. In fact I may say that I would have been glad to get rid of her, and that I repented very much of having anything to say to her."

"Of course."

"What do you go on saying 'of course', for Hanger? It is not 'of course'; for if I had found Linda de Chevenaux to be all that I thought her, I should have been constant to her. I thought her an angel."

"My dear Prince, that is always the case."

"What is?"

"Why, we think the woman an angel until she is our own, and then we find the angel a woman."

"Well, well, she had a son. I don't know what became of the child—not a bit. I might possibly find out. I do, indeed, think I have had some plaguing letters about him, from somebody who threatened that if they did not get some money of me, they would abandon the infant in some public thoroughfare. Now you know, Hanger, what brutes there are in the world."

"To be sure."

"Well, I paid no attention to the letters, and I should not at all wonder that they did desert the child."

"And it may have died of neglect."

"Well, that was their brutality, you know."

"After that little event, I paid no attention to Linda, for really her temper, which was never of the best, got to be quite unbearable, and she was put into a lunatic asylum to take care of her. Oh, I was quite willing to have every care taken of her."

"You were too good."

"Well, well, it is better to err on the safe side, Colonel. She was as I tell you, put into a lunatic asylum, to take care of her; and, to tell the truth, I had really forgotten all about her until that night when there was such a disturbance at the opera."

"The night of the masquerade?"

"Just so.

"From that night, then, I have known no peace from the persecutions of Linda de Chevenaux. By some means she had contrived to escape from the lunatic asylum in which she had been for so long confined, and she encountered me in a most uncomfortable manner at the Opera House. She seemed to be in league with, and to be supported by, bullies and bravoes; and she not only called herself my wife, but, in the most disagreeable way, began plaguing about her son. From that time forth she has haunted me."

"In the street?"

"Everywhere! Here—at St. James's Palace—wherever I am—wherever I go, she has some diabolical means of getting at me! I have found her in my own private rooms—in my very bedchamber! I must and will be rid of her!

"You may depend, then, Colonel, that if you do rid me once and for all of that woman, I shall feel you have done me a favour which can never be cancelled; and you can ask of me, at any time, whatever it may be in my power to grant to you."

The Prince had had too much conversation with Colonel Hanger about Linda not to know perfectly well what his meaning was.

His object was to get possession, in some seemingly easy and natural way, of his pistols, so that if in the course of that evening the invitation to Linda to appear should really be productive of her presence, he might rid his royal patron of her at once and for ever.

We do not mean for moment to state that his Royal Highness the Prince of Wales had made any agreement with the unprincipled Colonel Hanger actually to murder Linda de Chevenaux; but he did hope that the Colonel would be able to effect her capture; in which case she would once more have been condemned to some such a seclusion in a lunatic asylum as that from which she has escaped.

"She has been duly summoned," added the Regent, "to make her appearance here, in the manner that she said she could do so; for when I asked her how I should communicate with her, assuming that I wished to do so, she replied, 'that the air would convey the words to her,' or something to that effect."

"Yes," added Colonel Hanger, "and in pursuance of the orders of his Royal Highness, I say that I summoned this order to appear at this supper to-night."

"Just so; she comes not."

Willes, at this moment, shrunk back into the recess of a window; and if anyone happened to see his face, they would have been alarmed at the ghastly paleness that was upon it.

"I think, now, that it will be but a proper thing to summon by voice this presumptuous person."

The Regent said, in a louder voice that he had yet spoken in, "I can tell you all that it is a most curious circumstance that there are two thieves or housebreakers in Newgate now, who accuse this person, who calls herself the Dark Woman, of being the mistress of the gang of thieves called Paul's Chickens; and likewise of being identical with a person who has been in London the whole of the season, and who has called herself the Countess de Launy."

"Why—ah,—oh, dear!" said Brummel; "you don't mean to say, George, that the charming Countess de Launy is the Dark Woman, or the captain of a gang of thieves?"

"So it is said."

"Yes," added Colonel Hanger; "and if she should come here now on being summoned, I fancy it will have to be from a cell at Newgate."

"Summon her!—summon her!" cried several voices.

Colonel Hanger looked at the Regent for his approbation; and he replied to the look by saying, "I would gladly, once and for all, get rid of the troublesome persecutions of that woman. Let us now test her powers."

"Very good!" said the Colonel; and he rose from his chair.

There was a complete silence in the brilliant apartment. The guests disposed themselves in different attitudes of expectation of some remarkable event; and the Colonel spoke in rather a high and artificial tone of voice as he said, "In the name of the Regent, I summon Linda de Chevenaux!"

Willes looked out from the window recess, into which he had shrunk for shelter.

The French window that opened into the conservatory was dashed aside, and the Dark Woman made one step into the supper-room as she said, in a high, clear voice, "*I am here!*"

The Prince of Wales started to his feet.

"Ah!" shouted Colonel Hanger, "it is well done! Is she bullet-proof?"

Bang! went the pistol that he had held in his hand during the whole of this singular scene, and which he had possessed himself of with the sole purpose of taking the life of the Dark Woman.

The noise of the pistol's discharge, the smoke, the concussion of air in the room which made the drops of the chandelier rattle the one against the other, and the general shriek that came from the females present, as a sort of echo to the report, made up, for a few moments, a scene of great confusion.

But there stood the Dark Woman in a magnificent dress of black velvet, in precisely the same attitude she had assumed on first entering the room.

The Regent was pale as death, and kept his glaring eyes fixed upon the Dark Woman, while Annie clasped him in her arms, and seemed to be about to slide down to the floor in a swoon.

Her accents were of that high and exalted character which were sure to strike home to every ear and to every understanding.

"George, Prince of Wales," she said, "and Regent of England, I ask you for my son!"

The Regent shrunk from before her ardent gaze.

"In bed, or at the festive board—at home or abroad, in the veriest recesses of a palace, or beneath the thatch of a hovel—surrounded by the great or by the wicked, I will seek you, George, Prince of Wales, and ask you for my son! Where is my son?—where is my son?"

The Prince of Wales, in hastily rising, had thrown over his chair and did not know it, or had forgotten it. He reeled back to sit down, and struck against the chair that Annie had occupied, and half fell to the floor.

"Save the Regent!" cried a voice,—"save the Regent!"

A rush was made to support him, but he struggled to his feet, as he cried, "Seize her! seize her! Do not let her go! Seize her, somebody!"

"I will!" cried Colonel Hanger; and he made a rush towards the conservatory, and fell heavily over someone who seemed to be on his hands and knees, exactly in the way.

That was Willes, who in that attitude had crept round the room towards the conservatory, and then, before the Colonel could regain his feet, the Dark Woman had gone.

Willes darted into the conservatory still in the posture which he had assumed, to the discomfiture of the Colonel, and the moment he was past the threshold of it he pulled shut the half-window that had been flung open, and bolted it.

"Fly, madam—fly!" he said.

"I follow you," replied Linda.

Through the conservatory—out of that into the winter garden, and thence into the open air, went Willes, closely followed by Linda. There were some lights flashing in the grounds of the villa, in the direction of the ordinary entrance gates.

"We shall be seen," said the Countess.

"No, no!"

"But there are lights and people!"

"I have provided against all that, madam," said Willes; "and if you do not mind mounting a ladder, you may pass over the wall at this point, and you will find yourself at once facing the green."

Willes took from close under the wall of the villa garden, where it was most securely hidden, a light ladder that was used by the gardeners, and which reached to the top of the wall.

"Ascend, madam," he said,—"ascend, while I hold it."

The Dark Woman was on the wall in a few seconds.

Willes followed her; and then, with more dexterity than anyone would have given him credit for, he raised the ladder, and put it down on the outer face of the wall.

The Dark Woman was gone; and Willes swung the light ladder over the wall again, and hastily descended, and replaced it flat among the snow.

The Palace clock struck one.

A figure enveloped in a grey cloak, the hood of which was over the head;—a mysterious figure which entered the garden noiselessly, and closed the little door in the garden wall like one accustomed to it.

Familiar as she was with the route, it was not necessary for her to look to the right or to the left; but she reached a flight of four marble steps which led to a narrow door, which she opened with facility by the aid of another key she had with her.

It was one of her orders to Willes that this door should never be fastened in any way on the inside, and he had too much fear of her not to obey such an injunction.

It was a door which led very directly to that suite of apartments which might be said to connect St. James's Palace with Carlton House.

The Dark Woman had resolved upon a visit to the Regent, but she could not take upon herself to say exactly where he would be found.

But never had the Dark Woman entered those regal buildings with her mind in so chaotic a state, and her feelings so largely interested, as upon this occasion.

But how bitter was the disappointment which had swept over that passionate heart! How overwhelming was the crushing despair which now had taken possession of her!

She had found that son, and finding him, at the same time, all that her most liberal fancy had pictured him, she found in him an opponent to her dearest wishes.

No wild ambition racked his brain and heart.

The quiet domestic affections were, to him, painted in dearer colours than the regal state of a Court. She found him un-ambitious, and she found him forgiving; and worse than all, she found that he was ready to give credence to the commonsense view of his and her position, which no doubt, the fearful dreamy hours she had spent in the solitary agony of her confinement in a madhouse had banished from her forever.

But she would not succumb to these circumstances.

She told herself that she would perish in the assertion of what she thought her right, rather than she would forego that right for a single moment.

She shut her eyes wilfully and madly to all evidence that was contrary to that wild dream of her fancy.

She had believed herself to be the wife of the Regent when, full of hope and anticipation of a glorious future, she had left the home of her youth, depending on his love. She could not, would not banish that thought; and if its presence were madness, its absence would be death.

And now, upon a different errand to any which had actuated her upon any of her previous visits, she had made her way to the residence of the Regent.

Formerly it had been to demand him of her son; now it was to demand of him a recognition of what she considered her own rights, and that son's rights, to dignities that would raise them on a level with the Crown.

Paler and more spectre-like than ever, the Dark Woman made her way in silence through the passages and apartments which lay between her and those private rooms, where she expected to find the object of her search.

It was only now and then that some faint sigh, almost approaching to a moan, escaped her; for she felt that she was almost settling her life upon the hazard of that interview, and if ever insanity had taken possession of her brain, its darkening influence was that night gathering strength.

As she gained one of the long galleries which were on the side of Carlton House, communicating with the Palace of St. James, she heard a footstep in advance of her. It was approaching the direction where she now paused, and she hid herself in some deep shadows, cast by a row of columns supporting a portion of the roof.

The light was very dim in the gallery; for although the passages and thoroughfares, so to speak, of Carlton House and St. James's were lighted by oil lamps during the night, the illuminating power was very small.

It was a sort of twilight only that the Dark Woman found herself in, as she heard the approach of the footsteps hurrying towards her.

She thought, at the moment, that fortune was favourable to her.

It was Willes.

The Dark Woman laid her hand so suddenly upon his arm—springing out of the shadow in so spectre-like a fashion—that Willes, whose thoughts at that moment were anywhere but with her, uttered a cry of alarm.

"Peace!" cried the Dark Woman. "What is the meaning of this folly?"

"Madam, madam, is it really—can it possibly be you?"

"Since when have you doubted my identity? Dare you, creature of my bounty and forbearance as you are,—dare you, for one moment, seek to shake off your dependence upon me, and my authority over you?"

"No, madam, no! Certainly not; but—"

"But what? Speak out!"

"I was taken by surprise—the lateness of the hour."

"What are hours to me? Tell me, where is the Regent?"

There was a high tone of excitement about the Dark Woman which terrified Willes much. He feared she meditated some deed of violence, which would not only compromise her, but all persons who in any way had been instrumental in aiding her in her entrances to the Palace.

A terrible fear took possession of him. What if in her wild excitement she contemplated the assassination of the Regent? Would it be possible then, in the political and social convulsion that would take place, he should escape? Would it not be much more likely that he would be subjected to the fiercest persecution as an accessory?

A cold perspiration of fear broke out upon Willes's brow, He looked imploringly in the face of the Dark Woman. He clasped his hands, and bent forward abjectly. His tones were tremulous with fear and agitation.

"Oh, madam—madam, what good can be done? What good to you— to me—to anybody—would the death of the Regent do? Oh, madam— madam, reflect! You do not seem yourself to-night: you seem to meditate some dreadful purpose! Oh, do not—do not!"

"What do you fear?"

"I don't know what I fear; but I have a thousand fears!"

"I will answer one of them."

"One of them, madam?"

"Yes. I do not come here to kill the Regent."

"Gracious heavens!"

"That was your thought."

"It was—it was! Only, when the words are actually spoken, they sound so terrible."

"Lead on, then, now that this hideous fancy has left your mind,—lead on, and show me where he is."

It could scarcely be said that Willes felt quite assured of the sincerity of the Dark Woman, but he was compelled apparently to take her word, although he still trembled excessively, as he conducted her to the small supper-room in which he had left the Regent.

"Madam," said Willes, in a low tone, as he withdrew his head from a cursory examination of the small octagonal room in which the Regent was sleeping,—"madam, his Royal Highness if still there, and if you will permit me now entirely to leave you, you will confer a great favour upon me."

"I want no one. It is enough. *He* is here."

Willes made a gesture as though he had washed his hands of the transaction, and then went away as quickly as he could, leaving the Dark Woman's presence to explain itself to the Regent as best it might.

The Dark Woman stood in the doorway for a few seconds, as though she were striving to gather courage to enter and awaken the man upon the words of whose lips her life seemed to hang.

She clasped her hands nervously.

She muttered to herself.

"No, no, he cannot—dare not deny it to me! I have one threat to make which will surely move him. I have one last card to play which must bring alarm even to his breast. I will seek the mad King at Windsor, and in some lucid interval shall hear the truth from his own lips. He must—he did give the royal license to this marriage which has turned out so terrible a calamity."

The Dark Woman glided into the apartment.

The Regent was sleeping in a low chair, which was so contrived with elbows, arms, and back, and such a multitude of cushions, that it was almost like a bed.

He seemed to sleep profoundly.

The Dark Woman closed the door behind her, and turned the key in the lock. Then she paused to listen to some sound that came upon the night air.

It was the Palace clock chiming half-past one.

That sound, slight as it was, and penetrating but dimly into that apartment, seemed to have a disturbing influence upon the sleep of the Regent.

He moved uneasily.

The Dark Woman fixed her eyes upon him, and elevated one arm as though she meant to utter some exclamation that should at once attract his attention, provided he opened his eyes.

But the chiming of the clock was over. The Regent drew a longer breath, and once more subsided into deep repose.

Then the Dark Woman felt the necessity of putting an end herself to that slumber which might otherwise last far beyond the time when she could, with any regard to safety, remain within the precincts of the Palace.

She stepped up to him. She leant down so close to him that her breath fanned his cheek.

"Awake! awake!" she cried. "George of Wales, awake! Fate, justice, vengeance call out to you, awake!"

The Regent heard that terrible sound in his sleep. It seemed to him that some enemy had chased him to the brink of a precipice, and was calling out to him to awaken, that he might feel the full terrors of the situation.

But it could only be for a few brief moments that slumber could hold her sway in the presence of such sounds.

The Dark Woman did not have to speak again.

The Regent with an exclamation of dismay, opened his eyes.

Then he thought he still slept.

And well might he be excused for so thinking, since the first person he saw before him was a strange figure, attired in sombre garments, and in a threatening attitude.

There he was, to all appearance, in a room in his own Palace—a room in which, from its privacy, he should surely have been secure from interruption; but far from such being the case, he found a threatening apparition before him.

"George, Regent of England, awake!" cried the Dark Woman again.

Then the Prince knew who it was that thus, with such loud words and threatening gestures, assailed him.

"The Dark Woman!" he gasped. "The Dark Woman, again!"

"Yes," she replied. "I am the Dark Woman, and dark as Erebus are the feelings now of my heart."

"Help!"

"Ah! One word of alarm!"

She drew from the breast of her apparel a long glittering poniard.

"Guard!"

The point of the formidable weapon was placed within an inch of the throat of the Regent.

He turned as pale as death.

"So—so you have at last, Linda, made up your mind to murder me."

The Dark Woman gave a gasping sob as she cried out, "He calls me Linda—he calls me Linda! For the first time for so many years, he calls me Linda! Oh, heaven—oh, heaven!"

She dropped the poniard. It fell at the feet of the Regent, who made a movement with his right hand to pick it up.

The Dark Woman burst into tears.

The Regent let the poniard lie.

There was no further danger. He felt that these tears had at once, by their first gush washed away the desire to murder him, if in reality it had ever existed.

"What is the meaning of this?" he said. "Why is it that I am ever to live as the victim of those intrusions? Who is it, among all about me, that betrays me?"

"Betrays you?"

"Yes. By allowing you entrance to the Palace. I must—I will know!"

The Dark Woman stemmed the torrent of her tears, and with a certain air of dignity, she waved her arm, saying, "That is trivial—that is trivial!"

"What is?"

"How I came here. My errand to you overpowers all minor considerations!"

"What errand?"

"Ah, can you affect ignorance?—can you pretend not to know?—you have looked upon him—you who have seen into his eyes—you who have—who must have felt that you were father to that son?"

The Regent cast down his eyes. He fidgetted in his chair—he tremulously patted with his finger upon the table near him.

"Listen to me," he said. "Let me, for once now, speak to you calmly and rationally, and do you as calmly and rationally listen!"

"I listen."

"Sit down."

"Who—who? Sit down who?"

"Linda!"

"Linda again. Oh, heaven since when has this man's heart been made so gentle that he can again call me Linda?"

"Come, come! Let us be rational. Let there be no rhapsodies—no exclamations. I want for once, and for the last time, to try to treat you like a rational being!"

"Yes, I am calm now."

"You sent your son to me."

"Your son."

"Well, well."

"I did not send him."

"At all events, he came to me, and I was not disposed to disavow him. You should be satisfied now. In former times, when you made me submit to so much persecution from you, it was on the ground that you wanted what information I could furnish you in regard to the fate of your child."

"Our child."

"Well, well, have I not said that I am disposed to acknowledge the boy?"

"You have said it."

"And now you must feel that I really had no means of helping you to a discovery of what had become of him, since his appearance before me has been a complete surprise."

"Go on."

"I have very little more to say, but that now I hope, and trust, and expect, that by whatever extraordinary means you contrive to make your way into the Palace, your visits will cease."

"My visits will cease."

"You agree to that, then?"

"I do."

"That is well—that is well! I propose, then, to settle upon you and upon him a competent income; and if he would like to go into the army, why, of course, it will be open to him."

"The army?"

"Yes. It is a very honourable, and a very convenient, mode of giving a young man some social rank, and some addition at the same time to his income. I will see the Duke of York about it."

"One moment."

"Well?"

"You forget."

"What do I forget?"

"That the son of George Prince of Wales, and Regent of England, being by right a prince of the blood royal, holds such a rank, that—"

"What can you mean?"

"I mean that I, the Princess of Wales, address you, the Prince of Wales, about our son!"

The Dark Woman slowly sat down and looked in the face of the Regent with a fixed gaze, that at once alarmed and angered him.

The light that was in the room came from a group of wax candles; and in the quiet atmosphere, they burnt with a steady radiance, so that not a movement of the face of the Dark Woman, as the light fell full upon her, escaped the attention of the Regent.

She was now cold, resolute, and stern.

It was only about the eyes that there at times shone a strange, flickering, uncertain light, which showed how fevered was the mind within.

"You rave!" said the Regent.

"I rave? I rave, when I speak of our son—our own boy?"

"No—no! But—"

"Well, say on! Fear nothing!"

"Of course I fear nothing. What have I to fear? I can hardly believe that now you have found your son—"

"And your son."

"Well—well, I have admitted that. Why do you provoke me by reiterating it?"

"I was afraid that, having forgotten he was your son for nearly twenty years, it might slip your memory again."

"No, no! What was I saying? You confuse me. Oh, this was it! I fear nothing from you; because if you, the mother, were to contrive aught against me, the father, you would merit and have the hatred of him, the son."

"Ah!"

"You comprehend that?"

The Dark Woman trembled. She seemed at the moment about to clasp her hands with a feeling of despair over her eyes, for there was something about what the Regent said which chimed in terribly with some words that had fallen from the lips of Allan Fearon when he had been urging her to forget, or at all events to forgive, the past.

But she abstained from hiding the Regent from her sight even for a moment.

She had a fear of some sudden action on his part, if she did so, which would enable him to evade the remainder of the interview.

"I have heard you," she said,—"this poor heart had heard you!"

"Then you agree? That is, you consent to—to—take an annuity?"

She looked strangely at him.

"Do you persist in the story you told the boy?"

"Oh, you have seen him since?"

"Since he saw you."

"Very well, then. I told him the truth, and I hope that you feel as he does, that I have done all I can in the matter, and am willing for the future to behave as liberally as you can wish."

"George, Prince of Wales, listen to me."

"You consent?"

"Be not too hasty. You have asked me to be calm—I am calm. You have asked me to be rational—I am rational. But while one drop of life-blood warms this poor, suffering heart—while one throb of a sentient nerve lends vigour and thought to my brain—while memory and reason are left me, I never will abandon my claim to be your wife, nor the claim of my son to be a prince, by right of his royal birth."

"Mad! mad!" exclaimed the Regent.

"No, I am not mad. Dare you, can you deny it? Oh, look back upon the past, and then cast your regards upon the present! I, your true and lawful wife, present you with a son, who will be all to you that you will wish— who will be a credit, a pride, and a joy—a son who, when you are King of England, will be as worthy a Prince of Wales as was ever the admiration of a father, and the delight of a nation—a son who, when in the fulness of time, you, too, must shake off, along with the dust of mortality, the velvet and golden robes of monarchy, will most worthily succeed you."

"No no! All this cannot be."

"It is."

"Woman, it is not!"

"Ah! I am not Linda now."

"Because you rave."

"No, no!—a thousand times, no! Still listen to me, George of England. You have, it is true, contracted another marriage. You fancy yourself, or rather the world fancies, that you are yoked to one who you feel is a disgrace, and whom you never loved, even for a passing moment."

"Princes have little to do with love in their matrimonial engagements."

"But you did love me."

"You?"

"Yes. You cannot say you did not love me. Ah! surely there was a time when the old beeches of Dover Court echoed to the amorous sighs of a love-sick Prince, and when the name of Linda de Chevenaux was the sweetest music that could find its way to the heart of the Prince of Wales."

The Regent made a gesture of impatience.

"Linda—"

"Ah! you call me Linda again."

"I do."

"The memory of those days had cast its sunlight upon you."

"No. I was going to say that there is one thing, of all others, that it most aggravates a man to be put in mind of."

"And that?"

"That is the follies of his dead and buried passions."

The Dark Woman sighed deeply.

"It is true—it is true. I will speak to you no more of Dover Court, or of the Linda that was once there as gentle and as pure as a mountain stream. I will point to you the present. I ask you at once to relieve yourself of the disgrace and the embarrassment of this union which you have made with Caroline of Brunswick."

"How? how?"

"By at once proclaiming me as your lawful wife."

"Ha! ha!"

"You laugh."

"Because you are too extravagant for seriousness."

"Not so. Let all the world know that I am your wife. Then the union with the Princess of Brunswick falls to the ground, and her cause, with all its agitations, falls with it."

"I have a daughter."

"And a son."

"Yes. But the daughter is legitimate, The son—"

"No. Reverse the picture. The son shall be legitimate, and the daughter what your tongue would falsely proclaim him to be."

The Regent was silent.

"Think again, and think justly. Who and what is this daughter that you so madly prefer to the son providence has preserved for you? Dare you compare them? What is he? Is he not all that is noble—all that is great—all that a prince should be? Has he spoken to you angrily—has his voice been harsh in your ears—has his manner wronged or disgraced you? Speak—oh, speak!"

"No, no, no!"

"And the daughter? What is she?"

"Forbear."

"A thing of wild and wilful caprices—a creature who even now finds it difficult to fill up the circle of her attendants, from the natural dislike of those who are modest, honourable, truthful, and gentle, to endure the Princess Charlotte—"

"No more—no more!" cried the Regent. "I will not—I must not hear all this!"

"A daughter who has defied your authority—who has threatened you to your very face—"

"Peace, I say, or—"

The Regent's eyes flashed with passion, and he sprung to his feet.

"Peace, I say, woman; there has been too much of this, and I will hear no more. My intrigue with you of so many years ago has turned your brain. You are no more Princess of Wales than I am Emperor of the Moon. No other madbrain but yours would have for a moment hatched such rank absurdities. You will have again to find a home in some asylum, where you may rave to the walls, or to the ears of those who will be as indifferent to you."

The Dark Woman shook in every limb.

"You deny me" she said.

"Call it what you will."

"You deny him."

"Him? Who?"

"Your son."

"Woman, I tell you I admit an intrigue with you, for which I am heartily sorry; and I must admit that a young man who was here, and for whom I will, as he seems to be reasonable, adequately provide, is my son. That is what I admit."

There came a sharp rapping at the door of the room.

The Regent, when he rose from the chair, had, unobserved by the Dark Woman, placed his back against a portion of one of the panels of the room where there was the handle of a bell. With one hand behind his back, he had made two vigorous appeals to it.

It was Willes's duty to reply.

Willes was at the door.

"Come in!" cried the Regent.

The Dark Woman, however, had turned the key in the lock. There was the sound of the turning of the latch-handle, but the door was fast.

The Regent began to look frightened.

The Dark Woman advanced a step towards him; and he thought her object was to possess herself of the poniard that lay upon the floor, so he, too, advanced a step, and took care to put his foot upon it.

Her foot likewise accidentally fell upon a portion of the blade.

And so those two persons stood face to face with each other, each holding down to the floor a weapon that might have been most dangerous.

"George, Prince of Wales," said the Dark Woman, "I proclaim and denounce you as a false, perjured, and traitorous villain—as one to whom oaths are shams, and to whom conscience is a myth!"

"How dare you—"

"I will, in the open face of day, when the sun of to-morrow has climbed its midday height—when the eyes and the ears of all men are open to my works,—then, even then, I will tell the tale of my wrongs—of your villany!"

"Help! Hilloa, there! Break open the door! Here is a mad woman! Help! help!"

The knocking came more violently than before at the door.

The Regent now without disguise again appealed to the bell.

There would soon have been an alarm through the Palace.

THE WRONGED WIFE; OR, THE HEART OF HATE

Septimus R. Urban

Not much is known about this penny serialisation other than it was written by James Malcolm Rymer on his travels to America. Created under one of his many pseudonyms, Septimus R. Urban, this short tale of revenge first appeared in the *New York Mercury* as *The Vendetta; or, A Lesson in Life* in 1863. It was later rebranded as *The Wronged Wife* and published in *Frank Starr's Fifteen Cent Illustrated Novels* in 1870. Although it was published in America, it still maintains a mid-Victorian British setting and characters.

The tale begins with Sir Hannibal Murkington and his newly established "friendship" with the overindulgent and naïve George Wentworth. Acting as a friend and guide, Murkington deceives the youngest Wentworth son to infiltrate the family with the purpose of their destruction. Sir Hannibal Murkington, whose actual name is John Jeffreys, is a former soldier that was wrongly charged and almost executed by the Wentworth family. The near-death experience resulted in the psychological ruin of his wife, Agatha. Functioning as the vengeful guardian of the Jeffreys family, Murkington is instructed by Agatha's grandmother, known as Mother, who charges him with enacting the Italian "supreme vendetta" against the entire Wentworth family. Murkington takes his revenge on his initial assailant; however, post-assassination, Mother dies, Murkington fails at his final execution and is crushed in the subterranean tunnel, and Agatha, in her madness, meets her demise in the Thames.

Following the tropes of penny bloods, this tale, albeit shorter than most series, due to its limited popularity, branches into varied plots that deviate from the Jeffreys family purpose. This chapter, then, follows the story of both Agatha, a mirror of Charlotte Brontë's Bertha Mason, and Mother, the aged monstrous woman who is the true source of danger in this tale.

A T the extreme end of one of the old streets that leads down from the Strand to the River Thames stands a house with a balcony facing the river.

It is one of the oldest houses of all the neighbourhood—one of the Charles the Second houses, so few of which now remain (at least in anything like their original integrity) in London.

At high tide of the river the water flows completely under the balcony; and on those rare occasions when spring-tides take place, it has been known to lap up on to the stone flooring.

The lower part of the house—that is, the part which corresponded to the kitchens of other houses, was bricked up externally, and quite unused. The tide made too frequent incursions into it to render it at all tenantable. But the ground-floor, which was unusually elevated above the basement, was habitable. There was but one floor above that, and that was the floor from which the balcony projected. Above, to be sure, in the roof, there were two small rooms that would serve as box rooms, or store-closets, but that was all.

The house, though, was wide and deep.

On the ground-floor there were five rooms—on the upper floor, six.

A boat was always moored underneath the balcony, although no apparent means of getting to it appeared. Yet there it was, day and night, rising and falling with the tide, with its oars well secured in it.

Be assured it was there for a purpose.

The house had a strange and solitary look, so close to the great bustle of the Strand, and yet so still with no possible thoroughfare before its door.

The ceilings, too, were low, although the house was large, taking into account the superficial dimensions.

The time at which we would introduce the reader to this silent house by the Thames is, the decline of evening; and it was with a quick step that a darkly-dressed man made his way down the street, and hastily taking a key from his pocket, he opened the door, and entered the house—closing the door behind him so hastily, that it was evident he was well used to the amount of pressure required to snap a lock into its hasp.

Then this man—who was no other than Sir Hannibal Murkington—drew two bolts close into their sockets, and put up a heavy chain at the door.

"That will do," he said; "all is secure, and all is at peace here too. Peace! peace! O God! would that all were at peace here!" He struck his breast as he spoke. "My oath! my oath is registered in heaven. I will not leave one of the accursed race of Wentworth, whose life shall not be to him a burden; and in the process of so making it, I will enrich myself past all dreams of human avarice."

A strange unearthly sort of sound at this moment came from the upper part of the house. It was not a scream—not a shout—not a cry for help, but it was a something that might be any or all of these sounds, mingled together; and it seemed to fall upon the ears of Sir Hannibal Murkington like a lightning-flash of misery.

"There! There!" he said; "I hear her now. I can hear her now. Let me try to shut out that cry. It haunts me. It has found an echo in my heart, and I cannot chase it out. Oh, have some mercy, Heaven!"

He clasped his hands over his ears.

He sunk down on to his knees in the passage of the house, at a few paces from the street-door; and he swayed to and fro, and made a mournful murmuring sound, as though he hoped in its cadences in his ears to stifle any other sound that he dreaded to hear.

The strange cry from above had only sounded once. Then all was still again.

"Jeffrey! Jeffrey!" cried a voice. "Is that Jeffrey?"

"Yes, mother," said Sir Hannibal.

"Ay, ay! I may be old, but I am not deaf. Thank God, I have my faculties. It is Jeffrey."

"Yes, mother—it is I. I am coming. I thought—just not that—that I heard her."

Sir Hannibal had made his way rapidly up the stairs at the end of the passage; and on the landing above, clinging to the balustrades, was a very aged woman—so aged, indeed, that although Sir Hannibal Murkington called her "mother", the idea of her being in reality his mother was quite out of the question.

This woman must always have been small in person, but she was one of those who shrink with age, and at each year of a protracted life become less and less. It seems with these persons as if vitality were retreating to a centre, and disregarding the outward frame. Her hair was white as driven snow. Her face, a curious net-work of wrinkles; and yet there was a flashing brilliance about her eyes that betokened the lamp of life to be far from extinct within the brow.

With one long bony hand she clutched the balustrade of the stairs.

The other held a small hand-lamp.

The dress of this old woman was of an antique and long-gone-by fashion. It had never been English, either in its material or its out. It had a Spanish or Italian look about it; and, indeed, the complexion and the eyes of this aged woman seemed to bespeak her the native of a clime where the sun shines with bolder rays than in England.

"It is Jeffrey," she said.

"Yes, mother."

"Welcome, my son, welcome."

Jeffrey bowed before this aged woman. Jeffrey, as he was named in that house—Sir Hannibal Murkington, as he was known in the great world without it.

"Yes, mother, I am here. But was it imagination, or did I hear her?"

"You did. It is the full of the moon."

Sir Hannibal sighed deeply.

"Come," added the old woman. "Come. It is time you saw her."

"No—no!"

"But I say, yes—I say, yes!"

The old woman now showed that she was partially supporting herself by a stick; for she beat the end of it on the floor in an angry manner.

"Peace! Peace, mother," said Sir Hannibal. "I will see her since you wish it."

"Yes, I do wish it. Whenever I see you look as you look to-night, I wish it. Whenever I see you with sadness rather than anger in your eyes—whenever I see you drooping instead of raging—whenever I see you with indications that your heart is softening—"

"No—no! Do not say such things to me. Be assured that I will have vengeance—vengeance even such as you, mother, will say is sufficient."

"I am a Corsican!" said the old woman.

The singular being whom she called Jeffrey was silent.

"Yes, I am a Corsican! You, too, are an adopted brother of the band. The vendetta has gone forth. The Wentworths shall perish."

"They shall."

"I have sworn it—you have sworn it. There are but three of them now. There were four."

Sir Hannibal Murkington turned a shade paler as he looked into the glaring eyes of the old woman—hag we might almost name her, from the aspect at that time of her countenance.

Then again there came that strange and horrible cry from someone in the upper portion of the house.

Sir Hannibal again strove to shut it out from his ears; and the old woman struck the floor with her stick, as she said:

"Worse! Worse! Worse to-night!"

"Mother, tell me. Do you think that Agatha—that is, do you think that she is really worse when the moon is at the full?"

"I know it. Behold!"

The old woman moved with celerity, but yet in a sidelong sort of way, as though she were lame, toward a small window that looked out from the sort of corridor they were in toward the River Thames. She hastily drew aside a thick curtain that covered it, which made a sharp, rattling noise as the brass rings by which it was suspended ran on the iron rod. Just over the house-tops, on the Surrey side of the river, the full round moon was emerging.

The night was fine. We have remarked that the season was one of those exemplary ones that are at times found in England; so the atmosphere—considerably that it is of London we speak—was tolerably clear, and the beautiful disc of silver shone brightly over the masses of irregular dwellings, and warehouses, and shipyards, and pestiferous-looking abodes on the Surrey side of the river. On the rippling, heaving bosom of the Thames, too, they glistened and sparkled with metallic splendour.

"There!" added the old woman. "You see, my son!"

"I do—I do!"

"As the moon wanes, she will be better again. She will then begin to shed tears. The tears that have accumulated in her heart, they will come forth then, and she will calm for awhile."

"Alas! alas!"

The old woman turned fiercely upon him; and, with a strange sort of half-cry, half-exclamation, she clutched him by the arm in one of her long, bony fingers, as she said:

"Do you waver? Do you falter? Dare you?"

"No! Oh no!"

"And yet—"

"Yet what? Why should you doubt me now?"

"Your tone, your air, your manner! I fear you are forgetting."

"Never! Never! Can I forget? Oh! if I could only forget!"

"And if you could?"

"O bounteous Heaven! If the fabled waters of oblivion could, by a ghastly search, be found fathoms deep in the sea, or far down into the hot bowels of the earth, how gladly—oh! how gladly, would I quaff the delicious draught! Forget! No, no; there is no forgetting!"

"No. As you say, there is no forgetting," added the old woman; "but since your heart is sulky and since your purpose is half blunted this night, I claim the right that I have reserved by myself of reminding you of why it is you have sworn extermination to the race of the Wentworths."

"It needs not that you should do so. I will keep my oath."

"You are sure of that?"

"As I live—as I live. I have been at work in a way to please even you, mother."

"Ah, you shall tell me all that. But you will see her now?"

Sir Hannibal Murkington trembled.

"Yes, yes; I must—that is to say, I will."

"Come, then."

The conference we have related had taken place in a long kind of gallery or corridor that ran the whole length of the house on the first floor. At one end, this corridor terminated in the flight of stairs that led from the ground-floor of the house; at the other, it had the little window that looked on to the river.

The balcony that we have spoken of was in front of the windows that belonged to the largest room of the six that were on that floor.

A door to the left, after ascending the stairs, led into a small apartment, which, however, was handsomely furnished, and well-lit by a lamp suspended from the ceiling. The old woman and Sir Hannibal passed through this room at once into the longest of the suit—that one with the balcony, fronting the river.

It was a very singular apartment.

The whole of the walls were covered with hangings, in the same manner that windows are draped in modern houses. The effect, however, was good. The colour was a very deep crimson, and there were handsome tassels of yellow silk at intervals, that added much to the general effect. In this room, too, was a profusion of furniture of all styles and ages—in fact, the general effect was as if the fragmental portion of the furniture of some good mansion was bestowed in that one apartment.

A lamp, the metal work of which appeared to be silver, hung from the ceiling of this apartment, and lighted it but dimly.

"Mother," said Sir Hannibal Murkington—"mother, perhaps, after all, I had better not see Agatha."

"I knew it—I knew it!" cried the old woman. "I could see it in your eyes! I said I saw it in your eyes. Myself, even I! Vengeance! I am old—old. O my child's child! my Agatha! Lost—lost one forever! since the light of the mind, of the soul, has gone out! Even I will avenge you!"

"Mother," said Sir Hannibal Murkington, with gloomy firmness, "you mistake me utterly. I do not shrink; I do not falter; I do not waver. I will have vengeance, so deep, so dire that, although even now it would be easy for me, before twelve hours have passed away, to plunge a dagger to the heart of the hope of the Wentworths, I will not do it; because my vengeance would then be balked by the peace and the serenity of death."

"Ah, now you speak as you should. Now I know you as my child's husband—as my son—my Jeffreys."

"Mother (I call you mother because you are the grandmother of Agatha—of my wife Agatha), I am, as you know, not a Corsican, but I passed many of my early years in the fair island, and I have sworn, with you, the vendetta against the Wentworths. Be assured that I will keep my oath. And now I will see poor Agatha."

"Yes, I know you now; you are my son again. I know you now, Jeffreys."

The smile which the old woman lavished upon Sir Hannibal Murkington was fiendish in its expression, and he might well shudder as he looked at it.

And yet, if the human heart that beat within his bosom had its moment of relenting—if the direful oath of vengeance he had taken had in it at times a something that revolted his better nature—if, standing aghast and amazed at what construction the eternal goodness and forgiving mercy of God might put upon that wild human vengeance, it was here that the cause of the frenzy of the passions and the craving for revenge was one that might well excite the most morbid feelings of bitterness and hate.

What that cause was, we shall soon know. It was one which brought horror and mystery in its train, but it need not itself be hidden.

"Yes, mother, I will see poor Agatha," said Sir Hannibal.

"Take it," said the old woman.

She placed a key in the hand of Sir Hannibal. The cold touch of it appeared to send a shudder through his heart; but he silently bowed his head for a moment; and then, with the key in his hand, he walked to about the middle of one of the walls of the room, and held aside one of the hangings.

An ordinary room-door was immediately behind it, and the key that the old woman had given him opened the lock noiselessly. He passed on into another apartment, that was all in darkness.

"The lamp!" he said, as he returned and looked into the larger room.

The old hag did not reply to him. She was half-lying, half-kneeling, huddled up on the floor; and, by the muttering of her voice, he could hear that she was heaping imprecations on the heads of the Wentworths.

"Peace! oh, peace!" he said. "There will be enough of vengeance!"

She did not reply to him; and he took the small hand-lamp which the old woman had been carrying when she met him at the top of the stairs, and with it held above his head, he slowly and solemnly passed through the open door behind the hangings.

How deathly pale he was! What a sob of agony it was that came direct from his heart as he stepped across the flooring of that second room, and whispered to himself:

"She will not know me yet. No, no, no—she will not know me! Twelve long years—O God! O God! what misery! Am I, too, doomed to madness? No, no! Oh! spare me Heaven!"

Across this second room Sir Hannibal took his dreary way. There was another door in the opposite wall—a common room-door, in the lock of which the key was to be observed. It was turned so as to lock the door, but it needed but a touch to unlock it.

That door then was opened noiselessly, and then Sir Hannibal nearly fell, as a wild, unearthly scream came suddenly upon his ears. The strong man tottered, and had to support himself against the wall.

"Yes," he gasped. "It is the moon. She is worse—much worse to-night."

Then he staggered rather than walked on, until he reached the corner of this second room from the large one. In that corner was a smaller door. When opened, it disclosed a narrow flight of stairs. They must lead to those smaller rooms in the roof of the house, which, with their sloping ceilings, could scarcely be called apartments.

Up this narrow staircase, step by step, as if his feet had been led, went the heart-broken man. He reached a door—it was barred and locked. He knelt by its panels, and he called aloud, in heart-breaking accents.

"Agatha! Agatha! Agatha!"

Then hot tears rolled down his cheeks, and he smote his breast, and he spoke with a mournful tone at first, and then one that swelled into a torrent of indignation.

"Oh! what a wreck! what a wreck!" he said. "And it was permitted! O Heaven! look down upon her now, and pity her! Fiends might weep! devils show mercy! Agatha! Agatha! Agatha!"

A wild, mournful voice from within the room which that door communicated with, answered him.

"No!" it said, "no! The fire has gone back from my brain to my heart, and I can sing now!"

The tone in which the few words with which we concluded our last chapter were uttered by the mysterious occupant of one of those small rooms in Sir Hannibal Murkington's house, was so sweet, so soft, so tender, that one might have supposed it to come from some happy soul freshly awakened from a gentle sleep.

Sir Hannibal Murkington wept, and sobbed audibly.

"Yes, I can sing now," said the gentle tones from within the room. "I can sing, and my own dear Jeffrey shall hear me, and he will say: 'There is my Agatha cheating the hours of their sadness while I am away.' That is what dear Jeffrey will say.

'I sing of the floods, of the woods, of the vales;
Of my own dearest isle of the sea;
I sing of dear homes on our vine-covered hills;
Of the noble, the true, and the free.'"

"Oh! she no longer raves!" sobbed Sir Hannibal Murkington. "She no longer speaks with the double sense of madness. She will know me now! God be thanked! I will—I can forgive, if Agatha be but restored to me!"

He tapped gently against the door.

"Agatha! Agatha! Agatha!"

Oh! what a sound! Oh! what a cry! Sir Hannibal Murkington shrunk back on his knees as he was at the door, as far as in that attitude he could go, and horror was upon every feature of his face.

Some sudden change had taken place in the mood of the poor maniac within the room, and she had uttered one of those fearful cries that had appalled the soul of Sir Hannibal so frequently.

"Mad! mad still!" he cried, as he wrung his hands and wept. "She is mad still, I must see her. I will see her. I have said I would. I will! I will!"

He opened a small wicket that was in the upper part of the door. It afforded him, when he held the lamp so as to throw some rays of light through that wicket, a view into the room.

At its further end—and that was only about twelve feet from the door—was the poor maniac. Some string staples in the wall held thickly folded cloths, which were wound about her. They could not hurt her. A tender hand had placed them on her limbs, to save her from herself.

She was mad.

Long fair hair hung in wild disorder about a face and form of matchless beauty. The slender white arms were stretched forward supplicatingly, and then; with a rapid articulation and a vehemence of manner that were fearful to listen to, she spoke:

"No, no! A thousand times no! Fiend, I will not love you—you whom I may hate; you whom I may despise, but could never love. Save me, Jeffrey! save me from this man! Soldier! soldier! No! He is no soldier, for his first care should be, to protect the innocent! What is that? Condemned! For what? For what? Beware! I—I, his own wife will not smile upon her persecutor! No! It cannot be! Oh no! There is a Heaven above us which is too just for that. His jewels! His jewels that he brought from the East! What had my Jeffrey to do with his jewels? I am not mad, yet you see this; but it is for my husband I come to plead—not to plead! Oh no! no. I should not say: 'plead', for you see, gentlemen and officers, he is innocent. I tell you all, he is innocent, and if Colonel Wentworth persecutes him to the death, he still is innocent! I will tell you all about it. Let me think. Hush! What is that? A dream! a dream!"

"Agatha! Agatha!" cried Sir Hannibal, through the little wicket in the door.

She did not hear him.

The mind and senses of the poor maniac were far away in the midst of those awful scenes, the contemplation of which had made her what she was.

"Agatha! Oh, hear me!"

"A dream! a dream!" she said. "It is a muffled drum. The dead march. They take him out to death—my husband, my Jeffrey, and he's so innocent! Oh, spare him! Lightnings from heaven! Help! help! He is innocent! I, I proclaim it to this earth, to those trees, to that sunshine resting on the sea! Mercy! Oh, mercy! I hear the drum! I hear the drum! the muffled drum! Death! death! What is this? Fire! Is it fire? in my brain—in my heart! It is the fire of madness! They have killed him! Ha! ha! ha! And I am mad, I am mad! Ha! ha! ha!

> 'Pluck the vine, pluck the vine.
> From the slope of the hill.
> Pluck the vine, pluck the vine.'

Hush! What do they say now? That I am Corsican! Yes, oh yes; but you see I am fair. My poor grandmother is only left to love me now. A vendetta, say you. Yes, a vendetta! a vendetta!"

"Vengeance!" cried Sir Hannibal Murkington as he sprung to his feet, suddenly. "I will have vengeance! One has fallen. All shall fall."

Fencing with his clenched hands wildly in the air, he rushed down the narrow staircase and through the rooms below, nor paused until he had made his way on the balcony that looked upon the river, and he rested his head upon his hands, and groaned aloud in the bitterness and anguish of his spirit.

The clocks of the city began to strike the hour of ten, and it was strange with what an intense and seeming intent the wretched man counted the strokes, as though it were of vital interest to him to know that they all struck correctly.

"It is ten o'clock," he said. "Where is George Wentworth now? Ha! Ha! With the wine-cup at his lips, with sparkling eyes and radiant expression. The draught that he shall yet take will be one of blood! He is a Wentworth! And his father and his cousin; they are all that are left. They should whither from the face of the land like weeds rooted up by the husbandman."

Some sound from the street—from that dull quiet street, into which it was rarely that any vehicle found its way, and in which no footfall sounded except of someone bound direct for one of the houses, came upon the ears of Sir Hannibal Murkington.

He listened intently.

"Oh! The whine of some professional mendicant. That is all. I wonder, now, if happiness could be measured, as length, and breadth, and thickness may be, what would be the amount of that poor beggar's felicity in comparison to mine; and he, perchance, is without a crest or a home, while I have thousands and to spare."

Sir Hannibal came slowly from the balcony back into the room.

The old Corsican grandmother was there. She was active, vengeful, and her eyes were bright and glowing, as usual.

"Jeffrey, you saw her?" she asked.

"I did, mother."

"Is your heart stone—steel?"

"It is hardened."

"The boat?"

"Is still moored beneath the window."

"Ah, my son Jeffrey. When shall the mooring be cut loose?"

Jeffrey shook his head—

"I know not, but yet the time will come, mother."

"In my time?"

"Yes, in your time. I have an idea, a notion which has grown upon me for years, that you are preserved in order that you may know and see that vengeance if complete."

"I am ninety-eight years of age."

"A great age—a great age, mother."

"My daughter—your Agatha's mother, would be fifty-eight, were she living. Agatha is even now only twenty-nine."

"Oh, do not. Why do you say all this to me? Do I not suffer enough?"

"I have sworn."

"I know it well. The vendetta."

"And yet another oath, Jeffrey."

"Another?"

"Yes, Jeffrey; that is, that once in each year I would make you talk of the past to freshen your memory, lest dullness and forgiveness should find possession of your heart."

"But it is not yet time."

"To-morrow."

"Yes; I know the date well. To-morrow is the time."

"Jeffrey, you suffer much, now."

"I do."

"You have seen Agatha. Your heart is sad; your brain full of wild fancies; rest without the dread of what I have sworn once a year to say to you, and bear it now."

Sir Hannibal Murkington shook as with some powerful emotion, and his voice was thick and husky, as he replied:

"If it must be, let it be."

The old woman glanced at Sir Hannibal Murkington with her hawk-like eyes, as though she would pierce into his very heart, and read what was passing there in connection with all the most cherished feelings of his nature.

And from that terrible gaze he shrunk, as though too much light was firing into his eyes, and it was necessary to shield them from the glare.

"Speak, then," he said, in a low, wailing kind of tone. "If I must hear it, I will listen now."

"Then listen. Your name is Jeffreys. Hannibal is your Christian name. Your fortunes were poor, considering your birth and education; and the treachery and falsehood of a kinsman made these fortunes poorer still."

"I became destitute."

"You did, and in that condition you looked for the only occupation that you thought would not be repugnant to your notions of what shall I call it? aristocratic pride—what?"

"Call it what you will. I enlisted into the cavalry of the English army."

"You did. Well at that time, I and my daughter, and my daughter's daughter, Agatha—she who is above now—"

Sir Hannibal shuddered.

"We came to England, for a small patrimony which one who had wandered from his native Corsica had succeeded in laying up for those who were akin to him. We found the sum but a small one. The harpies of the law had been feeding on it, but, such as it was, it became ours. Then one night—"

"Yes—yes; one night."

"One night, in the neighbourhood of the city which is called Canterbury, when I and my daughter, the mother of Agatha, and Agatha herself were walking quietly to our temporary home in the town, we had to pass a lonely spot, close to a wood—"

"Yes. Yes; oh! I can see the place well now. It comes up before my eyes more vividly than a picture."

"It may well do so, Jeffrey."

"Go on; go on. I feel that there is to my soul a kind of fascination in returning to the recital of these incidents, although each one is so imprinted on my heart that I can never forget the minutest particular."

The hag continued, as though the last remark of Sir Hannibal Murkington had not reached her ears.

"Close to that wood we paused a moment to look at the sunset. It reminded us of Corsica. There was a blue and purple cloud, lying like an island, in the far West, and we likened it in its shape to our native land, to which we proposed soon to return."

"I saw the cloud."

"You did. I and my daughter were some paces in advance, when I heard a scream from Agatha. Two men had started out from the wood, and one had assisted the other to seize her, and bear her away. His unholy eyes of passion had looked upon her, no doubt, before, and we had not known that the baleful ire of such a glance was bent upon her."

Sir Hannibal made a sign to the old woman to go on with her narration.

"What could we do," she said, "against such strong men? I was struck down by him who commanded the other. We were powerless. Our Agatha would have been torn from us, when, at the moment when all seemed lost, a young soldier rushed to the spot, and with his sabre, he struck down one of the assailants. The other took to flight."

The faint gleam of a smile came over the face of Sir Hannibal.

"That young soldier was you, Jeffrey."

"Yes, yes."

"The man you cut down was a sergeant in your own regiment. The man who took to flight was your own Colonel."

"Yes; and his name was Wentworth."

"Wentworth! Wentworth! Oh, what a name that has been to me."

"Go on. I like now to hear you, mother."

"Yes. The purpose of your soul, the purpose of vengeance, is strengthened, by hearing from another the recital of your wrongs."

"It is. It is."

"Well, how could we be other than grateful to him who had done us such a service? You, the young soldier, were made welcome to our humble home, and soon you loved Agatha—"

"No—no."

"Not so? Ah!"

"Not soon, but at once, mother; at once. From that moment that I saw her, when I snatched her from the arms of Colonel Wentworth, I loved her."

"Well, well, it may be so; be it, I will say, then that soon the light of love shone from the eyes of my grand-child, and she loved her brave defender."

Sir Hannibal bowed his head, and tears stole from his eyes.

"She was but seventeen years of age," added the old woman; "but she had a brave and noble woman's heart, and when you asked her if she would be yours, and share with you your lot in life, she proudly placed her hand in yours, and consented."

"Agatha! Agatha! my poor Agatha!"

"We had the means of purchasing your discharge from the army—which we all believed would be easily obtained; for nothing was said or heard in the regiment of the adventure by the wood. The sergeant was weeks in the Military Hospital, and, when he came out, he had a scar which marked him for life."

"It was the dint of my sabre," said Sir Hannibal.

"It was. We did not look for revenge. We were simple-minded people, Corsicans though we were, and you and I, and my child—we all believed that neither Colonel Wentworth nor the Sergeant had been able to identify the man who had balked them in their villainy."

"Never by word or look," said Sir Hannibal Murkington, "did they betray that they knew it was by my hand they had been defeated."

"Well, you remember, Jeffrey, the first faint idea we had that something was amiss was the peremptory refusal of your discharge at any price."

"Yes—yes."

"But you were already married to Agatha, and very, very happy."

"Oh, so happy."

"And I would not separate those whom Heaven had united; so we all said, 'Farewell, Corsica,' and we settled in England. Well, things went on for half a year in peace, until, one morning, very early, there came a rumour that Colonel Wentworth had been attacked in the night, as he slept in his own rooms, at the barracks, by a dragoon, and wounded, and robbed of a small case containing jewels of great value, which he had brought with him from India."

Sir Hannibal Murkington smiled faintly.

"It was a hellish plot," he said.

"It was. A button was found in the Colonel's room—a button that had evidently been torn off a military coat. On examination of the regiment, it was found that one of your buttons was missing, and the shreds of cloth that was attached to the button exactly matched your coat."

"Yes—yes. I have no doubt whatever but that the Sergeant had managed to tear the button away and give it to the Colonel."

"There is no doubt of that. Well, in the garden of the little cottage close to Canterbury, where we resided, was found the Colonel's jewel-case, but empty."

"It had been thrown over the wall."

"It had. You were seized by the military; we, by the civil powers. Our house was searched, but nothing found but this jewel-case; and as you were supposed to be the principal offender, we were discharged. A court-martial sat on your case, not for what they called the robbery, but the attempted murder of the Colonel, as they styled the accusation against you. The button was produced. The Colonel said he could surely swear to you. You were pronounced guilty."

"I was—I was."

"And sentenced to be shot."

"I was shot."

Sir Hannibal Murkington rose and stood at full height, and faced the old woman.

"Let me continue," he cried out, "let me add the sequel to the tale. My comrades believed me to be innocent. You had been among them, mother, and spread the true story of my wrongs. There was one, Michael Shea, an Irish trooper, who spoke out boldly for me and he was imprisoned at once; but an impression had been made, and the firing-party who were told off for my execution put, with one exception, blank cartridges in their carbines."

"Yes. And Agatha was told that you would not be murdered."

"She was, and I, too; but we knew not of the one exception. That ball hit me in the neck, and I fell bleeding. Agatha saw me so fall. She believed me murdered."

"She did."

"And from that moment madness took possession of her. I lay fainting, and my supposed dead body was given up to you, mother."

"It was. I took you to our poor home. Your wound was not mortal. It was many, many months before you recovered; but we were at peace, for the regiment had changed its quarters. You looked up, at last. You were the shadow of your former self; but Agatha was a hopeless maniac."

"O Heaven! I think I could have forgiven all if she had been spared to me."

"And I. You had got your discharge. We would have gone home—home to our dear Corsica, and there, in the valley, where nestles our cottage, we might yet have been happy—oh, so happy!"

"It was not to be, mother."

"No—no. It was not to be. A learned man, a man well skilled in all that related to the wanderings of the mind, saw our Agatha. We gave him half the gold we had left for his opinion, and he said that her recovery was all but hopeless; and only not altogether hopeless because nothing is impossible with Heaven."

"He did; and then he would not take away with him the gold that he was to have for his journey and for the exercise of his skill."

"Heaven will reward him! But my time had then come, and I took the oath."

"The vendetta."

"Yes. The supreme vendetta."

"That means, mother, against the whole race of the person against whom the vendetta is proclaimed?"

"It does; it includes all. I took the oath, and you, too, Jeffrey, took the oath."

"I did."

"It was implacable revenge against all the Wentworths, man, woman, and child. It pledged us to the extermination, with such accompanying suffering, too, as we could inflict, on the whole race."

"It did."

"And it does still."

"As you say, it does still, Colonel Wentworth has fallen."

"He has. You did that deed well, my son Jeffrey."

"I found my way into his chamber in London. I shook him, and when his eyes opened, I screamed in his ears, 'Vendetta!'"

"It was well."

"I then left a dagger up to the hilt in his breast, with the words, 'Vendetta Supreme' on the hilt. The very case of jewels which I had been accused of taking, and for which false charge I had been shot, was lying on his dressing-table. I took them."

"You were right."

"Upon their product we live. We shall yet achieve all our vengeance with the means that have been supplied to us by our foe. Vendetta, vendetta!"

"Vendetta!" half screamed the old woman. "Vendetta supreme! The name is Wentworth!"

"The doomed race!"

"Ha, ha, ha! The doomed race!"

Sir Hannibal Murkington stood close to the door-step of his house by the Thames, and clasping his head with both hands, he uttered a scream of rage and anguish.

There came a howling cry from the maniac's attic. It sounded like the echo of his scream—that scream of rage which had been wrung from his heart at the idea that his mortal foe still lived.

"He lives, he lives!" shrieked Sir Hannibal Murkington, as he made his way into the lonely house by the Thames. "He lives yet! Are we all mad? Did we but dream of his death? I say he lives yet, and the vendetta has not even commenced. He lives—he lives!"

The wild cries, the excited gestures, the voice hoarse with passion: all made up such a picture of terror and despair that the old Corsican woman, from whose strange mental powers and furious passions had arisen the desire for revenge upon a race for the iniquity of one, shook like a leaf in autumn as she held by the balustrades of the staircase and looked down upon her raging kinsman.

She has hastily issued from one of the rooms on the upper storey of the house, for, late as it was, she was up and about. The existence she led was precarious and stealthy. She had none of the orderly and decorous habits of humanity, which prepare for the day's toils by the night's rest. She slept at all, at any time that she could snatch repose from that worst of toils, the yearning for revenge. Frequently for whole nights she would be about the house, like some "perturbed spirit"; and then, in the day-time, she would fall into a deep sleep, on the stairs,—in the hall—anywhere that she happened to be.

And so not only up and stirring was that old Corsican woman, but she was preternaturally wide awake and active. There shone from her eyes their utmost brilliancy, and notwithstanding her great age, no vestige of fatigue or weakness was about her.

But she was terrified as much as her cold, and vengeful, and unsympathetic nature could be at these terrible cries from Sir Hannibal Murkington.

And so she was looked down upon him as he slowly ascended the stairs, not with any precise object, but because in that direction he saw a light; and she shaded that light with her wrinkled hand as she called out:

"Who is that? What is that? Who talks of the vendetta?"

"I—I—I!" cried Sir Hannibal.

He ascended a few steps more, and then he saw the old woman, and some strange change took place in the state of his mind, for he burst into a laugh so loud, so ringing, and so awful, that surely the echoes of that ancient house has never before been awakened by such a mockery of mirth, and never would again.

"Yes—yes."

Even Sir Hannibal Murkington crouches down in terror; even the old hag trembles so excessively that the grotesque shadow cast by her own person on the wall by the light seems motioned with a strange life.

Another laugh rings through the house.

The awful reverberations of Sir Hannibal's mockery of mirth had reached the attic where the poor maniac was imprisoned, and the new sounds, infinitely more terrible than those were that Sir Hannibal had produced, came pealing through the place with horrible distinctness.

"That—that is Agatha?" said Sir Hannibal, in a faint tone.

"It is," said the Corsican mother; "and it is you who have awakened such sounds."

"Horrible! oh, most horrible!"

Raging in the still air of the night came the loud maniac laughter from above. It seemed as if the stricken creature had found some new pleasure in the terrible sounds which, such was their force and intensity, one might well wonder she had the strength to produce.

Sir Hannibal Murkington clasped his hands over his ears.

"Oh, this is terrible—this is too terrible! I, who have heard that voice in the soft accents of affection—I, who in still stillness of night have listened for the faintly murmured whisper of my own name in the happy dreams of that pure spirit—to hear her now, now, with such terrible laughter! O Heaven! O Heaven! May I not be spared yet? What have I done? what have I done?"

With one prolonged scream, the laughter ceased, and a stillness was in the house scarcely for a few moments more terrible than had been the previous sounds; for through that stillness there seemed to come a strange swinging cadence, such as is heard in the air after the deep tolling of a bell.

"She is at peace," said the Corsican mother.

Sir Hannibal looked up hastily.

"No, no! What mean you? Not—not—dead?"

"No. She cannot die yet."

"Cannot?"

"Not until the vendetta is complete."

Sir Hannibal shuddered. He had got over his first raging excitement.

"Listen, mother," he said. "That is the cause of my emotion. The vendetta is not only not complete, but it is not even begun. We, you see, thought it was. We thought that he, at least, had fallen—he, Colonel Wentworth; but that is not so."

"Not so?—not so? Did your knife fail you?"

"It would seem that it did. Only to-night have I been told, by one who knows him well, that Colonel Wentworth lives."

"No, no!"

The hag clapped her hands together as she let fall the lamp.

The staircase was impenetrably dark.

"Tell me; wither my heart and dry up my old blood with the news!"

"He lives! I can see it all now. At the time—I recollect now—there was a mystery about his death and pretended burial. He has recovered. The wound I gave him could not have been mortal. He lives!"

"And you live?"

"I?"

"Yes; you have seen your enemy, and yet he lives, and you live."

"Forbear your reproaches. I have not seen him; you did not listen to me. Dose now and I will tell you all. It was but one brief hour since that I would have answered to an angel from Heaven, had I been asked the question: 'Yes, Colonel Wentworth is no more. He fell by my hand.' But now I could not say so much, mother."

"Go on—go on."

"By accident I have overheard someone speak of him, one who knows him so well that he cannot be mistaken, a man whom I know well, too—an old soldier of my own troop in the regiment. He, this man, has seen Colonel Wentworth."

"Where?"

"Here, in London, only this day. No; not this day, for this is a new day. The dawn is coming of a new day; but he saw him yesterday. He is still in life, but with a dread of the vendetta—a dread which has been awakened in him by the words around the hilt of the dagger which must have missed his heart. He has changed his name."

"Ah!"

"But he still lives."

"That is well."

"Well?"

"Yes. Has he not suffered? Does he not still suffer? I say it is well. What ceaseless care he must endure! It is time yet for death. He shall die yet; but he has suffered while we thought his sufferings were over; so it is well, I say."

Sir Hannibal Murkington drew a long breath.

"I will seek him still," he said, "were it forty fathoms deep in ocean, or into the bowels of the earth, where men never dared to travel."

"His name?"

"His assumed name—General Smythe."

"You know that; and, therefore you can still strike him dead with terror, before again, you try the temper of a Corsican dagger on his breast."

"I can. I can."

"Go. It is your weapon; go now."

"Soon. I am weak and I want rest."

"Rest!" muttered the old hag. "He wants rest when revenge is shrinking in his heart. Degenerate race—O degenerate race. 'Tis well, Jeffreys; you want rest; and you must have rest."

"I am not strong."

"No, no."

"I have suffered so much, you know; and the one bullet that struck me when I was taken out to die, you are aware, is still deep in my breast."

"I forgot, I forgot, I am apt to forget all but vengeance. Rest, Jeffreys, rest. I will watch while you recruit the strength which you will need, but I will not regret this man's being still in life, for still to live means still to suffer."

"I know that as well as any man," sighed Sir Hannibal, as he went into the first room of the suite on the upper floor of the house and cast himself upon a couch.

In five minutes he was in a deep sleep.

The old Corsican mother found another light and stole into the room, and looked at him as he slept.

"Yes, yes," she said. "He is the avenger, and I will be mindful of his health and strength. He has suffered, but he will be avenged yet. The morning is at hand. I can feel the cool essence of the early day. The first stout ray of new light has shot out of the eastern sky. Oh, yes; we will have vengeance yet! The vendetta! Ha! The vendetta!"

The old hag placed one of the curtains of a window in the room in such a way that when Sir Hannibal should awaken he could not fail to see that it was daylight, and then she took her way restlessly about the house, muttering to herself and creeping up and down staircases and in and out of the rooms, with no apparent object.

It was broad daylight when Sir Hannibal Murkington opened his eyes again. The sun was shining brightly, and a ray had found its way through the gap in the curtain left by the Corsican mother, right on to the face of the sleeper.

It was that ray of light that awakened him, but yet he had slept for five hours.

Starting to his feet, Sir Hannibal looked hastily about him.

"Ah! yes, I am at home," he said. "But what a strange dream! I thought that on one of the bridges I met Michael Shea and his mother, the old camp-follower, and that—Hold! oh, hold! Vision!—dream, did I say. God, it was real!"

The old woman projected her head in at the door of the room with a hideous smile upon her wrinkled face.

"He lives! Ha! Ha! He lives! General Smythe!"

"It is not, then."

"What is doubtful in its reality?"

"I thought it was but all a dream; but now I know that it is not. Mother, I will make inquiries."

"For whom? About whom?"

A strange spasmodic smile came over the features of Sir Hannibal as he replied:

"General Smythe."

The old woman nodded.

"I have a scheme," she said.

"What is it?"

"You will discover where he is, and then I will tell it to you. Go, my son; go. Yours is the task yet. I only live to see it accomplished. When the vendetta is complete, I shall die; but not till then."

"The supreme vendetta?"

"You have said it. It is sworn."

Sir Hannibal Murkington bowed his head as he, too, added: "It is sworn."

In five minutes more Sir Hannibal Murkington was dashing along Regent street, and little guessed the passengers who turned to gaze upon that faultless equipage the heavy heart, so full of wild and stormy passions, that it carried.

Sir Hannibal drew rein at a fashionable bookseller's and alighted.

"A 'Court Guide', if you please, I should like to see for a moment."

There was a whole page of Smythe's, but there was one among them all that Sir Hannibal seemed, by a sort of instinct, to pitch upon.

"Smythe, Major-General, F. C., United Service Club, and No 97 Hanover Square."

"That is the man," said Sir Hannibal.

Sir Hannibal Murkington smiled blandly as he thanked the bookseller's assistant, and then he drove to Hanover Square.

*

Sir Hannibal Murkington, too, had work to do on that night of surprises and of terrors—work that, however unholy it might seem to one looking down upon his actions from some vantage-ground in the manner of a spectator of the tragedy of that man's life, yet recommended itself to him, for it grew from out of the ashes of his heart. His revenge was the only flower left in the ruined Eden of his existence. It bloomed with a baleful virility, and its fruit was to be death.

He was a Corsican. His was not the hereditary feeling which makes the natures of that rugged isle consider the vendetta in all its horrors a rational part of their existence. His vendetta was an acquired feeling, and his better nature revolted against while he obeyed it.

And now, as Sir Hannibal took his way to those new chambers that so closely adjoined those of the man who, although he knew it not, was all but a walking corpse—so near death was he—the idea of this supreme vendetta, with all its injustice, rose up from heart to brain, and he struck his breast, and murmured to himself, and groaned aloud, as he made his rapid way through the street.

"Let him perish—let him perish alone, and let the others suffer not for the crimes of one allied to them by the accident of existence. What have they done? How have they aided him in his deep iniquity? Oh no, no! It is wickedly unjust! it must not be! Yet—yet Agatha! my Agatha! Shall ordinary revenge appease the fair shadow of thy once pure and gentle spirit? Would I not, if such were possible, shake the great world to its foundation, cry 'halt' to all human footsteps, about a conclusion to all human affairs, so that the earth and all that it inhabit should be alive to the retribution my wrongs call for her!"

It was that time of the night in London when few people are stirring; there were no attractions in that square, with its tall, courtly houses, and its dim, shadowy trees, to arrest the footsteps of the ordinary passenger; so Sir Hannibal Murkington was alone; and he gradually recovered his composure—that sort of composure which he usually possessed, and which, to him, ever felt as if a cold hand was pressed upon his heart.

Sir Hannibal Murkington had no compunctious visitings about the deed he was now about to do.

The man upon whom he sought present and immediate vengeance was he who had actually done him and his all the direful injuries which had evoked the spirit of revenge.

There was an awful shadowy spectral look about Sir Hannibal Murkington now, as he trod those rooms, into which he had made his way as the avenger and executioner. A baleful light was in his eyes. He drew his breath in short, hot inspirations; and his attitudes assumed wonderful picturesqueness—if we may use the term—which did not usually belong to them.

Soft and stealthy was his tread, like that of one of the tiger tribe when it feels that it is in the vicinity of legitimate prey. He avoided the various articles about the rooms with a lithe and sinewy kind of dexterity, and then he stood in the centre of the apartment that adjoined the dressing and bed-room, and he gazed keenly about him.

In one corner were several swords: some that appertained to the military rank of the General, and might be worn in the field; others there were that had been made for occasions of courtly dress and ceremony.

A table, close to a window, had on it a desk. Opened letters lay about it; and as Sir Hannibal stepped up to it, he saw that a pen, lately used, lay carelessly over a sheet of unused paper.

Not a word did Sir Hannibal utter, but he took up the pen—not in the way one would take it up to write with it in the ordinary fashion, but by the quill end.

He dipped then the feather-end in the ink, and scrawled, in huge black letters, on the sheet of paper, the one word:

"VENDETTA!"

That done, he went to the corner where the swords were to be found, and he selected one—a long, straight blade, of moderate width. He drew it from the scabbard, and tried the temper of the steel upon the floor.

The blade bent strongly, and started back to its usual position freely. But not a word did Sir Hannibal speak.

Then he took the half-dry sheet of paper on which was the word "vendetta", and he thrust the sword-blade through its centre, and ran it up to the hilt.

He did all this so calmly—so coolly, and quietly, that one would have supposed him a gentleman amusing himself in his own apartments.

And the victim slept—slept without a sound, without a murmur, while the avenger was so near at hand, that with six strides he could make his way with that sword to his heart. How still the house was, likewise! Indeed, all London seemed to sleep. The noises of the good city were hushed in repose; or, if not wholly so, they came but faintly into that suspicious mansion. Then Sir Hannibal Murkington, with the sword in his hand, advanced into the bedroom of the General.

At that moment only a moan came from the sleeper, and it would seem as if with the avenger there came into the room an atmosphere of dread and pain to him.

A broad faint beam from the light in the other room streamed over the bed, and over the face of the man who so soon to die, and Sir Hannibal Murkington gazed long and fixedly at the features of his arch enemy—he who had been the bane, the blight of his existence, who lay at his mercy.

Mercy? No, no; no mercy for him. No mercy for such a man as Colonel Wentworth. He must not look for it in that seared human heart; he must not seek it in the chambers of that brain which he has disordered almost to madness. If mercy there be for him, it must be where mercy is infinite, and not on earth.

It is expiation now.

Sir Hannibal raised the sword in his right hand. He laid it edgeways over the throat of the General, and he gently, very gently (one would have thought him tender of his victim), he gently pressed it down, down until the cold steel must have indented the skin a little—down until in sleep some fearfully troublous dreams, concentrating in perhaps a moment's time (an age of agony to him who so dreamt), may have ensued.

The General tossed his arms to and fro. He moaned and sighed, but he did not awaken at the moment. Then Sir Hannibal bent low his lips to the ear of the sleeper.

"Vendetta! Vendetta! Vendetta!"

It was with a half-screaming, half-wailing cry that he uttered the word. That word, the most fearful one that he in whose ears it was screamed, could hear.

With a half-stifled cry the General awoke.

The edge of the sword pressed closer.

"Murder! God! Mur—"

He could not utter another cry. He convulsively clutched the bedclothes, and his staring eyes saw nothing but the upper portion of the hangings of the bed.

"Vendetta! Vendetta! Vendetta!"

Those terrible words, so repeated in his ears, told him of death. He uttered a scream—a scream in spite of the edge of the sword—a scream that was so strangely half-smothered in its utterance that it sounded as if it came rather than some other part of that room or the house than from the lips of that doomed man.

Then Sir Hannibal Murkington spoke.

"Colonel Wentworth. Colonel Wentworth."

"No," gurgled the Colonel, deep in his throat. "No—I—no—I am—not. O God!"

"Liar! Colonel Wentworth, would you live? Would you live yet? Would you avoid the tomb—the cold apathy of death—that sleep which, for aught we know, is haunted by dreams of agony? Would you live? Would you live?"

There was hope in these words—hope, dim, distant, and faint as the sea-bird's wing which the wrecked mariner believes a friendly sail on the far-off horizon.

The sword's edge, too, relaxed in its cold, stern pressure for a moment.

"Life! Life!" gasped the General. "It is all I ask. Life—oh! let me have life?"

"Ah! Then you are so very fond of life?"

"I am. I am. Oh! let me live. I know not who you are; but you are some Corsican—some kinsman of the—the—wife of—of him—who—"

"Well, go on."

"I need not. You know all or—or—"

"Or I should not be charged with the vendetta. It is well, Colonel Wentworth. Are you not a villain?"

"Spare me. I will enrich you. I have gold and jewels yet, although the greater part were stolen from me. Only let me live, and I will be such a friend to you."

"Let me see: you were a friend to poor Jeffreys, the trooper, and to his wife."

The Colonel groaned.

"Do you know what became of her?"

"No—no."

"Well, I can tell you. She is mad—a hopeless lunatic. When she heard the volley of musketry which by your machinations was levelled at her husband's life, and when she saw him fall, and blood upon him, she became what she is now: a thing of shouts, and cries, and moaning lamentations. She is mad. Her beauty—you know she had beauty, or you would not have been the serpent in her Eden—her beauty is gone. She would not tempt you now, Colonel Wentworth."

"My good Sir. My dear friend. Do not—I regret—indeed I do. Come now—you are, perhaps, a poor man—you would like to be a rich one. What, after all, is Jeffreys to you, or his wife either, eh?"

"But tell me, Colonel, one thing?"

"What is it?"

"Are you sorry that you had the poor fellow shot, on your testimony, when you knew he was most innocent?"

"Yes, of course. If—if he was—as I fancy he was—a friend of yours, you know."

"He was."

"Then I am sorry?"

"Would you give much to have been spared that deed?"

"I would."

"Your life?"

"Well, it cannot be helped now—what is done, is done; but if it would please you to hear me say so, I will say it—that I would give my life."

"To restore him to life?"

"Just so."

"You have said it!"

"You spare me, then; let me get up!"

"No; I am Jeffreys!"

"You—you—oh, mercy! Heaven does not perform miracles in the name of vengeance!"

"Peace! We are confidential now. I am Jeffreys. The men who were to form the firing party at my execution pitied me. My poor wife, you see, spoke to them, and convinced them of my innocence and your guilt. Well, they were to fire blank cartridges at me, and I was to be saved; but one was ill, and another man took his place. He fired a ball, and his bullet hit me. It is in my breast now. But I recovered, as you can see, and I sought you out and left a Corsican knife in your breast, from which you recovered, and here we both are."

The Colonel groaned.

"Jeffreys, Jeffreys—be human—be—be Christian! It is great to forgive. Leave vengeance for Heaven. My good fellow, you will not surely murder me now in cold blood? It is a long time ago, you know, Jeffreys, and I will make amends."

"What amends?"

"You shall be rich."

"I will make a bargain with you."

"For my life?"

"For your life."

"My good fellow—"

"Hush! Hear it out. You will restore to perfect reason and peace Agatha. You will remove this bullet from my chest."

"Oh! you know I cannot! You mock me! Murder! murder! mur—"

"There you see," said Sir Hannibal Murkington, "you are hurt. There is blood upon your neck!"

"Help! mercy!"

"Villain! murderer! suborner of justice! man with triple the crimes that should hurl you to perdition, on your head, if I thought that in that black and grimed thing you call a heart there dwelt the capacity for one hour's real agony of repentance, you should live!"

"Help! O Heaven!"

"Vendetta!"

"I will give you all! I will beg my bread—life—only life, vendetta."

There was one fearful plunge on the part of the General to rise, as Sir Hannibal Murkington suddenly removed the edge of the sword from his neck; but he was thrust back again on the pillow by a blow with the left hand of the avenger.

Then the sword gleamed in the beam of light from the next apartment, and it descended perpendicularly on to the breast of the General. Keen and sharp, its point penetrated the bedclothes, and reached the breast of the guilty man. The blade was impelled by hate. A wild cry of "Vendetta!" burst from the lips of Sir Hannibal Murkington, and, with a fearful strength, he thrust the sword through clothing, man, bed, mattress, and all obstructions, until the hilt struck upon the chest of Colonel Wentworth and the paper with the scrawly characters upon it rested broad and flat over his heart.

"Vendetta!"

"It is done," said Sir Hannibal.

There was one gasping sob, and the betrayer was no more.

A very few moments brought him to the door of that house by the river, into which he so seldom made his way until the shadows of twilight lent an additional screen of obscurity to the scene.

But now he felt impelled by a strong feeling to seek that house; for he had got the idea in his mind that he was a condemned man, and that, in some way, he was but nearing each moment, with a fearful celerity, his death.

With the master-key that he had, he opened the outer door and groped his way into the dark passage.

"Mother! Mother!" he called, in eager accents. "Mother, where are you?"

There was no answer.

"Speak! Speak! I have news for you. He is dead—dead now. When last I came, it was to tell you that he lived; but now the destroyer has been at work again, and I can tell you he is dead—dead!"

Sir Hannibal listened, but not a sound met his ear in that house.

"What is this?" he said. "What is this? Are they all dead here, likewise? Speak, I say, speak! Where are you? Why do you not answer me? You were always but too ready to awaken the slumbering fiend in my heart; always only too ready to fan the fading flame of my hatred to these Wentworths; and now, when I come to tell you they are dead—one of them at the least, and that, probably, before to-day's sun declines in the west, another will be no more—you cannot speak to me. Where are you? Where are you?"

The passage was very dark.

The staircase was very dark.

Sir Hannibal, with his hands outstretched before him, slowly ascended, still muttering to himself: "Mother! Mother, I say! Where are you now?"

He then thought that he heard a sound, as if someone was trying to get breath—trying to speak, and yet wanting the power so to do.

Inexpressibly alarmed, Sir Hannibal tore down the shutters of a small window in the corridor. The light of the young morning streamed in.

In a corner, propped up by the rectangular junction of the two walls, was the Corsican mother.

Well might Sir Hannibal recoil at the aspect of that hag-like woman, who, for so long had lived only on her enduring hatred to the Wentworths.

She had been seized by paralysis. The use of her limbs was denied to her, and she half lay half sat there by the walls, a corpse with a mind yet

belonging to it: a dead body, with one sentiment yet glaring from its eyes—
the sentiment of revenge.

"Mother, mother! What is this?" said Sir Hannibal.

She did not even try to speak. There was not muscular life sufficient left
with which to make the trial; but her eyes, like fiery specks, glared upon the
face of Sir Hannibal.

"She is stricken!" he said. "Alas! she is stricken! Mother, can you comprehend? Can you still know and feel the joy of the assurance that your foe is
no more? I have killed him—Colonel Wentworth. He is dead. He died in
agony. He knew the hand that dealt the blow. Mother, he is no more. This
time it was a sure thrust. He is dead! dead! dead!"

Sir Hannibal looked carefully into the eyes of the old woman, in order to
come to some opinion in regard to whether she really comprehended what
he said to her.

He could not tell.

There was the same eager but fiery look about the eyes, and that was all.
The intelligence might, possibly, have reached her, and she yet not be able
to give, by sign or token, an induction that it had done so. She was of this
world still, but that was all that could be said.

Then Sir Hannibal said no more to the hag who had hounded him on
to revenge for so many years, and who now, that there was no doubt of its
achievement, at least in one instance, had not the power left to appreciate
it. He slowly made his way along the corridor to one of those rooms which
we have before described, and opening a door that was behind one of the
tapestries, he listened intently.

The low, wailing voice of someone singing came to his ears.

Oh, how well he knew that voice! Oh, how each cadence of it echoed to
well-remembered strains in this heart!

It was Agatha!

She sang the Morning Hymn to the Virgin. In her native island that
gentle strain had often wafted its way to heaven; and now that a moment
of calmness and serenity had come to the poor, vexed spirit—come with

the early day, which ever brings with it some relief to the fevered heart and brain—the words of the hymn had risen up in her memory, and she sang the old and well-known strain with which the cottage-home in Corsica had been familiar.

Sir Hannibal Murkington shook as he listened to those strains, which spoke of gentleness and heavenly pity; and for a few moments, perchance, the fell purposes of his heart faded away before nobler and gentler impulses.

He even thought that if he could have but wept—if tears would only come at that moment, and after tears, sleep—that he might be satisfied with what he had already done, and that the vendetta, in what may be called its simplicity, and not the supreme vendetta, would suffice to allay the cravings of his bruised heart for revenge.

And it might have been so, but that the gentle and peaceful interval passed away, and a wild storm of madness took the place of the calmer feelings of the soul in poor Agatha.

She suddenly ceased singing, and uttered one of those fearful cries which had become to the heart and brain of Sir Hannibal so frightfully familiar.

He recoiled as if a shot had hit him.

"Help! Help!" he heard her cry. "Help! They kill him now, and he so good and so innocent. I know there is no help with man, but is there Heaven above us? Help! oh, help!"

Sir Hannibal struck his breast repeatedly. It was a habit with him when he was strongly moved, and then he said in agonised wails:

"Yes, yes. I need but that—but the sight of that wreck, to renew all the direful purposes of my soul. I will look upon her as she is now and think of her as she once was, when first I knew her, and told her that I loved her."

He passed through the small door behind the hangings. He ascended the narrow staircase that led to the maniac's attic.

But half-way up he paused, for so sweet a girl-like laugh had come upon his ears that, in the surprise of the moment, he had to cling to the front balustrade of the staircase for support, or he would have surely fallen.

Another varying mood had come over the poor mentally-stricken Agatha. That mood was one that surely should have melted him to tears.

But he was past weeping. The fount of tears was dry in his heart. But he listened that such agony of recollection took possession of him that he could hear no more.

Agatha had fancied herself in her native home; she had fancied that she was wandering in one of the valleys of Corsica, and that she had met with him—with him, Jeffreys, the young soldier who had won her heart. With all the charming coquetry of a young girl, she was speaking to him, and her fancy kept suggesting his remarks and replies to what she said.

"And so you love me. You say you love me; but you are not of our dear old island—you are not of old Corsica. How can I love you? Ah, you say because you love me. Ha, ha! Foolish, simple Johanis! Nay, I will call yon Johanis. Not that I love you, because, as you see, I do not love anyone. Oh no, no, no! I ought not to love anyone. I am of Corsica, you see, Johanis, and you are a stranger. Dear good Johanis. Shall I love you? Will you be unhappy, Johanis, if I do not love you. Come to this heart, then, my own dear. You weep. Yes; I hear your tears, although I do not look at you. I will love you—I do love you! So happy! oh, so happy!"

Sir Hannibal Murkington clasped his hands, and wrung them together in the deep agony of his spirit. He moaned and struck his breast then, and he looked upward, as to see if Heaven could be above him, and yet such wickedness in the world as he and his had been the victims of.

"Agatha, Agatha!" he sobbed. "My own, my beautiful, my Agatha! You know not—you never did know, how much I loved you, but you will know when you know all things in heaven!"

He sat down on those narrow stairs that led to the attic, and he walked to and fro, and moaned and sighed.

And he tried to weep.

But no tears came.

"No," he said. "This is a phenomenon. Time was when my overcharged heart would shed tear-drops like rain; and then there was relief; but they are all now turned to fire—to fire!"

Then he rose, and slowly made his way and purposes further up the staircase; and then he clasped his hands above his head, and he said, in accents that had in them a world of woe, and yet some touch of that feeling of gentleness that proclaimed that man, even in his uttermost fall, was near akin to heaven.

"Hear me, hear me, O Father of all mercy! Hear me now! Let me find this poor stricken heart only gentle and sad, and like some sweet harp, jangled out of tune, perchance but still with all fair music in its strains, though discords alone fall upon the ear. Let me find my Agatha, my love, my wife, my long-estranged, long-lost one—let me find her gentle, and I hereby renounce all bitter revenges, I hereby will cast from me the demon whose name on earth is vengeance, and I will seek peace, I will seek consolation, I will seek reconciliation with Thee, O God, in some other land, where Thy spirit shall encompass me and her. But oh, let me find her gentle! Let the false light that gleams from her disordered brain be faint but fair! I will see her now—I will see her now. Agatha, Agatha! my own loved Agatha!"

With moans and strange sobs, sobs that had no tears with them, that poor heart-stricken man utter these words which we can transcribe, but which we cannot accompany by the beseeching accents, the imploring gestures, and the world of supplicatory terror with which they were uttered.

Slowly, then, up the stairs he went. He paused at the attic-door. His hands trembled, and more than once he stopped to strike his breast one of those blows that made up a part of the physical expression of his grief.

A trick of nature, that was, which belonged to him. Another might wring his hands; another might clasp them, and cry out aloud. But he, that sufferer, when he suffered most, would strike his breast.

Pity him! oh, pity him!

Then he spoke:

"Agatha, my dear—my Agatha! It is I. You are so still, darling. Agatha! O my Agatha! my own dear girl! my maiden of the hill and the flood! My

Agatha! God bless you ever and ever! Do you know my voice? My dear, my pretty Agatha! Do you hear me? It is Johanis, your own Johanis. He thinks if you will speak to him, and say that you know him, that he will be able to weep, that the tears will come. That would be such happiness! Agatha, Agatha! my dear, dear Agatha!"

He knocked at the panel of the door.

A cry. O God, such a cry! Sir Hannibal Murkington echoed it. It came from the poor maniac in the attic. The soft and gentle mood had passed away. Twice-wild madness ruled the hour. Shriek came on shriek, imprecation fast on imprecation, yell on yell, howl on howl! O Heaven! it was dreadful to listen to.

He fled.

Down the stairs, across the room below, out into the corridor, past the corpse—yes, the corpse; for the Corsican mother was no more—down the staircase, along the dark passage, out of the house, and up the narrow street.

It was at midnight, when this rage of the elements was at its height—when flashed succeeded flash of lightning, and when the muttering thunder made the circuit of the heavens, that the door of the attic in the lone, sad house by the Thames, which had been the home of Sir Hannibal Murkington, was gently opened from within.

In the last visit, Sir Hannibal had himself drawn back the bolts, and turned the key in the lock; for he had, as we know, an intention of flying from England, and from a prosecution of further vengeance, along with Agatha.

It was only that sudden accession of raving madness on her part that had saved him from this purpose, and he had left the door unsecured.

And so at this midnight hour, the poor, lone maniac was left alone with no one to care for her—no one to tend her—no one to pity her, came forth. It was a quiet hour with herself. The strange light of insanity was in her eyes but she was gentle and sad.

"I am coming, Johanis," she said. "My dear Johanis, I am coming. Mother! Mother! where are you, too, mother? Oh, I remember I have heard you and Johanis tell me how to act when the time came. It has come now, dear Johanis. The boat! The boat!"

She crept gently and softly down the stairs. She reached the room with the balcony which overhung the river. The tide was high. The water raged in the storm against the piers of the balcony. The spray dashed against the window.

The boat, still secured to the railing, was there. It tossed to and fro on the agitated tide; but there it was, even as it had been for many months, waiting until the vendetta should be accomplished.

Agatha had, no doubt, often heard both Sir Hannibal and her mother talk of this boat, and how it was to be used as a means of easy and rapid escape down the river when the acts of vengeance against the Wentworths were completed; and now her idea evidently was, that the time had come, and that the door of her prison had been left open that she might accompany them.

"Yes," she said, gently, "I know, Johanis. The boat! The boat! All is well. I am coming—I am coming. You call me, and I come, dear Johanis."

She heeded not the vivid flashes of the forked lightning—she heeded not the reverberating roll of the thunder, but with her fair hair streaming about her, she went out on to the balcony.

The rain at that moment began to come down in torrents, and it hissed and splashed on the troubled waters of the river, but she heeded it not.

"The boat! The boat!" she said. "I see it now, and I see Johanis in it. Ah, he beckons to me. There is blood upon his face. He is hurt, is my Johanis, but I will tend him, and all will be well again. I come—I come!"

She drew the boat close to the balcony, and stepped into it. A large iron swivel, with a spring, held it to the iron-work of the balcony, and she released it by a touch.

The boat, with a whirl, swept out into the heaving tide.

"Johanis! Johanis!" shrieked Agatha.

She rose up, and stood in the boat. A bridge loomed large in the darkness. There was a crash, a cry, and the heaving water rolled over the fair form of Agatha.

The heart-stricken one had found peace at last.

THE END!

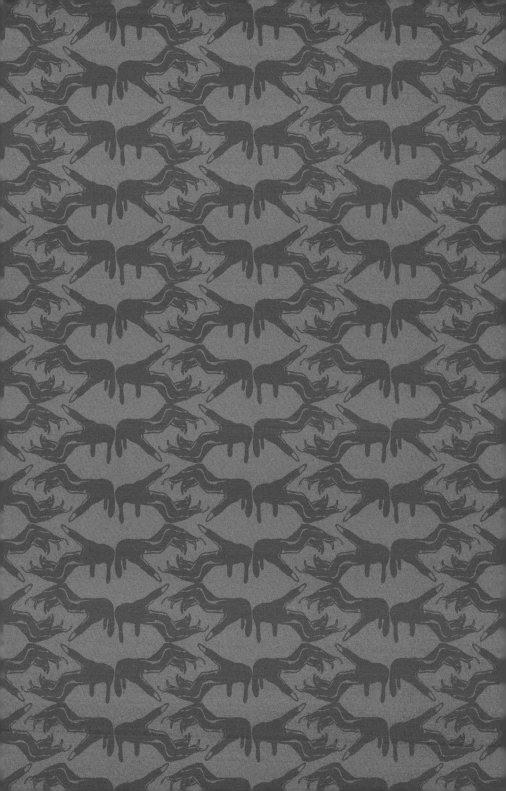

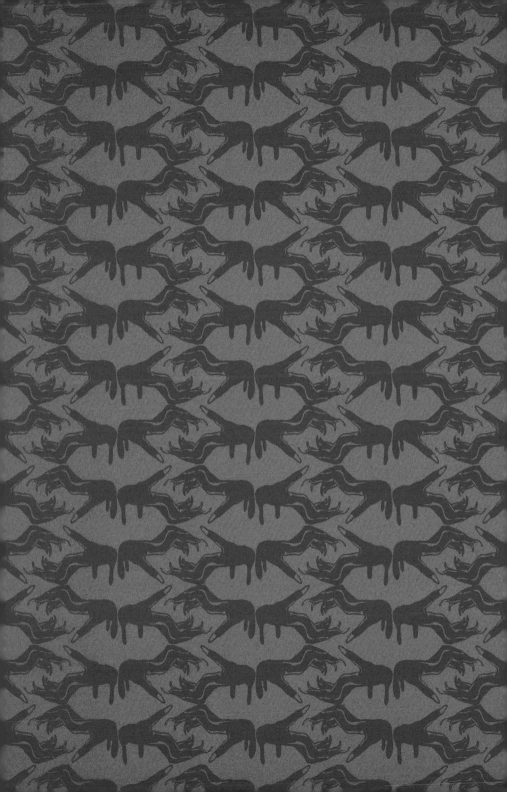